The Yorkshire Farm Girl

By Diane Allen

DIANE ALLEN

The Yorkshire Farm Girl

MACMILLAN

First published 2023 by Macmillan
an imprint of Pan Macmillan
The Smithson, 6 Briset Street, London EC1M 5NR
EU representative: Macmillan Publishers Ireland Ltd, 1st Floor,
The Liffey Trust Centre, 117–126 Sheriff Street Upper,
Dublin 1, D01 YC43
Associated companies throughout the world
www.panmacmillan.com

ISBN 978-1-5290-9310-0

1 3 5 7 9 8 6 4 2

A CIP catalogue record for this book is available from the British Library.

Typeset by Palimpsest Book Production Ltd, Falkirk, Stirlingshire
Printed and bound by CPI Group (UK) Ltd, Croydon, CR0 4YY

Visit **www.panmacmillan.com** to read more about all our books
and to buy them. You will also find features, author interviews and
news of any author events, and you can sign up for e-newsletters
so that you're always first to hear about our new releases.

To my grandson, Ben, I hope you never have
to endure the hardship of going to war and never
need to know the loss it brings. Love, Nanna.

Chapter 1

Dent, North Yorkshire, December 1938

Sally stood next to her mother, cold and ready for home, but she knew better than to say so as they both walked down the steep hillside of the graveyard to her grandparents' graves. Her long brown hair was damp and her winter coat barely kept her warm, and she shivered as they reached the graves.

Ivy Fothergill, still a good-looking woman for her age, looked down at the graves of her long-dead parents. Even though it had been more than ten years since her father had died, she still missed them both. She wiped back a tear and then smiled at her daughter Sally and put her arm around her, kindness showing in her blue eyes – the eyes that she had inherited from her grandmother, and which also reminded her every day of her loving mother.

'I bet you can hardly remember both of them, but they thought the world of you. Now what they would make of our Ben is another matter.' Ivy smiled and looked up to the ancient church doorway, where her youngest child, aged ten, was jumping up and down just outside the porch, without a care in the world. His blond hair was tousled and in a mess, while his mackintosh belt hung down, getting dragged carelessly on the ground.

'I can remember my granddad – he always had a bit of spice in his pocket for me. But I can barely remember my gran,' fifteen-year-old Sally said as she bent down and straightened the home-made holly wreaths they had laid on the two graves, to remember their loved ones at Christmas. Then she stepped back and sighed from the boredom of having to visit the gravesides yet again.

'Well, she was a good woman, and I wish she was still with us. You don't realize until it's too late that your mother is your best friend, and how much you'll miss her when she has gone. I could do with her now, that's for sure.' Ivy lifted her head and looked around the churchyard, which was filled with both her own and her husband Bob's family, and remembered happier times spent visiting family in the dale when life was easier. It was a churchyard filled with memories of better days, when things seemed not as hard and every day was warm and full of love.

'You've got me, Mam,' Sally chirped up, putting her arm through her mother's. 'As long as we have no more of those wreaths to make. My fingers are sore from bending chicken-wire and clipping holly to put into them. Look, my hands are fairly scratched.' She held them out and showed her mother the scratches on her hands from handling the prickly holly, which they had placed on six close relations' graves throughout the churchyard.

'That'll soon mend, and it's a small price to pay to show the love we have for our family, which is no longer with us at Christmas. My hands are just the same, and so will the hands of half the Dales folks be, looking at the number of wreaths around this churchyard.' Ivy glanced skywards. 'Look, you are getting a thank-you from heaven.' As she lifted her face up to the grey skies overhead, the first flake of winter fell down upon them. 'A white Christmas will be nice, as long as everybody gets to where they want to be, and folk have enough food in; otherwise it'll be a bind.'

'I knew it was cold – I've been cold all day. But I do so hope it is going to snow a lot, as I love Christmas when there is snow on the ground and we can go sledging.' Sally smiled and thought of pulling her father's home-made sledge up to one of the highest hills on their small farm and holding on for dear life, as it slid and bounced over the rough pastureland, eventually coming to a halt or throwing her into the icy snow; there she would lie, laughing, until the cold nearly made her cry and her clothes were sodden.

'Don't you think you are getting a bit too old for sledging? It's time you acted more of a lady. You'll be sixteen in June, and perhaps it's time to act no longer like the tomboy you are.'

'It's only sledging, Mam. Besides, I'll only be going with our Ben, and nobody else will see me,' Sally moaned. 'If I could wear trousers, like our Ben and my dad, it would make a difference. I hate skirts and dresses – I can't even ride our old horse without showing all my knickers when I climb on its back.'

'Sally Fothergill, watch what you're saying and stop moaning. You know your father would have a fit, seeing his li'l lass wearing a man's trousers. Now let's be away. What Ben is doing, jumping up and down on that grave-stone, I don't know! I'll have to give him a clip round the ear for not showing any respect to the dead.'

Ivy picked up her empty shopping basket and walked up the steep hillside of the churchyard to see what her son was doing, with Sally following her.

'Ben, stop that now. It's somebody's grave you are jumping on. Let them rest in peace.' She looked down at the flat stone, which was inscribed with the name of the person lying below it, and shook her head as Ben wiped his running nose on his sleeve.

'It's only the grave of the Dent vampire, Mam. I'm making sure he's dead. I don't want him creeping about at night and frightening us all.' Ben grinned and then pulled a scary face at Sally.

'That's a load of rubbish. I'm sure poor old George Hodgson, who's buried under there, harmed nobody. He was probably a lonely old man who folk made up tales about. Anyway, he was buried in 1751, so I think he is now well and truly dead,' Ivy said and grabbed Ben's hand.

'No, it's right, Mam, you know it is. Even my father has told me that once they had buried him, folk saw him wandering the streets at night, even though he was dead. And he came back as a black hare. That's why he was

4

buried again underneath the church path, for good churchgoers to walk over him; and then a stake was put through him and his coffin to hold him in place. Look, you can see where the stake went in.' Ben pointed to the metal end of the stake, which did indeed go through the gravestone and into the ground below.

'You are full of rubbish, our Ben. There's no such thing as vampires. You are supposed to be behaving yourself, else Father Christmas won't come. And he'll be hearing you telling tales.' Sally stuck her tongue out at her brother.

'It's right, I tell you. Mam knows, but she won't say 'cause she thinks I'll be frightened. I'nt that right, Mam?' Ben pulled on his mother's arm and looked up at her.

'Whisht now, Ben. I've enough on trying to remember what I want from the shop before we walk home, without you twittering on. I know Dinsdale's have delivered their order, but I've forgotten your Uncle Stanley's Kendal Twist, and I need some more plain flour. I'm glad Christmas only comes once a year. What with Stanley coming to stay, and your father trying to make a bit more money by raising turkeys to sell to the neighbours at Christmas, I'm jiggered.'

'Last time for plucking them tonight, Mam. Then it is mine and Ben's favourite day, delivering them up and down the dale with you and Father in Mattinson's van,' Sally said as they walked out of the churchyard and closed the wrought-iron gate, which creaked with age behind them. Then they walked on along the cobbled streets of Dent.

'Aye, if Jim Mattinson has let your father borrow it. We'll never get them all delivered by horse and cart, if he hasn't. Your father hasn't been able to say no to supplying half the dale with their Christmas dinner, not realizing the work that goes into it and quite how busy we women are at this time of year. All he thinks about is making enough money so that he can buy his own farm and stop lining old Turner's pocket with our rent. Your father can be so stubborn at times.'

Ivy took Ben's hand before he ran off to gaze in Dinsdale's shop window, which was filled with everything he had ever wished for, for Christmas.

'You can look, our Ben, but what you get in your stocking this year might not be what you want. Times are hard, my lad,' Ivy said as she let go of his hand and then watched Ben run across the street to Dinsdale's and place his nose as close to the window glass as he possibly could. She lifted her basket over her arm and looked at both her children. She didn't want them to come into the shop with her, as Father Christmas had one or two bits to be collected yet and she didn't want them to see the exchange. 'You stay here, you two, until I've done my shopping. I'll not be long.' She left both Sally and Ben gazing through the window at the Christmas displays.

The low whitewashed shop was a treasure trove of Christmas gifts, the two windows on either side of the main door being filled with toys and games and decorated with sprigs of red-berried holly, inviting people to gaze at what they could buy, if they had the money. Ben stared at the jigsaws and annuals, but most of all at the models of wagons and cars, which he knew he would never receive in his Christmas pillowcase. How he wished for the model of the Lancaster bomber that stood centre-stage in the Christmas display, with a price tag that was about a month's wage from his father's part-time job with Jim Mattinson. Ben knew it could never be his. Meanwhile Sally stared at the part of the window that for Christmas was displaying manicure sets, powder compacts, handkerchiefs and the item that she wanted most in her life: a pair of nylon stockings. How she longed for a pair of nylons to keep up with her friend, Marjorie Harper, who wanted for nothing.

'I really, really would love that Lancaster bomber, our Sally, and I've been so good this year – I've done all the jobs I've been asked to do, and I've washed behind my ears, just like my mam told me to.' Ben sighed and cupped his face in his hands and pressed his nose against the window.

'That's for well-off boys. Mam and Dad can't afford that. Whatever you get, be grateful for, as some children won't get anything,' Sally replied, her eyes lingering on a small silver compact and the pair of nylon stockings; she knew that they too would not be in her Christmas pillowcase at the end of her bed.

'It's not fair. Jimmy Banks at the vicarage and they at Whernside Manor get all sorts, and they don't behave at all. Well, not as well as me,' Ben wailed.

'Aye, but their parents are wealthy – that's the difference,' Sally said as she noticed Mrs Dinsdale reach over into the shop window and take out a box of Rowntree's Dairy Box, and then go to the side Ben was looking at and take out the copy of The Boy's Own Annual from under his nose.

'Oh, bugger, *The Boy's Own Annual* has gone now, and I really wanted that.' Ben pulled a face.

'Don't swear – remember, you've to behave.' Sally smiled. Her mother was always hopeless at keeping surprises at Christmas, but Ben still had to learn that she *was* Mrs Christmas.

They both looked up as the shop bell rang and out walked Mrs Banks from the vicarage, who smiled at both of them and carried her parcels of shopping off down the street.

'I bet Jimmy has even got the annual I wanted. He gets everything, and I always get nowt,' Ben said sulkily and folded his arms as he turned his back to the shop. The snow came down more steadily now.

'You never know – he might not have. You'll have to wait and see; you can always read it with Jimmy anyway. I wish Mam would hurry up. I'm frozen and we need to get home before this snow gets any worse.' Sally had no sooner finished her words than Dinsdale's shop doorbell went and their mam stepped out.

'Aye, Mrs Dinsdale likes to yack, and I think Jimmy's mother was buying half the shop up. They'll certainly not be going without over Christmas. Perhaps she and the vicar should practise what he preaches and show a bit of charity,' Ivy said and pulled her coat collar up.

'Yes, I bet it was her who bought the annual I wanted. Jimmy always gets what he wants.' Ben put his hands in his pockets and kicked a stone down the street as his mother winked at Sally and put a finger to her lips.

'Never mind, my love, you might be lucky and Father

Christmas might have heard your wishes.' Ivy quickened her step. There was a lot to do once they all returned home, and she hoped that the snow coming down would only give the dale a light dusting, else her and Bob's plans would be thrown completely out of kilter. And some families would have no bird on their Christmas table, if they were unable to deliver them because of the weather.

The two-mile walk home was cold and seemed much longer than it actually was. They finally turned the bend and saw their home in sight.

'Now, that's a relief – at least your father's got the van.' Ivy sighed as she walked up the rutted track to the farmhouse they called home and spotted the top of the black Morris van, which had been borrowed from fellow farmer Jim Mattinson.

'Good, as we would have been frozen sitting in the back of the cart delivering the turkeys. But I'd still have gone, as it is what makes Christmas. Everyone makes us so welcome,' Sally said. She smiled as Ben ran up the path home, heading for the outhouse where the sledge was kept. There was not enough snow yet, but she knew he'd be hunting it out and waxing the runners to make the sledge run faster for when there was. Both of them loved the first snowfall and sledging with their friends in the neighbouring fields, although this year she should be helping her mother, rather than playing like a child with her brother.

'Yes, well, I want you to help me and your father tonight, and let's hope this snow doesn't settle. You can bag up the feathers and perhaps clean a turkey or two, once your father and I have killed and plucked them.' Ivy walked quickly into the farmyard and entered the ancient farmhouse's porch, stamping her suede boots free of snow and opening the door into the kitchen.

Sally screwed up her nose; she hated cleaning the turkeys, pulling the innards out and washing the carcass in the freezing-cold water of the dairy. The stench turned her stomach, and more often than not she retched so much that her father got mad with her. 'Do I have to, Mam? Can't I do something else for you in the kitchen? Anything but help with the turkeys!'

'You listen to your mother – it's all hands on deck tonight. We have ten of the bloody things to pluck and prepare, before we can set off delivering them in the morning,' Bob Fothergill said sharply from the darkening recess, where he sat in his favourite chair waiting for Ivy to return and make him a cup of tea, before he went out on the final killing spree in the shed that held the fattening turkeys.

Sally said nothing. She knew that what her father said was law, and that she had no option but to help with the turkey cull – smell or no smell.

'How long have you been back, Father? I must say I was relieved when I saw the van outside, as the thought of going out and about, delivering turkeys in this weather, on the back of the cart was not that appealing.' Ivy pulled the kettle onto the backed-up embers of the coal fire and filled the teapot with loose tea, knowing that Bob would not have made himself a drink.

10

'Nobbut half an hour,' Bob said and lit his pipe, filling the room with the smell of tobacco. 'And, aye, Jim says we can have the van all day tomorrow, and I said I'd drop it off back at his house on Christmas Eve. That is, if I can. It looks like we might be in for a bit of snow, and then we will have to deliver the birds by horse and cart. The van would never get up to Hill Top and the Masons, and they've ordered the fattest bird we have.'

'I hope the snow stops. Once your brother is here and we have delivered everything, and my order from Dinsdale's has arrived, it can come all it likes. Until then, it had better hold back, no matter how much our Ben wants snow to go sledging on.' Ivy stood with her hands on her hips. 'Sally, put those potatoes that I peeled onto the stove. Once your father has had his brew, he'll be off to milk the cow; then we'll have some supper, and then we'll make a start on them turkeys. Lord, I will be glad when they are all done and dusted. Don't you get any more of these daft ideas about how to make money fast, Father. The turkeys have been nowt but work – work I could do without at this time of the year,' Ivy scolded him as she placed a mug of tea in front of her husband and tied her apron round her waist.

'You'll not be talking like that when we see how much brass we've made, and when you're putting it into the bank and can look at that miserable bank manager's face full-on. I'm not going to be renting this farm forever; I want my own, not just for me, but for all of us. I reckon nowt to renting. We will never have any money, paying leeches like our landlord,' Bob growled and took a quick sip of his tea.

11

'Aye, well, we'll see, but right now I could do without the work. I've our own Christmas to see to, and your Stanley makes work: the spare beds to be aired and extra stuff to be bought for his stay, and that's on top of all the comings and goings with the neighbours.' Ivy was flustered; there were so many things to remember in the run-up to Christmas, along with her normal jobs, that she felt a little swamped.

'It will all get done, so stop your wittering, woman. Our Sally is starting to be a grand help for you. Make more use of her.' Bob noticed the scowl on Sally's face as she put the peeled potatoes on the Belling stove top, which was the one luxury in the farmhouse kitchen. 'She could perhaps find herself a bit of a job next year – that would bring in a bit more brass.'

'Sally helps me about here; there's no need for her to find a job. She also, may I remind you, does a lot for you when you are out working for Jim Mattinson. You'll not be saying that when it's lambing and she's out in those fields, looking after our sheep when you haven't got the time,' Ivy said in defence of their daughter, who would never be forgiven by Bob for not being born a boy.

'Aye, well, Ben will soon be grown and then he'll be a grand help. Where is he anyway?' Bob stood up and pulled on his jerkin after finishing his tea.

'He's outside, looking for his sledge; he'll be wanting to go sledging.' Sally hoped that her brother had disappeared up the fields before her father nabbed him to help with something or other.

'Well, if he isn't, he can come with me and fodder the cow while I milk her. Have you checked for eggs today? The hens seem to have knocked off laying because of the cold weather. Perhaps it's time for some fresh'uns this spring,' Bob replied, making for the kitchen door.

'I picked up six – that wasn't so bad.' Sally pulled her coat back on, for her job of feeding the dog before the last hour of daylight.

'That means the other six of them aren't laying. We'll have one for dinner, come the New Year, Mother,' Bob said and went out, leaving the door ajar, for Sally to follow him into the grey December evening and the now bitter cold.

'It's stopped snowing,' Sally commented, hurrying to keep up with her father as he walked across the farmyard.

'Aye, but it's going to freeze.' Bob looked up at the sky. 'The stars are out tonight, so it's a good job I've wrapped up all the water pipes with lagging, else we would have problems. There's nowt worse than burst water pipes and trying to keep all the stock watered.' He opened the shippon door and walked across to the one shorthorn cow that kept the family, and a few of the neighbours, in milk. 'Where is that lad of mine? He's never here when I need him,' Bob moaned as he watched Sally go to the provin house, the place where they kept the dry feed for the animals, to get some Euveka maize flakes to give to the dog.

'I can feed Daisy before I feed my dog,' Sally said, turning back towards her father. She liked the warmth of the shippon and the smell of the summer hay, which

13

was kept in the adjoining barn to feed both the cow and the sheep through the winter. In fact she loved helping her father, but he never thought of her as the farmer in the family and never encouraged her, unless it was out of necessity.

'Aye, go on then, you'll manage that. But don't forget the dog, and then you'd better get back home and help your mother.' Bob picked up the milk pail and milking stool and sat down at the side of the roan-coloured cow, stroking her back as he did so and rubbing his hands together to warm them, before squatting down on the stool; he started to pull on each teat, slowly and steadily, as he had done since he was a boy.

Sally pushed past the ancient worm-eaten posts of the shippon and entered the barn, filling her arms with the dry green meadow hay that had been mown during the warm days of summer. The farm cat stretched and looked at her as she disturbed him from his slumbers on a pile of hay that acted as his bed, and the resident barn owl blinked and rotated its head, then decided to go back to sleep, recognizing her as no threat in the refuge of the old barn. She repeated the act four times, placing the hay in the byre in front of the cow, as her father carried on milking without saying a word. She then went back out into the cold and to the provin house, half-filling a bucket with the yellow maize flakes. She smiled as she saw Ben coming through the field gate, pulling his sledge along the frozen ground.

'You've not tried sledging on this scattering of snow, have you? I thought you were going to wax the runners?'

Sally said, with the metal bucket clanking at the side of her leg.

'I thought I'd get out of the way of my father, once I knew he was home, as he'd only find a job for me to do.' Ben placed the sledge on the end of its runners against the side of the house. 'I hate farming. When I grow up, there's no way I'm going to be a farmer,' he mumbled.

'You'll change once you're older – it's in our blood, Ben, our family has always been farmers,' Sally said as she opened the kitchen door and stood in the doorway, knowing that her mother would come with the boiling kettle and a wooden spoon to mix the maize concoction with whatever scraps were left for Spot, the sheepdog, who was kept in an old wooden kennel out in the farmyard.

'Never, our Sally. I want to be a pilot or a wagon driver, not a boring farmer.' Ben stomped past his mother as she poured boiling water into the mix and shouted at him to take his boots off, and wash his hands, before sitting at the table for his supper.

'Tell your father not to be long. The tatties are ready and the bacon frying, and as soon as we have eaten up, we'll see to them turkeys,' Ivy said, watching as Sally walked across the yard, with the steam escaping into the cold night air, and tipped the bucket out into the dog bowl for the grateful sheepdog to have for her supper, after patting her for a second or two.

'Mother says come straight away for your supper,' Sally commented as Ben watched their dad feed the cat, which had awakened from his slumbers, as usual, at the smell of fresh milk and in the knowledge that a

warm saucer was always there for him, once the cow had been milked.

'Aye, I'll come in a while. I'll just swill down the shippon floor and then get the worst bit done and pull the necks of the poor bloody birds. It isn't something I enjoy, but it's got to be done.' Bob leaned on the yard brush and looked at his daughter. 'Get yourself inside and then you won't hear the commotion and won't see me doing it.'

Sally nodded. She had no intention of stopping and watching her father massacre the poor birds, which were awaiting their fate in the stone shed next to the barn. She walked into the kitchen and washed her hands at the stone sink, then sat down at the table across from Ben and tried not to think about what her father was doing.

'Look, our Sally. I'm going to make an Indian headdress with this cardboard and some elastic. Save me the best turkey feathers when you are helping Mam and Father,' Ben said with excitement and put his hand on a box of wax crayons, ready to colour his headdress once supper had been eaten and the turkeys were being plucked.

'Grand – you'll look grand, I'm sure. Who are you going to be: Big Chief Sitting Bull or Crazy Horse?' Sally asked with little interest, as her mother placed a plate of bacon, mashed potato and fried egg in front of her, then moaned about Bob's supper having to be kept warm as she sat down at the table between them both.

'Neither. I'm going to be Big Chief Ben, and I'm going to make a bow and arrow tomorrow after we come back

16

from delivering the turkeys,' Ben said and tucked into his supper, grinning.

'You'll be going straight to bed. It'll be late by the time we get back, and the following night you'll be sharing your room with your Uncle Stanley and you'll be too excited to sleep, with it being Christmas Eve. So it will be an early night for you, my lad.'

'Oh, Mam, I'm not sharing with Uncle Stanley, am I? He makes such a noise in the night – he frightens me,' Ben moaned.

'He can't help it, Ben love, he's still got shell-shock from being in the trenches. Besides, he'll not harm you; he's only dreaming. Now whisht, your father's here and he'll not have a bad word said about Stanley.' Ivy rose from her seat and placed Bob's supper on the table. 'Is the deed done?' she asked quietly.

'Aye, it's done. And I've lit the paraffin lamps in the shed, so we can see what we're doing. It'll not take long.' Bob picked up his knife and fork.

Sally looked down at her supper, and at the blood on her father's hands. Suddenly she had lost her appetite; she only hoped she would be able to forget what she was about to do when she sat down to her Christmas dinner, and wouldn't remember every individual turkey that she had fed over the last six months. Perhaps Ben was right not to wish to be a farmer, because sometimes it was a cruel choice of work.

Chapter 2

'Stop arguing, you two, and sit still,' Ivy said sharply as she turned her head to Sally and Ben, who were sitting on either side of the back of the van on the wheel arches.

The van was filled with freshly plucked, trussed and cleaned turkeys, all with a ticket around their legs with the exact weight printed upon it and wrapped in grease-proof paper, awaiting delivery to the Fothergills' friends and relations. Ben and Sally were both excited, because they knew that with each delivery they would be made welcome and would hopefully receive a small Christmas present from each house they visited.

'If you don't stop annoying one another, you can get out here at Green Cottage and walk back home,' Ivy went on, as Ben kicked his sister's leg and she screamed.

'Whisht, else I'll take my belt to the both of you,' Bob said as he pulled in at the side of the road next to the small white cottage that was home to the elderly couple of Mr and Mrs Jackson, who were the first to have their

Christmas dinner delivered. 'You behave, do you hear? Mind your manners and watch what you say – none of your cheek from either of you.'

Bob put the handbrake on and opened his door, then pushed back his driving seat to let Ben and Sally out into the cold winter's air. Both of them were pushing and jostling to be the first out of the back of the van. They looked at one another and waited for their parents as they made sure they had the right turkey for the right house, then stood outside after knocking on the small, green-painted porch door and waited for an answer from within.

'Don't stand outside, you lot. Come on in, there's a good fire in the hearth and a drink waiting for you all.' Dick Jackson, smoking his pipe and with slippers on his feet, came and answered the door. 'Now then, Ivy, you'll have a drop of sherry for Christmas and I needn't ask you twice, Bob – a drop of the good stuff for me and you?'

Bob, Ivy, Ben and Sally walked past him into the small front room, which was warmed by a blazing coal fire that highlighted the tinsel hanging on the small Christmas tree in the corner.

'I see you've got your tree up, Betty? I haven't got round to putting ours up yet, what with all these turkeys to get ready.' Ivy sighed and smiled, looking up as Mrs Jackson passed her a small glass with a hunting scene upon it, half-filled with sherry.

'Only put it up yesterday, Ivy. I was late, in all honesty, and I've still my cake to decorate. But I can offer you a mince pie. Now, what will you two have to drink?'

Betty glanced at Ben and Sally. 'A drink of ginger cordial or blackcurrant? After all, it is Christmas, so you are allowed a treat.' Betty looked at Sally as she made her choice.

'Blackcurrant, please, for both of us,' Sally replied. It was the only time of year when they were ever offered the treat of cordial, and both had been looking forward to it all week.

'Aren't you two both growing up? It doesn't seem five minutes since you were born, and here you both are, growing up so fast. You are quite a young lady nowadays, Sally. And, Ben, I bet you are a good help for your father,' Betty said as she passed them both a drink, in the glasses from the sideboard that were obviously waiting for Christmas visitors, with its array of glasses and bottles of drink.

'Nay, he doesn't show much interest in farming, Betty,' Bob said as he followed Dick, after carrying the turkey into the kitchen. 'I'm hoping he'll change, because that's what he'll have to do when he leaves school.'

Ben bowed his head and Sally nudged him, hoping to keep her brother quiet and for him not to say anything in return.

'It's a grand turkey, Mother. We can feed half the dale or still be eating at it until the New Year. It's a good job our lad and his family are coming for Christmas,' Dick replied, seeing Ben blush and knowing that Bob would not be happy that his only lad was no farmer.

'It's grand that you've decided to keep breeding turkeys and deliver to us all again this year,' Betty said. 'I hope you'll be doing it again next year, because you can have our order already – God willing that we are still here then. The world's in a bit of a way with itself, and I've never known everything so dear. I've got to say I'm worried, especially when it comes to our lad.' She poked the fire to bring more life into it.

'It's not *that* we've to worry about – it's these other bloody countries that are rattling their sabres,' said Dick. 'Japan's all to hell, and that bloody Hitler is making bother in his own country, throwing out the Jews and bullying Austria into becoming part of Germany. That bloody Chamberlain has even let him get away with taking part of Czechoslovakia, and he'll not stop there.' Dick lifted up that morning's newspaper and put it down in front of Bob.

'Aye, well, it hopefully won't affect us up Dentdale. They can fall out all they like abroad, as long as they leave us alone and keep us out of it. We've only just got over the last war – we don't want another.' Bob glanced across at Ivy, hoping that she would soon drink her sherry, as he didn't want to become embroiled in politics, and he knew Dick would talk about the world's affairs for as long as he was there to listen.

Ivy knew what he meant and quickly swigged her sherry back, and looked at Sally and Ben sitting quietly on the sofa. 'Drink up, you two. We've a lot more houses to visit yet, and your father wants to get back in good time to attend the dominoes drive in The Sun tonight. And we have the tree to decorate before visitors start coming.' Ivy then turned to Betty. 'We've Stanley coming

21

to stay over Christmas; you can't let him stay on his own, poor man.'

'You are a good soul, Ivy. Poor Stanley, he's never been the same since he came back from the war. He does well, though, given that he was in such a state when he came back from the front. However, he wasn't the only one, that's the pity.' Betty stood up and took Sally and Ben's empty glasses and then walked through to the kitchen, returning with two small parcels in her hands. 'Now, don't you open them till Christmas. It's only a bit of something to put under the tree.'

Ben's eyes lit up as he saw the small present that was pressed into his hand, followed by a sloppy kiss, which he could have done without.

'Thank you, Mrs Jackson. We promise not to open them until Christmas Day, don't we, Ben?' Sally urged Ben to say thank you, and to stop shaking the parcel and examining it to guess what was in it.

'Yes, yes, we do, thank you,' Ben said as his father pushed him towards the door.

'We'd like to stay longer, but it's going to be a long day, as you are the first of many,' Ivy said and smiled at Betty. 'Have a grand day with your lad – it's a time for families at Christmas, and I bet you'll be glad to see him and his family. Is he still down in Norfolk and flying for the RAF?'

'Aye, he is. He's flying some new plane, from what I hear. I never thought my lad would be a pilot, but that's what he is. I miss him, though. I wish he was here, and then I could make a fuss of my grandchildren.' Betty sighed

22

and looked at Ben as he climbed into the van with Sally. 'It doesn't seem five minutes since our lad was that age. You don't realize how fast they grow up.'

'Not fast enough, in that one's case – he runs me ragged some days.' Ivy smiled. 'Have a good Christmas,' she continued as she climbed into the front of the van.

'Bob, see you at the dominoes match tonight in The Sun?' Dick asked quickly as Bob started the engine and was about to close the van's door.

'Aye, if I get finished in time. It's the highlight of the year, the doms match. I'll see you there for a pint or two of Christmas cheer, all being well. No rogueing, mind. We'll play a good game and give everybody a run for their money.' Bob grinned and closed the van door. The dominoes match was the highlight of Christmas for him: a night with good friends and a gill or two, and hopefully a prize for winning a game of bones.

'I hope you don't come back as drunk as you did last year – you could hardly stand up when you came home,' Ivy said, with a hint of annoyance in her voice, as they drove away to their next delivery.

'Whisht, woman, it's nobbut Christmas once a year, and surely I'm allowed one night of enjoyment. Besides, I always win something that comes in handy. Last year it was a tin of biscuits – they were a right luxury,' Bob retorted. He turned the van round in a gateway to make his way further up the dale towards the village of Dent.

'If you keep getting offered a glass of whisky, like Dick offered you, you'll not need any more tonight. My head feels light with sherry at eleven in the morning. I'll not have another, else I'll get nothing done when we get home.' Ivy turned round to look at Ben peeling back the red-and-gold wrapping on his present. 'Leave it; it'll give you something to look forward to, in case Father Christmas doesn't come. From what I can see, he might be a bit worse for wear by Christmas Eve.'

'What do you mean, Mam?' Ben said and looked at Sally, who just grinned at her parents.

'I mean he'll be tired, after delivering all those presents. He might not make it as far as Dent – not without help anyway,' Ivy said, then winked at Sally.

'He better blinking well do so. I've never been as good as I have been this year,' Ben exclaimed.

'Aye, well, you'll have to wait and see. Now, where's the next delivery to, Mother?' Bob said. 'The sooner we get home, the sooner I can take this van back to Jim Mattinson and then we can all concentrate on Christmas.' He kept his eye on the road as he turned up the hill onto the road to Gawthrop, knowing full well that the next delivery was at a farm called Dillicar, where they would all be made welcome again, as with all the drops that day.

'I'll be glad when we are back home and I can look after my own family, instead of making sure everyone else is right for Christmas. Next year, Bob Fothergill, there will be no turkey-rearing if I have my way,' Ivy said and closed her eyes. Sometimes Bob pushed her a little too far in his pursuit of possessing his own farm.

*   *   *

'Lord, Father, if you had supped another glass of whisky we would never have made it home,' Ivy lectured as Bob steered the van, rather erratically, into the yard at Daleside later on. 'I don't think you'll be fit to go out again – you want to give the dominoes drive a miss tonight. You'll not be able to count the spots, let alone know what's already been played.'

As they came to a halt outside the farmhouse they all breathed a sigh of relief, as the last few miles since the final stop at Hill Top, where Bob had been given an extra-large drink, had been hair-raising.

'There's nowt at all wrong with me, or my driving. You hold your noise and make sure my shirts are ironed, because I'm off out, no matter what you think,' he retorted as his family spilled out of the van and said nothing, except for exchanging quick glances, knowing that it was better to keep quiet than catch Bob's wrath after one too many drinks.

'It's already ironed and hanging up behind the bedroom door. Don't you forget you've to milk the cow, and you need some supper in you, if you will trail into Dent. Sally and me have enough to do, so don't rely on her to help milk tonight – nor Ben. He's to tidy his bedroom before your Stanley comes, and he'll want to decorate the tree this evening with Sally and me. It's a good job you brought it home the other day, else we'd have nowt to put up.' Ivy was cross with her husband; sometimes he could be so selfish. She was always scrimping and saving, never spending a penny that she shouldn't, but tonight Bob would think nothing of paying

25

for a round or two in the local pub while he played dominoes with his mates.

Sally looked at Ben as he struggled to carry all the presents they had been given, some of them wrapped and others hand-me-downs from children who had outgrown their use; and, best of all, a new brass threepenny bit or two to spend on sweets once Christmas had finished. She helped him carry the items through into the kitchen, and they both knew to make themselves scarce as they walked straight through to the main living room, out of the way of the argument that they knew was brewing.

'You could have said no to Matt Mason – you'd had more than your fill by the time we got to Hill Top. You could have killed us on the way back; you're not used to driving that van. What if we'd crashed? You would have been the first to moan at paying the bill to get Jim Mattinson's van mended,' Ivy growled as she saw to the coal fire and stirred the backed-up coals into life, before putting the kettle on to boil.

'I'm as right as rain, woman, so stop your moaning. I'll have a brew and then I'll get the milking done, have my supper and get out of your way. Then you'll happen be happy. You can get on with your Christmas. I don't know why you make such a fuss anyway – it's only another day,' Bob mumbled. 'You are never bloody happy.'

'Happen I'm never happy because this life is all about *you*. What if I'd like a night out with my friends, like I used to do before we were wed?' Ivy said and reached for the tea caddy from above the fire.

26

'Don't be stupid, woman. You are wed, and married women don't go to the pub. Now you are just being awkward. Forget brewing me a tea. I'll go and do the milking now, and you needn't bother with me any supper. There's pie and peas at The Sun tonight – it'll be better company there, and at least I'll not be lectured. Once I've milked the cow, I'll get changed and walk into Dent.' Bob stood in the doorway, not bothering to enter the kitchen. He knew he was the worse for drink, but he'd not let Ivy get the better of him. Best to go and keep out of the way until he'd sobered up a little or, better still, until he could have another drink with his mates.

'Suit yourself. I'll go and see to the decorations, which Ben and Sally can make until supper time. When you come back in and have had your supper, you'll find a new carbolic soap next to the wash jug. You'll have to take some hot water from the kettle, if you are having a shave. Mind you, don't cut yourself when you're looking at yourself in the mirror – I'd think you'll be seeing two of yourself, the state you are in,' Ivy said, with sarcasm heavy in her voice.

Bob said nothing as he closed the kitchen door and walked out into the dimming light of the winter's evening. He'd go and find an hour's peace in the barn and shippon, where no wagging tongue would bother him. It wasn't as if he drank that often; never usually through the day, and only on a Friday evening to be sociable and catch up with Dales news. Ivy didn't know how good she had it; she got to visit Kendal twice a year on the bus, and the nearby market town of

Sedbergh when he had business to do there. What more did she want? he thought, as he sought solace with his head resting on the side of the cow, while he mulled over his lot and tried to concentrate on the job of providing milk for the evening.

Ivy sat down in the chair next to the fire and looked into it as she supped her tea. Her mother had warned her Bob Fothergill had a mind of his own, and that she would never have a penny to her name once she got married and had children. However, she had been too head-over-heels in love with him to listen to her mother, who she thought knew nothing of being young. Had she not seen how handsome Bob was, with his dark hair, standing six foot two, with the bluest of eyes and more ambition than any other farm lad in the dale?

She wiped away a tear that was running down her cheek, remembering when her mother had bought her a winter coat and had commented that once family came along, Ivy wouldn't be able to buy herself one, which she had scoffed at. How true those words were. In fact the coat her mother had bought her sixteen years ago was still being worn and had just been taken off, after her ride up the dale. She'd been young and foolish back then, swept off her feet by the handsome Bob; and then she found herself pregnant by him – the pregnancy being a disgrace to the family, if he hadn't offered to marry her quickly.

Ivy remembered that her father had not talked to her for weeks, which had broken her heart, as she loved

28

her father and they had been so close until Bob entered her life. She remembered wondering why he hadn't been able to see that she was ready to be a wife and have her own family, even though she was only seventeen. She realized now why both her parents had been disappointed in her; she could have done so much better than marrying a farm lad with no farm of his own. After all, Jim Booth had offered to walk her home from many a dance in Dent Memorial Hall, as well as Ted Brunskill, and both owned their own farms, but they didn't have the looks or cheek of Bob Fothergill.

Ivy took her handkerchief from her pocket and blew her nose, then wiped away her tear. It was no good thinking of what might have happened. She had two wonderful children and a hard-working husband and she should be thankful for that, she thought, as she got up from her chair and headed for the pantry, bringing back with her enough potatoes for the three of them; after peeling them and putting them on to boil, she returned to carve seven slices of bacon from the flitch of home-cured bacon that hung from a hook in the pantry's ceiling. It was the family staple, as a pig was reared in the hull outside every year, and was slaughtered to keep them fed throughout the year. Along with the rabbits that both Bob and Ben caught, and the mutton they had to eat when Bob butchered a long-in-the-tooth sheep, that provided their main meals. With vegetables grown in the garden, and butter and milk from the family's cow, they were nearly self-sufficient.

However, as Ivy placed the rashers of bacon in the frying pan, she thought how lucky some of her friends were, who got treated to dinner in Metcalfe's tearooms down in Sedbergh. The closest she got to that was when she was waiting for Bob, when he had done his dealings at the auction on a Friday. She'd sit with some of her friends in the outside, partly protected meeting place – which was nicknamed the Monkey House because the seats in the small alcove were surrounded by metal bars, making the people within look like caged chimps – as they watched well-off locals giving Metcalfe's tea rooms their business. Occasionally Ivy would shop in there, especially at Christmas, for her spices and dried fruit, which Metcalfe's also supplied; and she always loved the smell of the freshly ground roasted coffee that customers frequently bought. She wished she could have a drink of that, instead of cheap Camp coffee, a thick black liquid of chicory and coffee beans, with a picture of a soldier in uniform upon it and an Indian standing by his side, from the days of the Raj. That she only used to make coffee cake, as she didn't enjoy the chicory that was the prominent taste and was nothing like real coffee.

Ivy stopped feeling sorry for herself as Sally walked in from the front room. Sally looked at her mother; she knew that sometimes she found life with her father hard. Words between them could often be heard through her bedroom wall, when Sally was trying her best to get to sleep. However, talking to her friend Marjorie, she had decided that it was not unusual for parents to argue. After all, making a living in the Dales was hard, and that was what her parents were usually arguing over. She smiled and tried to look unworried as she came into the kitchen.

'That's the paper chains made, Mam. Where's the drawing pins at? I'll stand on the chairs and pin them up. Same as last year, do you think? From corner to corner of the room, meeting in the middle at the ceiling light?' Sally asked. She watched her mother, knowing that the words said between her parents had been sharp and to the point. 'My father has set his head on going out, hasn't he, Mam? Although I'm glad, as he usually brings something home with him that he's won from playing dominoes. A nice box of chocolates would be more than welcome.' She hunted for drawing pins in the drawers of the oak dresser that stood along the back wall on the stone-flagged floor of the kitchen, while her mam pointed to where they could be found.

'Aye – and lines the landlord's pocket. Father would have something to say if I did the same. I suppose I shouldn't moan, as he isn't the heaviest drinker in the Dales and it is Christmas,' Ivy said as she turned the bacon in the pan, while it spat and shrank to half the size as the fat upon it melted. 'Lay the table, our Sally, before you put the paper chains up, there's a lass, and then after supper I'll help decorate the tree. Has Ben blown the balloons up? He usually likes that job, even though he sometimes looks like he's going to burst himself, with all the puffing he does. He can go and get some twigs of holly for the windowsills in the morning; it will keep him out from under our feet, as we will be busy all day. The holly tree up in the top field is laden with berries, so he's not far to go.'

'He likes that job, and it gets him out of our way, because I know you'll be busy and will need my help,'

Sally replied, as she took the knives and forks for their evening meal out of an old stoneware jam jar that had doubled up its usage, after being emptied of the four pounds of damson jam it had once held. She started to set the table.

'Aye, I'm hoping you will make me the stuffing and the apple sauce in the morning, and then I've not that to worry about on Christmas Day. And perhaps you could ice the Christmas cake? Lord knows, I'm late with that job this year.' Ivy reached for the potato masher and drained the potatoes, mashing them liberally with a knob of butter and a splash of the rich, creamy milk from the jug that Sally had placed on the table.

Both women looked at one another as the kitchen door opened and Bob walked in.

He placed a tin pail full of frothy new milk down by the sink. 'There's the house-milk, and the rest is in the kit for me to take to Pratt's in the morning. Are there any spare eggs I need to take with me?' Bob turned to his daughter.

'No, my mother will need them all over Christmas; the hens are not laying as well, with this cold weather,' Sally said quietly as she placed the salt and pepper from over the fireplace onto the pine kitchen table, which was scrubbed clean by her mother every morning. And she watched as her father pulled out his chair at the head of the table and sat down, deciding now that he would be better with some supper inside him before going drinking.

'You are sure none are laying where they shouldn't? We could do with an extra bob or two, especially now.

Although why you make such a big fuss of Christmas, Ivy, I don't know. It's just another day. Waste of hard-earned money, if you ask me,' Bob moaned as Ivy hastily laid another place and put the small amount of mashed potato onto his plate, as he sat in readiness for his supper, with his knife and fork in hand. 'Pour some of that bacon fat over my tatties – don't waste it woman,' he growled, as Ivy finished frying the eggs and put the frying pan to one side.

'It's fatty enough, without you adding more. Perhaps next year you'll think of killing the pig a bit earlier and then the bacon's a bit leaner,' Ivy said, then yelled through for Ben to join them at the table for his supper.

'I'll take mine and sit and eat it in the front room on my knee,' Ben said quietly, knowing that his father would not agree, but wanting to keep on blowing up the balloons out of his father's way.

'You will not – you'll sit and eat your meal with us. Just like the family we are. The kitchen table's here for eating on, and nowhere else is, do you hear me?' Bob said crossly and stared at Ben, as he pulled up his chair to the table and sat with his head bowed.

Supper at the kitchen table was eaten in silence, as everyone knew better than to challenge Bob. Both children watched as he ate every mouthful and they hoped for a quick escape.

'Have you two finished now?' Ivy asked. 'If you have, then pass me those plates and get yourselves into the front room and start to decorate the tree, while I wash up.' She knew they wanted to get away from the atmosphere in the kitchen. 'I'll be in with you in a while. Leave the fairy for us all to put upon the top of the tree.' She smiled and watched as both Sally and Ben left the table and went into the front room as quickly as they could.

'Bob, you take the water that's boiled in the kettle up with you for a wash, and then I know you are done and can be on your way. I'm going to put our turkey into the fireside oven for an hour or two while the fire is decent. I like to make sure it is well done – there's nowt worse than blood running out, when you cut into it, and thinking that you are going to be poorly after eating it.'

Ivy walked into the pantry and reckoned to be busy organizing her shelves as she heard Bob's chair getting pushed back, and the creak of the stair floorboards as he made his way up to his bedroom to wash and shave. She'd make herself busy until he had left the house. Tomorrow, when he had had his fill of drink and knew that he'd only half a day to work for Jim Mattinson, she hoped Bob would be in a better mood, else Christmas was going to have no joy in it.

She looked at the turkey gazing at her from the slate bink of the pantry. She didn't fancy eating it, but hopefully once it was cooked she'd forget the smell of its innards and what it had looked like when it arrived as a chick. She sympathized with Ben; he was the softer of her children, he took after her, and she'd have to make sure his spirit was not knocked out of him by Bob's hard words. She knew that he loved both his children, but Bob could be hard and unforgiving; and no matter how he tried, if Ben was no farmer she knew that Bob would always hold it against him, no matter what.

Ivy carried the turkey into the kitchen and placed it in the large roasting dish that was only used at Christmas; it had been a present from her aunty on her and Bob's wedding day and was of good quality. It was cream enamel with dimples in the bottom, which were supposed to help tenderize the meat, with handles and a lid that had green piping around the edges. It was really heavy, and felt even heavier as she placed into it the turkey that would keep her family fed. Pulling up the loose skin on the bird and filling it with butter, she then covered the turkey with slices of cured bacon that she had sliced from the flitch. She placed the lid over the bird and carried it to the fireside oven. Soon the whole house would smell of roasting turkey as it cooked, long and slow. The Belling oven that she used for everyday cooking was not large enough to handle the Christmas bird, so Ivy was glad that there was still the Yorkshire range in her kitchen, which she often used especially for meat and milk puddings that took no watching.

'Right, I'm off. I'll not be late – I've work in the morning and our Stanley will be landing, so it'll be a few late nights over Christmas.' Bob stood and put his trilby on his head.

'Right, see that you aren't, and don't get too drunk. And if there's a box of chocolates in the raffle, choose them, although I've already got one box for our Sally, but Ben would like a box as well.' Ivy straightened up from putting the turkey in the oven. Looking at Bob, she still saw the handsome man she had fallen in love with, standing washed and shaved, and dapper in a clean shirt and best breeches. His hair was starting to grey, but so was hers – life and children did that to you.

'Aye, I will. If there's owt that I think might suit them, I'll choose that. I've taken a pound out of the turkey money, and all the rest is in the tin box under the bed. We've made a pretty penny, lass. I know it's been work for both of us, but it's been worth it,' Bob said as he made for the door. He hesitated for a minute and then turned. 'I couldn't do all this without you, Ivy. We will have our own farm one day. And I only got a bit drunk – if you think about it, it'll have saved us money tonight. I'm not right bothered if I have a beer or two or not, this evening.'

'I'm sure you'll manage an odd'un. Now get yourself gone, as the codgers will be waiting for you, and I and the children have a tree to decorate.' Ivy smiled; that was as close to an apology as Bob would get, and well she knew it.

'Aye, don't wait up, but I know you will.' Bob stepped out into the sharp winter's air to the village of Dent and the warmth of The Sun inn, where he and his cronies would sit in the snug and play dominoes, and join in the raffle in the hope of winning something to make their Christmas more special.

Ivy watched him go and then turned to join her children. No matter how poor the family were, they would make this time special, with paperchains hanging from the ceiling and balloons in bunches in each corner of the room, and the Christmas tree taking centre-stage, decorated with glass baubles and silver tinsel and standing tall next to the window.

'By, don't we look grand. You two have been busy.' Ivy smiled. 'It looks like I'm just in time to put the fairy on the top of the tree.'

Sally picked up the fairy, which was looking a bit worse for wear, after she had made it from a cake doily when she was several years younger. 'Yes, Mam, we've kept it just for you to place, and then we know it's Christmas.

'Then here, let's do it. The tree's a bit smaller this year, so I can easily reach.' Ivy took the hand-made fairy and carefully balanced it on the upright spike of the fir tree and then stood back. 'There, she will look after us all Christmas now. Let's light the fire and, Ben, you get the Snakes and Ladders board out of the cupboard. I've time to join in a game before you go to bed.'

'Are you sure, Mam? We never light the fire in this room unless it's a special day.' Sally looked shocked, as Ben rushed to the drawers where the only game they owned was kept.

'I'm sure, as your father's having a good night out. We can sit in warmth and enjoy ourselves – after all, it's nearly Christmas. And I'll make us all a good mug of cocoa to go with a biscuit before bed. I've been thinking, Sally, do you want to go to the dance on New Year's Eve at Dent village hall? You've got to that age when it's time to go out and meet new folk. I was about your age when I spotted your father for the first time,' Ivy said quietly as she watched Ben place the Snakes and

Ladders game out on the table while she scrunched up newspaper and placed kindling sticks upon it, and a few pieces of dry coal from the scuttle, before putting a light to it. And then she smiled at the look on Sally's face.

'Really, Mam, do you think I could? What would my father say? Marjorie asked me to go with her, but I said no because I didn't think I'd be allowed.' Sally beamed.

'Never mind about your father – leave him to me. It's time for you to go; he forgets how old you are. There's a dress in my wardrobe that I'll alter this next evening or two. I've hardly worn it and if I take it in at the waist, you'll look really grand in it. And you can borrow my pearls as long as you don't break them – not that they are real or worth much,' Ivy continued. And then she felt Sally's arms around her, when she bent down and hugged her mother as she watched the newly lit flames leap and make the front room fill the home with love and warmth.

'Thanks, Mam, I did really want to go, but daren't ask. Nearly everybody my age is going and I didn't want to be left out.' Sally stood up with her mother and felt her heart beating fast: her first dance; how she had wanted to go, but daren't even mention it to her parents.

'Are you two going to join me and play Snakes and Ladders or what? I'm red, by the way, and I've already thrown a six,' Ben said and looked at his mother and sister getting excited over what he thought to be a stupid dance.

'You have not, you little cheat. You can start again with Mam and me, and we will watch you like a hawk,

38

so count the squares correctly, else we won't play with you,' Sally replied quickly.

'I don't cheat, and I have thrown a six, so there.' Ben stuck out his tongue.

'Never mind. Come on, my turn, and no more cheating,' Ivy said and tousled Ben's hair as she sat down at the table to take part in the Christmas party game. Tomorrow she would be busy preparing food and seeing to everyone's needs, but tonight she would enjoy being with her two children in the warmth and comfort of her home.

'Your feet are as cold as cobbles, Father,' Ivy commented as Bob slipped under the bedcovers next to her and warmed his feet upon her.

'Aye, it's a bit parky out there – there's a frost on everything. It's a good job I've lagged all the outside water pipes,' Bob said as he put his arm around her.

'Have you had a good night? Was there many at your dominoes drive? You smell of whisky!' Ivy replied as she turned and patted her pillow and looked at him.

'Tha'll say I've had a right good night: I won top prize in the dominoes. Our Ben will be over the moon. I've won that aeroplane he's been talking about in Dinsdale's window, and the vicar's wife had donated it, of all people. I've put it on top of the wardrobe out of his way, along with a pair of silk stockings, although they'll be no good to anybody.'

'You've done well, and you are wrong – our Sally will love the stockings. I've told her she can go to the New Year's dance; she's at that age, Bob, she's growing up.

That'll make them both have a good Christmas.' Ivy hoped that Bob would not argue about their daughter going to her first dance.

'A dance at her age! Bloody hell, where's the years gone, Ivy? I remember looking at you across that dance hall, and now our lass is going. And to make things worse, I've still not got my own farm – you could have done so much better for yourself. Are you sure she's old enough to go? She's still only a young lass to me.'

'She's old enough, Bob. And you'll get your farm one day. Now stop your banter and go to sleep. Morning will be here all too soon.' Ivy sighed.

Bob looked up at the ceiling. Life was going too fast for him; his family were growing up and he seemed to get no nearer his one ambition in life. To make things worse, everybody had been talking about how hard things were, and the worsening times abroad, at the dominoes match. Bad times were coming, and he would have to protect his family even more if they were to survive.

Chapter 3

Christmas Eve was a busy time, which Ivy hated for being hard work but also loved. It enabled her to show the world how much she cherished her family and to display her cookery skills. The kitchen was awash with the smells of Christmas as Ivy made sage-and-onion stuffing and apple sauce, and finished off cooking the turkey in readiness for that evening's supper and for the Christmas Day dinner.

Ben had already been up to the back pasture for the holly needed to decorate the windowsills. The holly berries, shining red and ripe, balanced on each downstairs window ledge and he had also hung a bunch from the front door's knocker, before he was sent to collect the much-needed eggs for all the baking that was taking place in the warm, welcoming kitchen. Knowing that he was only going to be in the way of his sister and mother on his return, he had decided to go and collect some sticks from the nearby hedges for kindling, for the house fires. At least that way he would be in his father's good books for once.

Sally was busy icing the Christmas cake that her mother had covered with almond paste, but now it needed the crowning glory of a make-believe snow-scene upon it, with painted children sledging and skating in strategic places, along with a small, wiry Christmas tree edged with snow, and gold-paper lettering wishing everyone a 'Happy Christmas'. She loved the feel of the kitchen, and was warm and content as she stood back and surveyed her handiwork.

'There, what do you think, Mam? Do you think it looks good enough?' The icing had been made especially thick, so that the snow peaks stood up strong and proud, as if the figures were sledging through snowdrifts.

'It looks grand, Sally. There's a cake ribbon in the top drawer of the dresser to finish it off. Fasten it with a blob of icing in between the layers.' Ivy watched as Sally went to the drawer, which held all sorts of bits and bobs that were occasionally used in the kitchen, and fished out a green-fringed paper ribbon with a gold band on it, which had been used in previous years, and wrapped it around the cake. 'That's another job done. Now, do you fancy making some mince pies before your Uncle Stanley descends upon us? He's rather partial to a mince pie. I usually make at least three batches before he goes home.'

'And he likes pickled onions. Can you remember when Ben watched him take the last one out of the jar and told him, in no uncertain manner, that he had eaten them all. I thought Father was going to lose his temper, but in the end he just laughed. Especially when Uncle Stanley took the onion out of his mouth and offered it to Ben.' Sally reached across the table for the flour and salt, and started to mix the pastry that was needed for the mince pies. 'Then he took out his false teeth and grinned at Ben. I'll never forget his face, because he thought Uncle Stanley's teeth were real.'

'He teases Ben, as he knows he can get away with it, poor man. It's a wonder Stanley has a bit of humour left in him, after what he's been through. Left for dead in the trenches of the Somme and then found by the Germans, who put him back together as best they could, before making him a prisoner of war. He'll not have a bad word said about the Germans; he said they were all cannon fodder, just like our lads were. Not that Stanley mentions the war to hardly anybody,' Ivy said as she creamed the butter and sugar together for her trifle sponge, then put her hands on her hips as she reached for one of the eggs that Ben had brought in.' She sighed. 'Your father has made me short of eggs for my baking; he took what there was in the house this morning, along with the kit of milk, to Pratt's at Sedbergh. If there is a penny to be made, he'll make it, despite us having to go short.'

Sally smiled as she put the home-made mincemeat into her tarts, after rubbing in the pastry and rolling it out thinly, before cutting it with the biscuit-cutter, which she hazily remembered her grandmother showing her how to use when she was small. 'I heard my father come back

43

in last night. He didn't sound worse for wear – not like when he came back from delivering the turkeys.'

'No, he'd have to spend money to get that drunk again, and he'd not do that.' Ivy grinned. 'I did take advantage of him being a bit merry to tell him you were going to the New Year's dance at Dent. Surprisingly, he hardly argued, so he must realize that you are old enough to go nowadays.'

'I thought he'd not let me go, and I'm so glad he is going to. I'll run across and tell Marjorie when we have finished the baking. She will be so glad we are going together, although I hope she doesn't leave me standing like a gooseberry, as she's sweet on Jonathan Birbeck, and I think he is on her. I don't know why – I think he is awful.'

'There's plenty of time for lads, Sally. You are not sixteen until June, and that Marjorie Harper has only just turned it. Neither of you should throw yourself at the first boy who comes along. I sometimes wish I had listened to my mother and gone for money, not for looks; good looks don't pay the bills or keep a roof over your head. So think on that, when you are giving your heart to the lad who will no doubt come along all too soon.'

Ivy stopped short as the kitchen door opened, and decided to continue her conversation with her daughter when they were both alone.

'I didn't expect you home so soon – it's not even eleven yet,' she exclaimed as Bob entered the kitchen and took his cap off, then pulled a chair up to the kitchen table. 'Jim Mattinson must be going soft in his old age.'

'I'd done all there was to do. I'd cleaned out his calf sheds and foddered his sheep, so he said I could get away. It's not as if I've nothing to do here myself. I borrowed his van again to pick up our Stan; it saved him walking here from Gawthrop, as he's getting worse at his walking and it wasn't out of my way, as Jim asked me to pick up some hen feed from Dent. I dropped Stan off at the bottom of the lane and then took the van back to him.'

'So where's Stan now?' Ivy asked as she put a pot of hot tea in front of her husband and hoped that both men would not get under her and Sally's feet too much before they had finished the baking.

'He's out in the yard with Ben. You'll never guess what he's brought us for Christmas, the silly bugger. I've told him that he must have more brass than sense. Lord knows how it's going to work, as we have no plugs.' Bob shook his head and looked at his womenfolk.

Both Sally and Ivy stared at Bob. 'What? What has he brought?' Ivy asked as she stopped in her tracks.

'Stanley's brought a radio, Mam, and he says it's ours to keep – look, look, isn't it posh. That's the best Christmas present we could ever have.' Ben nearly fell into the kitchen, followed by Stanley, who was carrying the latest technology in the form of a Philips radio.

Stan, standing tall and immaculately dressed as ever, took off his trilby hat and smiled. Years of serving in the army had made him careful of his appearance, but his face told another story: the pain and hurt of his past life had made him look older than he was. 'I thought it was time I thanked you for all the times you have had me

45

here over Christmas, and I know you will all enjoy listening to it.' Stan placed the box of delights upon the kitchen table and the whole family stared at it.

'What does that dial do?' Sally asked.

'That's for the sound and volume, and that one is for the different radio stations. Look, you can pick up the BBC Broadcasting Corporation national programmes and even international ones, if you can understand a word they are saying. You just turn the dial until you find something you like,' Stan said as they all gazed at the piece of technology in disbelief.

'That's all well and good, our Stan, but we've no plugs. When we rented here, old Turner had only put in the electric light and a box for a cooker, as he wasn't going to spend any more money than he needed to. So it's not a bit of good,' Bob replied and sat back down in his chair.

'That's where you're wrong, Father. Uncle Stanley has put this lead on, so that we can plug it into the light socket.' Ben grinned as he showed everybody the lead that connected into the light socket. 'We can listen to the radio all day. It says in this magazine that Uncle Stanley has brought with him that there's *Snow White and the Seven Dwarfs* on just before bedtime tonight. Can I listen to it, Mam, please? Please, I really want to.'

'We'll see, Ben. It might not work.' Ivy held her breath while Stan, even though his legs were badly injured from his war experience, stood on one of the kitchen chairs, took the light bulb out of its socket and plugged in the radiogram.

'Switch it on, Sal, let's see if it works,' Stan said as she made for the light switch. And then he turned the on-and-off knob and stood back, as a posh London accent filled the humble kitchen. 'Just missed the eleven o'clock news, but in time for the weather – listen, Bob. Sounds like we are going to be in for some snow.'

'It'll be wrong; he's talking about London, not up here, and they take fright at the first snowflake.' Bob was determined not to show any interest in the new toy that his brother had brought the family.

'Doesn't he talk posh, like he's got a mouthful of marbles?' Sally said and looked at her mother.

'That's the Queen's English, my lass – posh folk talk like that,' Ivy replied. 'Here, listen, he's telling you the farming weather, Bob. That'll be a good help for you.'

'It will if he gets it right. I keep telling you, woman, he'll not know owt about up here,' Bob said, but took a sudden interest when he heard the presenter announce heavy snow along the back of the Pennines and into Scotland. 'I'll just gather and look at my sheep and bring them down into the top pasture. I was thinking of doing that anyway, before we had dinner. That's nowt to do with what he has just said.'

He stood up and shook his head, as he observed his family trying out the many stations they could find, instead of offering to help him or getting on with their own jobs. Nowt would get done now, he thought, as he closed the kitchen door and whistled to his sheepdog, Spot, to gather up the small flock of forty sheep and bring them down nearer the house. He'd have done it anyway, without a posh voice in London telling him what the weather was going to bring. The clouds had looked threatening all morning and he'd known snow was coming, without being told by someone who he doubted had ever set foot in Yorkshire.

'There will be no making sense of that lot in there now, Spot.' Bob patted his faithful dog as she ran around the corner of the barn and stopped by his side. 'Let's be away. I'd rather be up the fell than listening to the rubbish that will come out of that box. I'd have thought our Stan would have had more sense – it'll have cost him a bob or two to buy, and it'll cost me electric and all.'

Spot gazed at him faithfully with her doe-eyes and then ran ahead up the fellside, as Bob strode out, opening the gate and following the well-trodden path that led to the top of the fell and to the allotment where the sheep that were already in lamb were grazing. The climb was steep, but Bob was wiry and fit and used to the walk. The sheep were grazing in singles and groups, as Bob sent his dog to do the job of herding them.

'Get out, lass.' He whistled directions known only to the shepherd and his dog as the sheep were rounded up into a manageable group. Except for one, which stood her ground and stamped her foot in protest at being moved from her eating ground. 'Get on, you stubborn old bugger. You'll thank me when there's six inches of snow up here and you are safe down in the pasture.'

Bob watched as Spot snapped at the awkward old ewe's heels and got her to toe the line and wander down the same way as the rest, knowing where they were going, after years of the same route, down to better eating in the pastures. Bob leaned on his walking stick and watched

48

as his faithful sheepdog kept them all in line. A snowflake fluttered down onto his face and he pulled his jacket around him. The air was fresh and biting, but the view from the fell top was one he'd never tire of. The Lake District hills were already covered with snow and, looking up towards Dent and Cowgill, he could see that the sky was heavy and grey and that snow was already falling further up the dale. It was going to be a white Christmas – and a noisy one, thanks to his brother. He'd have been more at home up on the fell than having to join in with all the frivolity of the season.

Spot barked as the flock reached the gateway to the pasture, reminding Bob to get on with his job.

'Aye, I'm coming, lass. It seems a man can never have any peace, not even from his dog,' he growled as he walked quickly down the fellside and opened the gate that led into the bottom pasture for the sheep to pass through, with Spot barking at their heels. 'Aye, get in, you old devil,' Bob said to the ewe that had shown her own mind. 'You'll be thanking me in the morning, you'll see.'

He tied the gate and whistled for Spot as he walked back towards home. Just the milking of the cows to be done now; the next few days would be a welcome break for him, too, he thought as he placed Spot in the aged beer-barrel that was her kennel and entered back into the warmth of the family kitchen. Peace had been regained, and Ivy looked up from her baking as he walked through the door.

'Got the sheep down alright, have you? Sally said she would have helped, if you'd asked.' Ivy patted her hands free of flour and looked at her husband.

'Nay, it's right – me and the dog managed. Where is everybody at?' Bob asked as he sat down in his chair and unlaced his boots, emptying the many hayseeds onto the hearthside pegged rug, as Ivy scowled at him. 'It's going to come some snow. It looks like a blizzard further up the dale.'

'Ben is with your Stanley, and Sally won't be long; she's just gone across the field to Marjorie's house, to tell her she's allowed to go to the dance,' Ivy replied as she put the last batch of mince pies into the electric oven to bake. 'Both are over-excited, and that radio Stan brought has made their Christmas. They've plugged it into the light socket in the front room now, and at least there it is out of my way, here in the kitchen.'

'Are you alright? Have we got everything we need, if it comes a lot of snow? Our Stanley can take some feeding, as you know.' Bob sat back and lit his pipe with a spill taken from the holder in the fireplace; he felt contented as he watched his beloved Ivy in control of the kitchen, and smelt the comforting aroma of her Christmas baking.

'Aye. The pantry is full, and if worst comes to the worst, we'll live on turkey and bacon, because we have enough of both. Although I'm short of eggs at the moment. You shouldn't have taken what we had to Pratt's this morning, as I needed them for my baking. Ben could only find four.' Ivy sighed, then sat down at the table and looked at Bob.

'They paid me for what they owed for the milk and eggs this morning. They also asked me if I wanted to drive for them, collecting milk up Garsdale to take to the dairy at Hawes, starting in the New Year.' Bob watched as Ivy started to tidy her table and then decided that what her husband was saying was more important.

'And what do you think? You can't farm here, work for Jim Mattinson and Pratt's. It just can't be done, and you'd be jiggered.'

'I know, I thought I might leave Jim Mattinson. Once I've collected the milk from up the Dales in a morning, the day will be my own. It makes more sense, although I don't really want to let Jim down, as he's been good to us all these years.'

'Well, at least you've got time to think about it over Christmas. The extra money would be welcome, but you'd be tied to your job every day. What if we had a sheep lambing and in trouble this spring? You'd be needed then, and you'd be no good halfway up Garsdale in Pratt's milk wagon.'

'Ben's growing up, and there's you and Sally to help. It's too good to turn down, but I need to think about it. So don't say owt to anybody yet.' Bob noticed the expression on Ivy's face; she was not happy with the news, but it would mean more brass and more security.

'Sometimes money isn't everything, Bob. You've got a steady job with Jim Mattinson and he's good to us. There's not many that would have lent their van and given you this morning off. I think I'd think twice about working for Pratt's dairy. Our Sally would relish the chance to help more, I know she would, but if there's a difficult lambing she might struggle.' Ivy checked the oven and hoped that, for the family's sake and not for the money, Bob wouldn't take the job he'd been offered.

'Aye, well, I'm thinking about it. Whatever I do, it'll be for the best for all of us,' he replied, putting an end to the conversation as he stirred the fire with the poker and added more coal.

'I never thought your father would let you go to the dance. Your mother must have really stuck up for you,' petite, blonde-haired Marjorie Harper said to her best friend, Sally, in the front room of Beckside, the neighbouring farm to Daleside, as she manicured her nails.

Marjorie was, as Ivy called her, a little forward. Although only six months older than Sally, she already had her head set on catching a wealthy farm lad; or, if not wealthy and local, one who could sweep her off her feet and show her the wonders of the world.

'Well, he has, I can't believe it myself. I must admit, I'm only going to believe it when I'm in that hall and I'm enjoying myself. Anyway, Uncle Stanley has made Christmas for us already – he brought a radio with him. You should have seen my father's face. It'll never be turned off, when he's not about.' Sally watched as Marjorie blew on the tips of her fingers after filing them and crossed her legs, copying the famous film stars that she gazed relentlessly at in *Film Weekly*, an expense that Sally's parents would never allow.

'We've had our radio for nearly a year now. There's never anything I like on it. Now, if we could pick radio stations from America, I might listen to it more. Jonathan says that I shouldn't listen to that rubbish, but I don't care; he knows nothing about music anyway,' Marjorie said. She crossed her legs again and looked at Sally.

'I thought you were sweet on Jonathan. That he could do no wrong, no matter what he says?' Sally commented, flicking through the latest copy of *Film Weekly*, which was on the table next to her.

'He's alright, apart from he smells of carbolic soap all the time, and mothballs when he wears that awful green jacket his mother dresses him in. Anyway, never mind me. When are you going to find yourself a boyfriend? I've seen Harry Huddleston looking at you and you've completely ignored him. Maybe this will give him the chance to ask for a dance with you, and then who knows where it could end.' Marjorie grinned and squashed up next to her best friend on the settee, then glanced at the film star Sally was looking at. 'Isn't James Cagney so handsome? I wish Jonathan looked like him. I would happily put up with the smell of carbolic and mothballs to be on his arm.'

'Harry Huddleston is far too old for me, and besides he's courting Susan Winn. I don't want a boyfriend yet anyway.' Sally turned the next page of the magazine, to a picture of Clark Gable. 'Now he's handsome – a lot better than James Cagney,' she said as she showed Marjorie.

'Oh, he'll never be anybody. I've never heard of him. You have the most terrible taste in men. You need to be looking at them, Sally, else all the best ones in the dale will get snapped up. And let's face it, you could really do with one who has money,' Marjorie said with a hint of malevolence. Sally was always getting compliments from the boys, despite not taking care of her looks. Unlike Marjorie herself, who went to bed every evening with night cream on her face and kept her nails immaculately. In fact if she could have her own way, she might even have a perm done for the New Year's Eve dance, and then she would look exactly like one of the actresses in her magazine.

'I tell you, I'm not interested. And I'd better be getting home. It's dinnertime and my father and Uncle Stan are there; my mother will be waiting for me.' Sally pulled on her coat, which she had put on the chair back. 'Hope you have a good Christmas – your house looks ready for it anyway,' she said, as she noticed the bowl of fruit and the bottles of drink out on the sideboard, and the many decorations bedecking the walls. The Harpers were much better off than her family, owning their own farm and never seeming to go without anything. 'I've brought you this; don't open it until tomorrow, though.' Sally reached into her pocket for the small parcel covered in Christmas wrapping paper. 'It's only something I made, but it's pretty. I hope you like it.'

'I'm sure I will, and here is my present to you.' Marjorie reached for an apple from the fruit dish. 'A lovely rosy apple. My mam said they cost a fortune at Dinsdale's, so I hope you enjoy it.'

'Thank you, I'll keep it until tomorrow,' Sally said graciously. That was typical of Marjorie, who'd not bothered with a present, even though they were best friends. Hers might only be a home-made brooch, created out of a fir cone with the skeletons of dried-out holly leaves glued onto it, along with a safety pin and some glitter, but it had been made with love. A lot more love than an apple taken from a fruit bowl. Perhaps she should listen to *Snow White and the Seven Dwarfs* on the new radio tonight; happen she could find some similarities between the Wicked Queen and Marjorie, she thought, as she put the apple in her pocket and ran across the adjoining fields, with snow falling heavily and covering the surrounding hillsides. It was how a Christmas should feel, Sally thought, as she entered the warmth of her home and sat down with her family around the table, while her mother served the cold sliced ham that had been cooked specially for Christmas.

The evening soon descended. Bob went about milking the cow and checking his sheep, and Ben and Sally sat down in the front room with the fire lit and the radio playing. They had all enjoyed a special supper and now, as their father returned from his jobs, and their mother finished hers for the day, with Uncle Stanley joining them in the glow of the firelight, it did feel as if it was truly a magical time. Even Bob was enthralled by the radio pantomime and did not reprimand Ben for being late to bed, as the programme finished and Ivy gave the order for him to get to bed, before Father Christmas caught him still up and awake.

'I'll take you up the stairs to Bedfordshire,' Stan said as he got up from his chair and winced because his legs had gone stiff with sitting. 'I've still some stuff to unpack, so I'll do it while you are getting to sleep.'

'Thanks, Uncle Stanley, I'd like that. Do you think you could tell me a story while I get to sleep?' Ben said and made for the stairs, with Stanley following him.

'Happen tomorrow night – it's late enough; you need to get to sleep,' Ivy shouted as she watched the two of them go up the stairs. There was enough to do once Ben and Sally were in their beds, and the sooner that came, the better.

Once in his pyjamas, Ben quickly got into his bed. The lino underneath his feet was cold, and there were already the creeping fingers of Jack Frost on the bedroom windows, so he pulled the blankets up around him and watched Uncle Stanley unpack his small suitcase for his few nights' stay with his brother. Stanley placed his spotlessly polished shoes underneath the washstand, and arranged his soap and flannel over the washing dish and urn, along with his cut-throat razor. Then he placed a small box containing his new clean shirt collars; he would fit a new one each morning on his round-necked shirt with a stud. Uncle Stanley was a man of habit, taught well by the strict rules and regulations of the British Army. His shoes were always polished, he was clean-shaven and his shirt was clean and ironed. He was the exact opposite of his father, Ben thought, as he watched his uncle place his suitcase under the bed across the other side of the bedroom, then sit on the bed, raising his trouser ends and rubbing the legs that gave him so much pain.

'They are a right mess, aren't they, lad? Scars of war. That's where the Hun put a shell in me and then dug it

56

out again,' Stan said as he saw Ben watching him from under the covers, noticing the half of his leg that was virtually missing. 'Still, it's better than being six foot under, like some of my mates are. Be thankful for small mercies – that's what I say – and let's hope that the idiots who run the world learned a lesson, but I doubt they did.' Stan pulled his trouser legs back down and stood up. 'Now get yourself to sleep, else there will be nowt at the bottom of the bed, if the big man can't deliver your presents,' he said softly. He looked down at his nephew and hoped he would never have to go through what he himself had experienced on the Western Front.

'I will, Uncle Stanley. Goodnight. Can you leave my little paraffin lamp on until I've gone to sleep, as I don't like the dark?' Ben looked across at the blue paraffin lamp that was always kept alight, until he knew no different. It was his comfort in the darkness of the night.

'Aye, I'll keep it on, lad. I'm not keen on the dark myself, so you're alright. Now to sleep.'

'I never heard your Stanley last night. He must have had a good sleep, thank heavens, else he would have woken Ben, and then he'd have seen his pillowcase of presents too early,' Ivy said to Bob on Christmas morning, as he got out of bed while she pulled on her skirt. 'Ben must still be asleep, else he would have wandered in here by now, especially with that aeroplane you got him. I can't wait to see his face, and that of Sally when she sees her stockings.

'Stockings at fifteen! I've been thinking about what you said. I think she's a bit too young for going to that

57

dance – she might get up to all sorts.' Bob pulled up his braces and walked to the window, then rubbed a small patch of the pane free of frost. 'It's come some snow through the night, by the looks of it. I'd better get a move on; everything will be twice the work this morning.'

'You let her go, Bob, and don't you be spoiling her Christmas,' Ivy said, as he pulled on his jumper over the top of his shirt and then put on his jacket and grunted in reply. 'I'll go down and light the fire and get everything warm, before everybody else is stirring, and make some porridge for breakfast. It's lovely when they both come down and open their pillowcases in front of the fire – I love seeing their faces.' She watched as Bob led the way downstairs, then sat and put on his boots while she stoked the fire into action.

'I'll get the cow milked and then I'll be in for my breakfast before I check the sheep. The water outside will be frozen over, so that's going to make things harder, watering and feeding, so I might be a bit longer than usual.' Bob shivered. 'By, its bloody cold this morning, even in here with the fire banked up.' He reached for his kitel, the leather over-jacket that hung on its peg, and shook his head as he went to the door, opening it to let an icy blast come into the back kitchen, plus the sight of a good three inches of snow all over the yard and the surrounding fields and dales. 'It's a firesider today, so the sooner I get all done, the better. It's a good job that it's Christmas Day and nobody is stirring about the dale, and everything's down in the fields near home or inside.'

Ivy sighed as Bob went out of the door. She hoped he wasn't going to change his mind about Sally going to the New Year's dance, as she'd promised her daughter and she wasn't going to go back on her word. She cleared the ashes of both fires quickly, then started the new fire going in the sitting room for the Christmas Day frivolities, and built up the smouldering fire in the kitchen before starting to make the porridge for everyone's breakfast. It was just what they needed on a cold day to keep warm, until the house warmed through. As she laid the kitchen table she heard footsteps running about upstairs. The fun was about to start, as she heard Ben yelling and running into his sister's bedroom.

'He's up and he's full of it,' Stan said as he entered the kitchen quietly and sat at the kitchen table. 'I've never heard a voice so loud, when he ripped into his main present and found the box with the Lancaster inside it. I'd have liked that, when I was his age. It must have cost a bit; our Bob must have hated paying with his brass for that.'

'He didn't pay for it – not that Ben knows, but Bob won it in the doms match at The Sun, along with a pair of silk stockings for our Sally. Although he thinks she's not old enough for them.' Ivy smiled and put a cup of tea in front of Stan.

'She's growing up; they both are. Time goes so fast.' Stan smiled at his sister-in-law. If his brother hadn't courted her, he would have been sorely tempted, for Ivy was a good woman – too good for his penny-pinching brother, who was not adept at showing his affection to anybody. If it had not been for the war he had been drawn into, Ivy would have been *his* wife, of that Stan was sure. 'It doesn't seem that long since we were both her age, and I was looking at you from the other side of the dance hall, dancing in my brother's arms,' he said and touched Ivy's arm lightly.

'I know. I sometimes wonder where the time has gone, and what I would do if I had it back again,' Ivy replied softly and looked at Stan, who she knew had always been sweet on her. If only she hadn't been engaged to Bob when Stan's girlfriend left him high and dry because of his injuries, things might have been so different. Sometimes she did wonder if she had married the wrong brother, for Stan was a lot more caring than Bob. But life was what she had made it, and she had to get on with her lot.

'You know I'll always be here for you, Ivy. I know things are not happy sometimes between you and my brother, but you understand that I cannot come between you both,' Stan said quietly and watched the flush come to his sister-in-law's cheeks. 'Whoo – gird your loins, here they come!' He grinned at the sound of heavy feet running down the stairs.

'Mam! Mam, guess what Father Christmas has brought me? Look, Mam, look! I bet everyone at school will be jealous of me. Tommy Brooksbank really wanted it, and so did Roger Clough, when we all saw it in Dinsdale's window.' Ben ran around the kitchen, ducking and diving with his aeroplane in his hand, making engine noises and pretending its guns were firing. 'I can't believe it's mine. And Father brought me a new box of dominoes and an apple and orange. I've never had such a good Christmas.'

He ran into the front room and swooped around in there, before coming back to sit down at the breakfast table, and grinned at his Uncle Stan.

'Tha's been spoilt rotten, young man. That can only have been made not long ago, as it's only just come into use in the RAF. Planes have come a long way in the last few years, but then again our lads might be needing them, the way the world is looking,' Stan said softly and looked at Ivy. 'It's a good job he's this young, Ivy; at least he'll not be asked to join up or enlist.

'Whisht now, Stan, it'll not come to that again. And let's not talk about such on Christmas Day.' Ivy scowled and then lifted her head and watched Sally as she came downstairs into the kitchen. 'Morning, love. Has he been to you and all, or did he forget you this year?' Ivy winked at her daughter, knowing full well that Sally still played along with Father Christmas visiting, to keep things special for her brother.

'Yes, he's been, Mam, and I'm so happy with the stockings he has left me. I don't know if I'll ever dare wear them, though. And the small bottle of Devon Violets perfume is lovely, as well as the chocolates, which I'll share with everyone.' Sally blushed slightly as she mentioned the stockings in front of her uncle.

'You are growing up, lass. I'll be coming to your wedding before I know it, but not too soon, I hope.' Stan winked and watched as his niece looked out of the kitchen window.

'It's come some snow, and it has been so cold through the night. Will my father want any help out there?' Sally asked and looked at her coat, hanging up behind the back door. But really she wanted to go into the living room with her bowl of porridge and open the small presents still awaiting them under the tree.

'No, he's right, our Sal. He's only doing what needs to be done and then he's coming straight in. All's seen to and safe. Once he's milked and fed all, he'll be in, as even your father believes in enjoying Christmas Day. Now sit down and I'll give you your breakfast. And then go into the front room; the fire is lit, it'll soon warm through and then we'll stay in here and there for most of the day. The kitchen will be the warmest place in the house when everything gets cooking for our dinner.'

'Can we not go into the living room and have our breakfasts, please, Mam? It's what we usually do,' Sally said, as her mother spooned the steaming porridge into bowls and put it in front of them all.

'Yes, can we, Mam? I always like just me and Sally opening our presents together and then you, Father and Uncle Stan coming in to look at what we have got from other folk,' Ben said. He stopped revving his aeroplane for a moment.

'Go on then. I'll sit with your Uncle Stan and wait for your father. And then I'll have to start thinking about our Christmas dinner. The turkey's cooked, but all the rest is to do, and I need some leeks and sprouts from out of the garden. There won't be much joy in picking those in this weather.' Ivy picked up her spoon to start eating her porridge and smiled as her two children nearly tipped over their chairs and ran into the living room to see what awaited them under the Christmas tree.

'I'll pick your vegetables for you. Sprouts, leeks and the usual turnip, is it? There's nothing I like better than that, mashed with butter and pepper on it,' Stan said and sat back in his chair. 'I might as well make myself useful while I'm here. I've also got those two a crown apiece, to spend on what they like. I'll give them it before dinner.'

'Aye, well, they've a present for you as well – not a lot, but it's given with love.' Ivy smiled. 'Christmas wouldn't be Christmas if you weren't here with us. I hope you know that, Stan?' She remembered the look on Stan's face when Bob had announced their forthcoming marriage. The feelings were still there simmering, in Stan's case. Both knew how the other person felt, but both of them were loyal to Bob, the brother and husband whose heart would be broken if he knew how Stan really felt.

'You are a good woman, Ivy. Our lad is lucky to have you.' Stan patted her hand tenderly and looked at her, before spotting Bob coming towards them, through the window. 'Lo and behold! Speak of the devil and lo, he appears, even on Christmas Day.' Stan stood up as Bob entered the kitchen. 'I'll go and get you those vegetables and let you feed your man – he looks half-frozen.'

'Aye, it's a bit thin out there, but the water supply isn't frozen up, thank heavens. Hopefully the snow will not be down long – just over Christmas, I hope, else it will make life hard for everyone. Put my top coat on, else it will upset your chest,' Bob yelled as Stan looked out into the cold yard, with a colander in his hand and a sharp knife, and thought twice about leaving the warmth of the kitchen.

'It'll be my fingers when picking the sprouts, but they always taste better with a bit of frost on them. Right, I'll be back in a while.' Stan pulled his brother's thick overcoat around his shoulders and braved the cold northerly that blew outside.

'He'll not be long, if I know him; he never did like the cold, our Stan didn't. I notice he must have slept last night, or I never heard any noise anyway. Happen his shell-shock is finally leaving him – that would be a blessing,' Bob commented as he sat and ate his porridge.

'That would indeed be a blessing. He deserves a bit of peace, he's a good man,' said Ivy. She remembered the look in Stan's eyes – the look he had given her for years, although he knew better than to say how he felt towards her. She knew she could always count on Stan and his unrequited love for her; but Bob was her husband, and she had vowed to be loyal to him, come what may.

'I think I'm richer than the King of England,' Ben said as he sat at the Christmas dinner table after eating the main meal of the year and finding the lucky silver sixpence inside the Christmas pudding. His money was piled up at the edge of his plate: a crown from Uncle Stanley, plus various threepences and sixpences from neighbours and friends; all that he would save to spend in the coming weeks on toffees or a comic, when allowed. Along with receiving a book or two, Ben had indeed had a good Christmas.

'Well, I'm so full, I don't think I can move.' Sally rubbed her stomach and sat back in her chair.

'Aye, that was a good dinner, Mother, you've done us proud yet again,' Bob said as he went to the fireplace, took down his pipe from its rack and lit it, while he looked at his family, sitting happy and contented. He'd managed to provide yet again what they had needed, and that was what mattered at that moment in time.

'We have finished just in time for the King's Speech on the radio. Have we to go through to the living room and listen, and then I'll come back and do the washing up afterwards?' Stan said; he didn't need to say it twice, as all the family moved into the living room and the warmth of a blazing coal fire, which looked so welcoming in the fading light of the winter afternoon outside. They gathered around the radio, listening intently to every word the King said and feeling deeply patriotic, as George VI wished every one of his subjects a peaceful Christmas and a happy New Year.

'He don't half talk slow,' Ben said as his father turned off the radio and sat back in his chair.

'The poor man wasn't expecting to be King, and he's a quiet soul,' Ivy replied to her son. 'His brother, Edward, was supposed to be King, but he gave up his throne because he loved the wrong woman to have by his side and become Queen.'

Ben looked puzzled.

'She was a Yank, lad, and she'd been married before, as well as being a commoner. Not a drop of royal blood in her. She couldn't have sat on our throne of England,' Bob explained and then stoked the fire.

'He must have loved her, to stop becoming King for

the sake of her,' Sally replied and thought about how deeply they must have loved one another.

'He'll regret it one day. Women are ten-a-penny, but kingdoms aren't. Never mind, we are in good hands with George, as he's far more sensible. And his wife is from good stock, being a Bowes-Lyon – not American rubbish.' Bob yawned; he'd just close his eyes for ten minutes and he noticed that his brother Stanley had the same idea, as he sat slumped in his chair. This was what Christmas was all about: good food, family and a day or two to take things more slowly.

Ivy put down her knitting, which she had been doing while listening to the speech, and put her finger to her lips to quiet her two children as they played dominoes on the table. She'd do the washing up. Stan did always offer, but as usual he had conveniently gone to sleep and forgotten, like every Christmas. There was no stopping the work for women at Christmas – unlike for some people.

Over the coming evenings Ivy pinned and tucked, and added a band of lace to the red velvet dress that, when younger, she had loved to wear, but that she was giving with love to her daughter now. Stanley had gone back to his cottage in Gawthrop, and the family was working as usual.

All that was left of the celebrations was the big event in Dent, the New Year's Eve Ball, although it was really only a dance in the village hall. But it was the place where many a couple had met, and then gone on to marry and have children. It was one event where all the generations mixed with one another, and enjoyed a waltz or a foxtrot with the person who caught their eye.

Ivy smiled as Sally came down the stairs and stood in front of her mother. Her long, dark hair shone and the dress, altered with love, fitted like a glove when she twirled around, as she asked if her precious silk-stockings seam was straight on the back of her leg. Ivy's heart filled with pride; this was her daughter, her beautiful daughter, going out for her first big night at a local dance.

'You are as pretty as a picture. I don't think anyone can outshine you, my love,' Ivy said and walked over to Sally and hugged her tightly. 'Now you'll behave yourself – you know what I mean,' she whispered. 'Don't be led astray by that Marjorie, although it's good of her father to give you a lift up to Dent and bring you back. I hope he's sober enough to drive back from Dent alright, after having supper and seeing the New Year in with the Dawsons. Your father would never forgive me if owt happened to you because of me agreeing that you could go with Marjorie.'

'Mam, I'm not like her. She might be my friend, but we are not the same. And yes, I know what you mean!' Sally beamed as she saw the lights of the Austin van owned by their neighbours light up the kitchen as it turned into the farmyard, and heard the horn being honked by Brian Harper, who was not about to get out of the van into the cold night's air.

'Enjoy your night. I've put you an extra shilling in your handbag – I thought you might need it.'

'Thanks, Mam. Now stop worrying, I'll be fine.' Sally gave her mother a kiss on the cheek and ran to the van, while Ivy stood at the kitchen door and watched her daughter turn the handle on the back of the van and climb in. Those stockings will be laddered before Sally's got to Dent, she thought, as she waved at the Harpers and hoped they would take good care of her daughter.

'Is that her gone?' Bob asked as he entered the kitchen from the living room. 'I reckon nowt to her being pals with that Marjorie – she's always being talked about in The Sun, chasing after that Birbeck lad. She's no shame.'

'That's Marjorie, not our lass, Bob. Sally will have to grow up and leave us sometime,' Ivy said and sighed.

'Aye, but not yet. I'll be watching that clock every minute until she's back. I purposely didn't come to see her, all dressed up, before she went. Stockings at fifteen – what the world is coming to!' Bob growled and went back into the living room.

'And bright-red lipstick,' Ivy whispered and smiled. What the eyes didn't see, the heart wouldn't grieve over.

Jonathan Birbeck sat at his family's supper table and looked at his four sisters, none of whom were married. No wonder, he thought, as he swigged his mug of tea and sat back in his chair. They were bossy and ugly and would like to rule his life, if given the chance. Already they had scowled at his choice of jacket, and had made him change back into the drab green one that he wore every day of his life. His eldest sister took his supper plate from under his nose and regarded him with disdain, as she walked across the starkly furnished kitchen and placed it in the stoneware sink to wash.

68

'I suppose you'll be going down into Dent to celebrate the New Year? All that drinking and frivolity! You want nothing of it, our Jonathan. You should be here with your parents and us to see in the New Year respectfully.'

Their father and mother, sitting next to the fire, said nothing. They knew their son was the wild one of the family, no matter how hard they tried to rein him in.

'Aye, I'm off into Dent. It'll be better company than sitting here, listening to Bible verses and tales of days gone by, which nobody but my family remembers. Things have changed in the world, except in this house. You'd think we were still in the last century, the way all of you act.' Jonathan pushed his chair back as he reached for his coat and made for the door. The coat that would hide the jacket that his sisters insisted that he should wear even though it was at least twenty years old and had once belonged to his uncle.

'You'll bring no sin back in this house with you, my son, on your return. You can at least promise me that,' his father said as he looked up from the fire, recognizing the wild look in his son's eyes as he opened the kitchen door.

'I'll do what I want, Father, because I'm not part of this family and have no wish to be. You never pay me for my work on the farm, or favour me like you do my sisters. I think I owe it to myself to make the best of what time and life I have to myself.' Jonathan spat and shook his head in despair at his family, who still followed to the letter the teaching of the Quakers. Those days were gone, and he was planning to go forth and enjoy a good night and not care about the consequences.

Tonight he would set his sights on one of the Dales lasses who had caught his eye; he wasn't bothered which one, just as long as she would do as he said – unlike his sisters – and not boss him around.

'Listen to that. Oh, my feet want to dance even now,' Marjorie said as she and Sally waited at the door to get into the village hall with various other dance-goers.

'I know, but at the same time I feel quite sick, as my stomach is full of butterflies. I've never been anywhere like this on my own,' Sally replied as she recognized the man on the door as being in charge of the post office through the day.

'Now then, young ladies. Have you come to see the New Year in and have yourselves a dance? We've a full hall tonight, I'll tell you that.' Alf Sowerby took the money for their tickets and watched both girls enter the bustling hall; he thought it hadn't been too long ago that both had been visiting the post office in their prams. Life didn't go fast enough when you were young and then, in a flash of the eye, you were looking at leaving the planet and regretting what you had not done in life. He hoped they both enjoyed the evening and made the most of it, because he would do so, if he could turn back the clock.

Sally linked her arm into Marjorie's as they both walked across the immaculately polished wooden floor and went to sit on two empty chairs in the corner of the room. On the stage the Beresford Band was playing the latest tunes and the singer was crooning and trying to look at his best, as the older ladies smiled and regarded him, commenting on how handsome he was and how he kept tune with the band.

'I don't reckon much of him; he's old enough to be my father,' Marjorie said as she looked at the lead singer, dressed in a sharp suit, with his dark hair smoothed back.

'He can sing, though, and everybody here is enjoying listening. Anyway, like you say, he's far too old for both of us. He is more for our mothers, as you say. Not that my mam would ever look at another man,' Sally added quickly.

'My mam does, all the time. She often says when she finds somebody attractive; she says it's only normal and as long as she doesn't touch, then there's no harm in it.' Marjorie pulled her compact out of her handbag and patted her nose with her powder puff. 'Just admiring the view and making sure I look right. I can't disappoint Jonathan if he turns up; and if not, then I can take my pick. He can be a bit dark and moody, but that, in a daft way, is what attracts me to him.'

Sally said nothing. She wished she had as much confidence as Marjorie, although sometimes her friend thought a bit too much of herself. As for Jonathan Birbeck, he was – as Marjorie said – dark in looks and in mood, so she was welcome to him. Sally smiled as she looked across at a group of farmers and their wives from further up the dale. She knew them all well, and once they had spotted her across the other side of the hall, they gave her a wave; then she watched, as they obviously talked about her while they smiled at her. And then the women

71

folded their arms and leaned closer to one another to be heard, when the band started to play louder.

'Oh, my favourite, a St Bernard's waltz! Come on, Sally, stand up and look interesting. We need to get ourselves someone to dance with, because I'm not looking like a lemon and dancing with you,' Marjorie said. She pulled on Sally to stand up and join her, as she walked like a glamorous model on the catwalk around the edge of the hall, swishing her skirts and smiling at each boy who took her fancy, but with no success, as Sally followed behind her.

'Sally, it's lovely to see you here.' Edward Riley stepped in front of her and gave her a smile, coming in between her and Marjorie as she paraded herself to the young men of Dent.

'It's good to see you as well, Edward. I didn't think you'd be here tonight. I thought that you'd be at home with your mam and dad, seeing the New Year in.' Sally felt a slight tingle as she looked at the lad she had gone to school with and had always liked. Then her gaze was taken up by Jonathan Birbeck entering into the hall and making a beeline for Marjorie, who almost looked disappointed at his appearance as she chatted to a lad from Sedbergh.

Edward smiled. 'No, my mother said I'd to get myself out, instead of sitting in with them both. That now I'm twenty-one, I'd better get on with some courting, else I'll be a lonely old man before I know it. I must admit this is not exactly up my street; for a start, I've two left feet, and I don't know any of the music and songs they are playing. It's my first dance.' Edward put his head down, only to raise it again with flushed cheeks.

72

'It's mine, too. I'm not a dancer, either,' Sally said, trying to concentrate on Edward as she watched Jonathan Birbeck take Marjorie's hand, which drew Edward's attention.

'Ugh! He's here. I'm surprised, as his parents won't be in agreement with him attending the dance. They are old-school and keep themselves to themselves.' Edward followed Sally's gaze and watched Marjorie and Jonathan talking.

'No, I'm not keen on him, either. He's a bit dark in his ways, but I think that is what Marjorie is attracted to – more fool her.' Sally looked up at Edward, giving her opinion on her best friend's choice for the night. 'I can manage this dance, if you want to try,' she said and then realized that it should have been Edward asking her. 'Sorry, I'm being a bit forward.'

'No, not at all. Shall we?' Edward held out his hand for Sally to take.

'I'd be delighted,' she said with a laugh as she took his hand and they joined the other people and started to dance.

'One, two, three, stomp, one, two, three, stomp,' they both counted as they laughed in one another's arms. And neighbours and friends smiled at them, a young couple enjoying each other's company and joining in the evening's entertainment.

The music stopped and Edward and Sally looked at one another. 'Have we to try another?' Edward asked and smiled.

'Yes, I'd enjoy that,' Sally said and let him put his arm around her. She felt happier than she had done for some time, as in dance after dance Edward and she got to know one another and enjoyed each other's company while they whisked around the hall together. They held one another tightly. She'd never viewed Edward Riley in the light that she was now seeing him in. He was perhaps not the best-looking young man in the room, but he was polite and entertaining, and he could make her laugh as he tripped over his own feet on the dance floor. She remembered how Edward had comforted her when she first started school and was crying alone on the steps, even though he was the oldest boy in the school. However, now she realized quite how attractive Edward was, and she smiled at the lad on her arm.

Sally watched Marjorie and Jonathan Birbeck as they passed them doing the foxtrot. Neither of them looked happy. Marjorie would never be happy, Sally thought, as she watched them stop dancing and walk out of the hall onto the dark streets of Dent. Marjorie always wanted more than any young farm lad could give her; her head was full of film stars, and Jonathan Birbeck was merely the wild lad of the Dales – one she could compare with Errol Flynn or his like.

Edward and she stopped dancing and stood hand-in-hand. Sally couldn't help but think that if Marjorie didn't come back in soon, they would miss the countdown to midnight, as the band stopped and the singer started to tell everyone to make a circle to sing 'Auld Lang Syne' as it was nearly time to welcome in the New Year.

'Sally, come on, cross your hands and grab hold of mine and Mrs Burton's next to you,' Edward said as the circle around the hall grew, with everyone there taking a place and waiting for the hour to strike. Sally felt her heart thumping as the leader of the band started counting down the seconds in time to the hands on the hall's clock, until both hands were exactly at midnight. Everyone cheered and then started to shake their crossed-over hands and sing the Robbie Burns song to usher in the New Year. The hall was filled with hope and joy for the new year of 1939, as everyone turned to the people next to them and hugged and kissed one another.

'Happy New Year, Edward,' Sally exclaimed and looked at him, feeling a little awkward, but noticing her heart beating fast.

'Happy New Year, Sally. I've never had chance to say how bonny you look tonight.' Edward put his arms around her and kissed her tenderly, taking her by surprise.

'Oh dear. Thank you. I've enjoyed our time together,' Sally replied quietly as everyone around her partied. But she was lost in the world of Edward and herself, with his arms around her, as he kissed her again.

'Aye, I have too. We'll have to do it again sometime – go to a dance down in Sedbergh perhaps?' Edward said. Then he stood back as he saw who was making his way through the cheering crowd.

'That's enough of that, lad. She's going to come home with me; she's seen the New Year in – time she was back home,' Bob Fothergill said and looked down at his daughter. 'Get your coat. I've the horse and cart waiting for us outside. Them Harpers will not be back before dawn, if I know them. And besides that, I've just seen

75

Marjorie and a lad I didn't quite recognize up the side of the hall outside. I'll not have you following her example.'

Sally blushed. How could her father show her up like that? She was nearly sixteen. Edward would think she was still a child and had to do whatever her father said. However, she hoped her father had not seen her and Edward kissing, else there would be hell to pay when she got home.

'I'll see you, Sally,' Edward said, as he knew not to argue with Bob Fothergill.

'Yes, thank you, Edward, I've enjoyed your company.' Sally smiled and said nothing as she walked to the doorway of the hall, and to the pile of coats on a table, which she looked through for hers. Hopefully she'd get to see Edward again, she thought, as not a word was said between her and her father as they left the hall into the frosty night's air and the waiting horse and cart. From around the side of the hall, Sally heard Marjorie's familiar giggle and her father said quietly, 'That lass is a trollop. She can't help it; her mother was, too. I'll not have you going the same way. Happen you could do worse than that Riley lad. They farm up at Rayside, and his father is right enough.'

Sally wrapped her coat around her. At least her father had not lost his temper with her, even if he had perhaps seen her kissing Edward.

Chapter 4

Sally had not slept all night, as her head was full of the New Year's dance, Edward's kisses and the look he had given her as they parted. She'd never felt that way before, and she snuggled down under her eiderdown and tried to forget her parents' raised voices, which she had heard through the night. She worried that it was about her kissing Edward Riley, but soon realized it was more than that, when she quickly dressed and went down into the kitchen to find her mother and father not talking to one another. Her father slammed the kitchen door to go out and do the daily jobs of milking and cleaning out the byres.

'Men – they think of nobody but themselves. Don't rush into finding yourself a boyfriend, as he will only break your heart and make your life unbearable.' Ivy swore under her breath as the bacon in the frying pan spat at her.

Sally said nothing but, noticing the table wasn't yet laid, she reached into the knife-and-fork drawer and set it,

77

as her mother's face got redder and redder with both the heat from the frying bacon and her temper. 'What's up, Mam? Is something wrong?'

'No, nowt's wrong – nothing that you can do owt about. It's just your pig-headed father; he's decided to finish working for Jim Mattinson and to work for Pratt's, collecting milk and eggs from up the dale and Garsdale. He says he can manage looking after here and work for them. He thinks far too much of money, does your father. He'll be milking the cow an hour after he's gone to bed, if he's not careful, along with lambing the sheep. Now look, that egg yolk's cracked, with me being rough frying it. I can't give your father that, as he doesn't like them split.' Ivy sighed as she placed the split egg onto a plate for herself. 'Stubborn, that's all he is!'

'He must think he can do it, Mam, else he wouldn't even be thinking about it. And I'm at home all the time now that I've left school. I don't mind working outside, you know I don't.' Sally reached for the salt-and-pepper pot, which was kept dry in the damp house above the fireplace. Her heart raced; this was her chance to prove that she was the farmer in the family. If her father was not going to be at home, then she would have to do the farm work.

'I wanted better for you, Sally lass. You can barely make a living on these farms up here in the Dales. I didn't want you to wed a miserable tight farmer like I did, but to make something of your life. And now you'll just be working at home. Not that Father'll give you any credit for anything you'll do,' Ivy replied and placed the

78

breakfasts on the table, then yelled at the bottom of the stair for Ben to get out of his bed.

'It might not be forever, Mam. Father might be back with Jim after a week or two, if he thinks it's not worth his while. You know what my father's like: full of schemes on how to make money. He's set his heart on having his own farm, that's all,' Sally said, with the wisdom of an older person in her head.

'Aye, and we all have to suffer for it. Who else wears knickers made out of flour bags because he watches every penny? My mother said I'd never have a penny to my name and she was right.' Ivy went to the bottom of the stairs again and hollered, 'Ben, breakfast! Get yourself down here fast. Your father's in a bad mood, and you are best out of his way until he's calmed down.' She then went onto rattle the plates in the sink awaiting a wash.

Ben's footsteps echoed like a giant's as he ran quickly downstairs and pulled his chair out at the table, looking across at Sally as she cut the rind off her bacon to give to the dog, which she'd go and feed as soon as she'd eaten. 'Happy New Year, our Sally,' Ben said quietly and looked at her.

'I don't think it's that happy in this house. Do you want to come with me and feed the dog and hens when you've eaten up, and then we are out of the way when my father comes in,' Sally whispered. 'Mam and father have had words!'

'Aye, and we'll stop in the barn for a bit until they've run out of things to argue about.' Ben quickly ate his rasher of bacon and fried bread.

'Ben's coming with me to collect the eggs and feed the dog. We'll both offer to take some fodder to the sheep in the front field, if Father will let us,' Sally said and looked across at Ben, who nodded his head in agreement.

'Yes, and I want to look for some kittens in the barn. I'm sure our cat has had kittens,' Ben added quickly.

'That'll be a first: a tomcat having kittens in winter! Still, you must tell me if you find any.' Ivy's mood lightened, knowing that both her children knew to stay out of the house until peace had come between her and Bob. 'Don't stop out there too long – it looks like more snow is on its way. And wrap up.' Ivy wound Ben's scarf around his neck and watched as Sally took the bucket of food scraps for the dog, before nearly pushing Ben out of the door. She was at her wits' end with Bob; in fact she was the closest she had ever been to walking out and leaving him. Stan would welcome her with open arms, she knew that. However, she could never be that cruel to Bob, and she could never leave her children behind.

'Kittens! What did you have to say that for? You know our cat's a tom,' Sally said as they trudged across the farmyard towards the barrel that housed Spot.

'I couldn't think of another excuse fast enough,' Ben replied as they approached the ageing dog, which came out as far as her chain allowed her to and wagged her tail, knowing that breakfast was about to be served. 'Sorry, Spot, no Euveka flakes this morning. I'll bring some later when all has gone quiet at home.' Sally patted the old dog, which wolfed down the small offering in one gulp, then she watched as her father came out of the shippon and went into the barn. Poor Spot, even she was suffering from her father and mother's falling-out, she thought.

'Go and tell Father that we will feed the sheep. He's just gone into the barn to get the cow some hay,' Sally said to Ben and looked at the face that he pulled, not wanting to go.

'I'm not telling him – not if he's in the same mood as our mam. Besides, I can do nothing right, you should know that,' Ben replied and kicked his sister for good measure.

'Chicken, chuck-chuck-chuck,' Sally said and kicked him back. 'I suppose we will have to go together.' She watched her father come out of the barn and go back into the shippon with a pitchfork loaded with hay for the milk cow. 'It's best they get their arguing over this morning and then perhaps we can have a decent New Year's Day. I don't want to freeze out here all day, and I've better things to do with my time.'

'Well, at least you didn't hear them arguing all last night. I heard them down in the kitchen as soon as you had gone out of the house. I thought it was all about you going out with Marjorie, but then I heard mention of Pratt's and a new job, and my mother crying,' Ben said, with his hands deep in his pocket as he kicked a stone across the yard and they both entered the shippon together. The smell of last summer's hay made them both remember the days when, in the meadows at Daleside, the grass had been mown and made lovingly into hay for days. Summer days were always easier, when the sun

81

shone, the skies were blue and the swallows and swifts flew and screeched overhead. Winter was hard in the Dales, and the worst two months were about to be endured, Sally thought as she walked up to her father while he shook the hay out into the rack for the cow to eat her fill, now that milking had taken place.

'What are you two doing here? Has your mother sent you?' Bob asked as he picked up the bucket full of milk, with a few hay seeds floating on the top, and headed for the open doorway.

'No, I said I'd see if you wanted the sheep foddering, and Ben said he'd help. I thought that could be my thank-you for picking me up from the dance last night. Seeing as Marjorie deserted me, it was just as well you did,' Sally said, lying through her teeth. She was secretly angry at her father arriving just as she was starting to get to know Edward.

'You want as little to do with that lass as you can – she's not up to much. As for the sheep, I've fed them, so you needn't bother yourselves.' Bob looked at them both, knowing full well that Ivy had sent them out of the house until the differences between himself and her had been settled.

'Then we'll go and collect the eggs. Mam says to tell you your breakfast is ready and the tea is brewed.' Sally followed her father out of the door, with Ben trailing after her, saying nothing as he closed the shippon's door behind them all.

'I'm going. She knows how long it takes me to fodder everything, and she shouldn't have made it so soon.' Bob walked towards the low-roofed farmhouse with the bucket of milk, and both Sally and Ben watched as he placed it down and brushed his hobnailed boots with the yard brush, before closing the kitchen door behind him. Whatever was going to be said between their parents, they were best out of it, Sally and Ben decided, as they made for the barn, to be out of the way of the arguing that was certainly going to take place.

They both lay back in the warmth of the hay-filled barn and looked up at the rafters where the resident owl was sleeping after his night's adventures.

'I didn't know my father came up to Dent and picked you up from the dance. I never heard him leaving,' Ben said as he chewed on a piece of hay and lay beside his sister.

'Well, he did – right after the New Year had been rung in and I was just getting to know Edward. Poor Marjorie will have wondered where I got to. I hope somebody told her and her parents that my father saw me home.' Sally sighed.

'Edward – who's Edward? Not spotty, stinky Edward Riley from Rayside at the top end of Dent? You weren't with him last night, were you?' Ben rested on his elbow and looked at his sister in disbelief.

'He's neither spotty nor stinky. Edward was my perfect dance companion last night – that was until our father came in and spoilt it.' Sally gave another sigh. 'Father always spoils everything, but you didn't hear me say that.'

'Well, I'm glad he spoilt it. He didn't kiss you, did he? Ugh . . . a kiss off Edward Riley! I think I'm going to be sick.' Ben puckered his lips together and made kissing noises while laughing.

'Stop it; it wasn't like that. It was just to see the New Year in. But thank heavens my father must not have seen, else his job wouldn't be the only thing being argued about this morning.' Sally lay back and thought about her first proper kiss with a boy, and how it had made her feel. She was also hoping that her mother and father were going to give her the chance to prove that she could farm as well as any lad, if given the chance.

Ben lay back in the hay, thinking about Edward. 'Edward Riley – well, at least he's got a good Raleigh bike. I could happen borrow it and see what it is like to ride, if he comes courting,' he said, looking on the bright side of things.

'He'll not be coming courting – he never said he was going to, anyway. Besides, his bike will be too big for you to ride, you idiot.' Sally secretly hoped that Edward would be whizzing down the dale on his bike to court her, if he dared face her father and his temper.

'Your head is set, isn't it? No matter what I say, you'll still go and tell Bernard Pratt that you'll be starting work for him next week.' Ivy stood at the kitchen sink, looking out of the kitchen window with her back towards her pig-headed husband.

'It makes sense, Ivy. We'll not just be shillings better off, but pounds. And I'll be back by one every day. In summer that will be a godsend. For God's sake, woman, you'll manage without me. You or Sally can milk the cow, and that lad of ours will just have to turn his hand to helping out around the farm when he's not at school. I'll be at home in an afternoon and evening to see to the sheep, and you'll manage through lambing time, I'm sure.' Bob was annoyed that Ivy couldn't see that his new job would be to everyone's advantage, and that it was him who would be working longer hours than anybody. He banged his mug down upon the table. 'At least let me try it for six months and then, if it's too hard work for all of us, I'll pack it in.' Bob swore under his breath.

'Six months then. And you make it right with Jim Mattinson, because like I say, he and Mary have been good to us. And don't come moaning at me and the children if it's not right for you,' Ivy replied and then carried on washing up. She wasn't happy, but six months would make or break Bob and would hopefully bring him to his senses. If things got worse, it gave her time to settle her thoughts. An hour or two working for Jim was a lot different from working so early every day of the week for Pratt's and their milk-and-egg delivery firm. Bob had lost any bit of sense that he had; and it wouldn't be the only thing he would lose, if he wasn't careful.

Snow had threatened and been in the clouds ever since the new year had come in, but now, in the second week of January, the sky was heavy with snow. Sally knew that a blizzard was approaching as she walked across the farmyard after milking the cow.

'We are going to be in for some snow this morning. It's warmed up and is not as icy – that's a sure sign snow is on its way,' Sally said as she strained the milk for the house through muslin, then placed it in the pantry, along with the few eggs that had been laid.

'At least your father should be nearly at the top of Garsdale by now. He'll just have to drop at the creamery in Hawes whatever milk he's collected and then make his way home,' Ivy said and looked out of the window. 'I'll be glad when he is. I don't like him driving that wagon, and he's never driven owt as big as that before.'

'He'll be alright, Mam. It will not snow that much before he's home. I keep hearing Father leaving the house long before it's light in the morning. He's working long hours at the moment – no wonder he falls asleep every night in his chair,' Sally replied, showing sympathy for her father, unlike her mother.

'On his own head be it. He would have his own way. The money is good, but we'd manage without it, and then you wouldn't have to be doing all his jobs.'

'I don't mind, Mam; you know I like outside jobs. I love milking the cow and seeing to the sheep. Just as long as it doesn't come too much snow. I know the sheep are in the home pasture, and everything else is in and looked after, but snow will make everyone's life and jobs harder. Foddering everything is hard enough; I can only carry so much hay at once.' Sally looked at the new blisters that had appeared on her hands, from using the pitchfork and shovel on a daily basis. Marjorie Harper would never have hands like hers, she thought. Not that she had seen Marjorie since the New Year's Eve dance. She had probably taken huff at Sally not returning with her, as she was like that.

'Aye, your father has just not thought this through. First he doesn't want your help, and now he can't do without you. It's amazing how money changes his mind,' Ivy said and then gasped. 'Oh Lord, here it comes – look at them flakes falling.'

Sally observed her mother as she watched the snow falling through the window.

'We've had nowt really yet; just that sprinkling of snow before Christmas, but this looks like it's going to settle. And the weather man on the radio yesterday said there would be snow on the northern Pennines – not that your father believes a word that comes out of the box.'

'At least our Ben is safe at school and they'll send him home, if it snows a lot. Old Mrs Bentham, his teacher, will not want to get stuck in Dent. The first bit of snow and she'll send the children home, as she's to walk up to Bridge End at Deepdale,' Sally pointed out, as her mother looked more and more worried as the snow fell more heavily. She knew Ben would be alright; he'd play snowball fights with his mates, no matter how bad the weather was, on his two-mile walk home. She had done it many a time herself and it was more of an adventure than a chore when walking home with friends from neighbouring farms. Although poor Bill would have to walk the last quarter-mile on his own, living at the last house down the dale.

'Get some coal and wood in from the coalhouse, Sally. Best get ready for a wild day and night. Both your father and Ben will come in frozen to the bone and will want drying out,' Ivy said as she finished kneading the bread.

'At least we've got plenty to eat, in case we get blocked in. It's just as well I make my own bread,' she went on, as she placed the dough in a greased tin and left it to rise near the fire. Ivy was always prepared for whatever the weather threw at them; it was amazing what she could make, with a bag of flour and the ingredients found readily on the farm. Her mother had taught her well, showing her how to make pastry and cakes and, above all, how to be thrifty in hard times; this was what every farmer's wife had to be for some of the year, and Ivy had in turn shown Sally. She watched as her daughter went back and forth, filling up coal scuttles and building up the log pile next to the fireplace. She was proud of her; Sally was a good worker and a grand lass.

'Lord, this snow has come down quickly. Thank heavens I had some snow chains for the van's wheels, else I'd never have got home.' Bob stamped his feet and shook his coat before entering the welcoming warmth of the kitchen. 'I only just made it home, coming down the hill near The Gate, as the van got a right slide on and I nearly hit the wall.' Bob saw Ivy and Sally both looked worried.

'Well, that's one of you back. Now we just need Ben back. I hope Mrs Bentham has sent them all home and not been stupid enough to have kept them at school. Surely she will have done. The snow looks a few inches high now, and the wind is getting up and making it drive into drifts.' Ivy looked at Bob. 'You don't fancy going back out and seeing if Ben's coming down the road, do you, as the weather is that fierce out there?'

'Bloody hell, Ivy, I've been up since four and am frozen

to the bone. He'll be on his way somewhere,' Bob said and then thought better of it; the boy should have been home by now, if the school had sent him back. It was only a two-mile walk and the snow had been falling for more than three hours. 'I suppose I'd better make sure he's alright, else you will only moider me until he turns up.' Bob started to put his coat back on, to go and see where his missing son was. That was until all heads turned as the kitchen door opened and Ben came in, covered from head to foot in snow.

'Thank the Lord for that. Your father was about to go and look for you. Have you all been sent back home from school?' Ivy asked as she walked over to Ben, took his balaclava off his head and shook his coat free of snow, leaving puddles on the stone flags.

'Stop fussing with him, Mother. He's not a baby anymore.' Bob took his own coat off and hung it on the back of the kitchen door and looked at Ben. 'Tha looks a bit frozen, lad, you had better sit next to the fire for a while.'

'It's my fingers that hurt the most – look, they are blue!' Ben tried to bend his frozen fingers.

'Put them in hot water in the sink, then they will soon come to life,' Sally suggested, knowing that usually did the trick, although the pain when the circulation came back into them was terrible.

'Aye, put them in here with the tatty peelings. I'm about to put some potatoes on for dinner, so I'll peel another, now that I know you are home.' Ivy quickly walked to the sink, took her sharp knife and dunked a potato into the water, before peeling it and pushing Ben to warm his hands in the water. His face had turned from a frozen blue to a bursting red now, and he yelled and made such a fuss as his fingers came back to life in the warm water.

'It's that Robert Mason's fault – he would pick a snowball fight on the way home, and I hope his hands feel like this,' Ben said and nearly cried with the pain.

'You've been playing about instead of getting yourself home! There was your mother and Sally worried to death about you, and you were fooling about with that Mason lad. I should take my belt off to you, then it wouldn't just be your hands that hurt,' Bob growled.

'Aye, Father, whisht! You did exactly the same when you were a lad – we all did. Besides, we are all home now and everything's fed and watered, thanks to Sally. Nowt is coming to any harm. Now sit yourselves down and we'll have some dinner.' Ivy shook her head. Bob often threatened to take his belt off to wallop either Sally or Ben, but he never had done. His raised voice was enough to put them in their place, and he knew it.

Later that night Sally lay in her bed and listened to the wind howling around the eaves. The snow had never stopped falling; it was piled up on her window-sill and had whipped up into tall drifts around the yard and in the fields. Her father had quickly milked the cow and done the jobs that he was able to that evening, and now everything would just have to survive, no matter what the weather was like outside, until the morning. When she was younger she had enjoyed the snow, like Ben, but now she realized that too much snow endangered their livelihood. The sheep in the home field were down from the fell, but the snow had fallen so heavily and had whipped into such drifts that there would definitely be some caught in it, sheltering underneath the walls, with snow covering them. Would her father attempt to drive to his work at Pratt's or would he stay at home in the morning and help her search for the buried sheep? She hoped the latter as she fell asleep, hearing the soft voices of Ivy and Bob discussing what would take priority in the morning, while the snow lay heavily over the dale. Whatever happened, it was going to mean hard work. Her last thoughts were of Edward, and she hoped that his flock was safe and well on his farm.

'I can't get down to Sedbergh – our farm lane's blocked, not to mention the main road,' Bob said as he dug the snow from around the back door and pushed the shovel like a miniature snowplough across the yard, to make a path to the main buildings. He stopped for a second and leaned on his shovel. 'The water troughs are frozen up, and so far I've only managed to count twenty-four sheep, when I shouted to them at the low-pasture gate with a bucket of sheep nuts. That reminds me. Thompson's salesman will be calling next week, so we'll have to see what we can afford and make him an order. But never mind that. Right now it's time to get our lass out of bed, and Ben; if he doesn't want to do anything else, he can break the ice in the troughs.'

'Will they pay at Pratt's, if you don't show up? And what will all the farmers do with their milk, if you don't pick it up?' Ivy said as she stood with her hands folded in the kitchen doorway, looking at Bob in the still, grey winter morning's light.

'Nay, I'll not get paid if I don't go in. But I'll not be on my own. And the milk to be picked up will be alright for a day or two in this weather. It would be a different matter if it was the middle of summer.' Bob shovelled another path of snow and then took another rest. 'It's a good job I put their van in the barn last night, else it never would start; it's a bit temperamental anyway. Needs at least four or five turns of the handle. He glanced across at the snowdrift up the side of the barn door. 'Get them two out of bed, Ivy. I need Sally to look for any sheep that are under the drifts, after I've milked the cow.'

'Sally's up. I heard her upstairs a minute or two ago, and Ben will be down shortly; he'll not stop in his bed if he knows there is that much snow. He's been waiting with his sledge all Christmas.' Ivy stepped back into the warmth of the kitchen and closed the door. It was going to be a day and a half: there would be a constant stream of wet clothes to dry, after shovelling the snow, and they would all have to be fed and kept warm. She hated winter, when there was little or no money coming in and everything took so much work – not to mention the cold that seemed to get into every one of her bones even more each year.

'Hey up, Mam, does Father need my help?' Sally asked as she walked into the kitchen and reached for her winter coat from behind the door. She already had several layers of clothing on: a vest, a liberty bodice, an underskirt, a knitted thin jumper and a home-knitted cardigan, over the top of a pleated tartan skirt and red knitted tights, which her father always commented on, as he thought they were a bit brash for a lass of her age. Today she hoped he'd say nothing, because they kept her legs warm and that was all that mattered.

'Aye, he's some sheep missing and the farm lane is blocked. It will have to be dug out if he's to go to work. The council men should clear the main road eventually, but all the dale will be blocked, I bet, so it might be some days, and I know your father won't want to wait that long.' Ivy turned and smiled at Ben. 'You are up then. Before you disappear with that sledge of yours, your father wants you to smash the ice on all the drinking troughs. The ones in the barn, the yard, the shippon and the home field.'

'Oh, Mam, do I have to? I've waited all Christmas for this snow.' Ben screwed his face up.

'Yes, you do. Come on, I'll see to the dog and hens and you break the ice, and then both of us will help Father look for the sheep that are missing after we've had breakfast. Now stop moaning,' Sally answered for her mother and pushed her younger brother out into the yard, after he had pulled on his boots; she dragged him behind her to the farm buildings. 'There's too much snow to sledge on anyway, and it's that soft stuff. It needs a good frost on it before it's fit for sledging upon,' Sally said to her brother as he stood and looked around him, at the sight of the dale and the surrounding farms covered in a blanket of white.

'You know nowt, our Sally, I could sledge on this – you know I could,' Ben shouted as he walked to the barn to see to the first trough.

'I know this: Mam and Father need both our help this morning, so stop moaning and get on with your job. There will be plenty of time to go sledging with your mates. All this snow is not going to go anywhere fast, that's for sure,' Sally replied as she picked up the tin bucket to be filled with Spot's dinner and passed Ben a hammer from the barn's wall for him to use to smash the ice. 'Here, get on with it, and don't blubber if your hands get cold this morning. We'll all be cold today. At least you can wear trousers – Father won't let me.

'Lasses don't wear trousers; sometimes you talk simple, our Sally. Dad's right, you'd look a right tuttle,' Ben said as he swung the hammer at the thick ice in the drinking trough. It was quite a decent job, he thought, as he watched the inch-thick ice start cracking and the water begin seeping through: one trough down, only a few more to go. He crossed to the yard trough and stuck his tongue out at his bossy sister. She knew nowt: the snow too soft – how daft was she?

Dinner was eaten in silence by all four of the family. They knew what was expected of them, and even Ben had decided it was only right that he helped look for the sheep that were buried in the high drifts.

'They'll not be dead, will they, Father?' he asked as his mother cleared the table.

'No, their breath and body heat melt the snow and give them enough air to breathe for a long time. They'll be fine, once we have dug them out. I remember when I was a lad your age, my father and I found a sheep in a drift still alive after three weeks up on the fellside. She'd survived by eating her own wool; she was bare and wobbly on her legs, but she went on to live and carry lambs for a few more seasons.' Bob pushed back his dinner plate. 'Right, we'll get Spot. Take those three long walking sticks and let's get the sheep sorted. And then we'll make a start on digging our lane out, so that at least when they have cleared the main road I can get back to work.'

'Walking sticks – I don't need a walking stick!' Ben said as he pulled his coat on, along with his mother and Sally.

'Aye, tha does. It is how you'll find the sheep: you prod the stick into the drifts and then, when it hits a sheep, you can tell by the feel. You didn't think we were going to turn every drift over, did you? That would take all day. Thank heavens we are only missing sixteen, as there will be other folk with a lot more sheep buried than us,' Bob said as his family, all dressed for the weather, and he walked into the home field and looked at where the snowdrifts lay.

The sun had come out and the sky was bright blue above them. The snow glistened as if covered by diamonds, and the trees that were laden with snow kept letting loose their loads from their branches as the sun melted it free, making a noise in that unusually silent world.

'Now, isn't that bonny, just like a Christmas card?' Ivy said as she gazed across at the other side of the dale, which was coated in snow and shining in the sun.

'Aye, it is, if you haven't to work in it.' Bob pushed the field gate through the snow and looked around him. 'Right, the sheep will be more than likely in groups, so if you find one, there will be another next to it.' He whistled to Spot, who was already sniffing along the wall side. 'Seek, lass, seek them out,' he said, as the four of them walked to the deepest drifts and started probing into the snow, with the twenty-four existing sheep standing in a huddle, worried that the dog was in their field and that some of their group were missing. Spot started barking and scratching at the snow, excited by the smell of sheep under the drift.

'Good lass, I knew you'd find them.' Bob quickly started shovelling snow away from the bodies that lay underneath, uncovering the woolly body of a Swaledale ewe and then pulling her head clear of the snow and helping her to her feet, as she gazed around her, bewildered at the commotion.

'There's another here and all, Dad. I can feel it with my stick,' Sally yelled, making her mother come to her side with a shovel and dig, along with Sally and Ben using their hands. 'There's two or three here – they've been taking shelter behind this limestone wall.' They all dug deeper, freeing the sheep from their snowy tomb. Soon all of them were accounted for, and Bob and his family were simply glad that he had brought the sheep down from the fell, else it would have been a different matter.

'That's a good do. Now we've just to tackle our way out onto the main road,' Bob said as he and his family stood together and looked around. 'I hope the council will soon get the main road cleared, and then I can get back to working at Pratt's. We need the money.'

'If you hadn't packed in working for Jim Mattinson, we wouldn't have had that worry. You could easily have walked there,' Ivy commented as she headed back to the farmhouse.

'Will you hold your whisht, woman. I've missed a day, that's all, and I'll not be the only one. Folk will be blocked in. Pratt's will know that. I'll be back there as soon as I can.'

'You'll be back tomorrow, Father. Look, I can see the smoke from Brian Harper's tractor coming along the road, and he's turning up our lane. He'll soon get our track cleared.' Sally smiled, hoping that Marjorie would be with her father.

'I wish we had a tractor instead of horses. I could learn to drive it then,' Ben said and went to the field gate to watch the Ferguson tractor coming up the lane with no bother, as it made tracks through the drifts and filled the air with the smell of its diesel oil, as it pushed and slid along, making the way to Daleside more accessible.

'Now then, Bob, I thought I'd save you a job. You can do anything with this machine. You need to get yourselves one.' Brian jumped down from the vehicle and patted it. 'Built by Harry Ferguson, an Irishman, but made here by David Brown and it's worth every penny I paid for it – there's nowt it can't do.'

'Nay, I'll put my faith in my horse. You can keep your monstrosity; it costs too much for this house.' Bob watched as Ben walked around it, looking at the tractor's workings and wanting to sit on it.

'Go on, lad, sit in the seat. It'll not set off unless you turn the key in the ignition.' Brian smiled as Ben climbed up and wrapped his arms around the steering wheel, then looked at the pedals and throttle on the black iron work-horse. 'That's the way to go, lad – be interested in mechanics and how it all works. It will be all there is in another few years.'

'Tha can think again. He needs to learn farming first,' Bob scowled.

'Aye, well, happen he's not that way inclined, just like our Marjorie. She never helps out on the farm, nor her mother in the house, come to that,' Brian sighed.

'Has she not come with you, Brian? I know Sally here would have liked to see Marjorie,' Ivy asked, glancing across at her daughter as she watched Ben.

'No, she's blotted her copybook. She's been told to stop at home until I tell her different,' Brian replied sharply, but added no more.

'Are you coming in for a drink? I was just about to put the kettle on,' Ivy said and made her way to the house, leaving the men standing there and Sally joining her.

'Nay, I'll not bother, thanks, Ivy. I've my stock to feed and if I don't get back, the wife will have something to say,' Brian Harper shouted and picked up Ben from the tractor. 'Here, sit on my knee and have a ride down to the bottom of the track with me. You can steer if you are careful. Just mind the big drift at the bottom of your lane – even this struggled to get through for a while.' He jumped onto the tractor and turned the key, making the engine spring to life and the chimney puff out smoke, filling the farmyard as the wonder in engineering shook. Ben beamed as, with Brian's guidance, he turned the wheel and moved slowly out of the yard.

Bob shook his head. 'More money than sense,' he muttered as he brushed his boots and went into the warmth of the kitchen. And that lass of theirs was nowt but a trollop – that's why she had been kept at home, he thought, not that Brian would ever admit that.

Chapter 5

'The world's going mad. I just don't know what we are going to wake up to each morning,' Ivy said as she glanced at the headlines of the newspaper Bob was reading, while she was mixing her Yorkshire-pudding batter for their usual Sunday dinner. If it isn't the Irish, it's the Jerries. Why anybody wants to be always fighting, I don't know.'

'The Irish always have been awkward, but you can't blame them for wanting Home Rule. But bombing spots like railway stations is not the way to go about it. Bombing Tottenham Court Road and Leicester Square will not get them any English sympathies. Thank heavens there were no dead, only injured, although it doesn't say how badly injured some are.' Bob sighed. 'There'll be worse yet, with these bloody Jerries. This Hitler isn't building up his navy for nothing and, not content with holding Austria, he's marching on the rest of Czechoslovakia, so there's going to be bother yet. Our government will be daft enough to get us involved, that's for sure.'

He folded his newspaper and sat back and lit his pipe.

'Dick Jackson told us this was coming when we saw him just before Christmas. He must be worried to death about his lad. I wouldn't want any of mine in the forces right now, or a lad that was the right age to enlist. Times are worrying now, my lass, but I don't doubt they are going to get a whole lot worse.'

'We've just got through one of the worst recessions, and now I hope to God we're not facing another war. My father used to say that a country always went to war when its coffers were empty, and perhaps he was right.' Ivy bent down and took the sizzling patty pans, filled with dripping, out of the oven and covered them with the batter, before placing the puddings back in to cook.

'Your father was no military man, but perhaps he was right. This country is in a bad way, but if that bloody Hitler comes knocking anywhere near our door, then he'll have to be put in his place. I only hope he waits until after we've had our Sunday dinner because that lump of beef that's cooking in the oven is too good to waste on fighting him.' Bob grinned as Ivy flicked her tea-towel at him.

'You silly bugger! I don't think he'll be bothering us somehow,' Ivy laughed. And then both of them gazed at the door as it opened with a thud.

'Bloody hell, he's here. Be careful what you say next time, my Ivy,' Bob said as Sally came in, after balancing against the door to take off her wellington boots.

'What are you two laughing at?' she asked and looked dismayed at so much mirth in the kitchen on a Sunday morning.

'Nothing really; just making the news a bit lighter, because it couldn't be any darker.' Ivy smiled. 'Now look at them: aren't they bonny? Spring must be around the corner,' she said as she appreciated the bunch of snowdrops that Sally held in her hand.

'Yes, I picked them out of the orchard. It's covered with them in there, like a white carpet, and they look so bonny. I'll place them in water and put them on the table.' Sally bent down under the sink to find a vase from the various collections stored there. 'Dinner smells good, Mam, I can't wait for it. I love my Sunday dinner,' she said as she placed her snowdrops in pride of place on the kitchen table in a small cut-glass vase inherited from her grandmother.

'Aye, I'm about to dish it up. Go and get Ben; he's listening to the radio in the front room. I've lit the fire, seeing as it's Sunday, so he's taking advantage of the warmth.' Ivy watched as Sally went and got Ben. Her daughter was growing up, and each time she looked at her she thought that Sally had grown another inch and had filled out in all the places that young women should be filling out at her age. She only hoped that would make the most of her youth and eventually – but not yet – find a good man to marry, when she was ready.

She shook her head as she heard Sally shout, 'Dinner's nearly ready, so stop listening to all them foreign stations that you can't make head nor tail of. If one's German, they'll come and get you.'

Ivy shook her head again. If Ben had been five years older, she might be having to send him to Germany, the way the world was looking. The enlistment of young men would be something the government would do straight away, if there was a threat of war again. Thank the Lord Ben was too young. Still, it might not come to that. She sighed as she uncovered her piece of beef brisket, which had cooked long and slow in the fireside oven. It might be a cheap cut of beef, but it was tasty, if cooked long enough and given sufficient reverence. The rich gravy from it was the added luxury that made her Sunday dinner enjoyed by everyone. And there was always enough of both left over for Monday's dinner, finely sliced, when the beef was cold; with mashed potatoes, it was liked by all.

Ivy was dishing out her Sunday dinner when all heads turned, as there was a knock on the kitchen door.

'That bloody Hitler is persistent today,' Bob said as Ivy wiped her hands on her pinny, after placing the last plated dinner in front of Ben.

'I'll get it – you tuck in, don't let it go cold,' Ivy replied. Bob scowled, wondering who was daft enough to come at Sunday dinnertime. She walked to the door and opened it, to find a fresh-faced Edward Riley standing on the step, looking sheepish at the thought of calling on Sally for the first time. He struggled with his words as he looked at Ivy.

'I just thought I'd call and see Sally, if that's alright, Mrs Fothergill. I hope that it isn't inconvenient?' Edward said and wished he could escape back on his bicycle, which was propped up against the side of the house, as he saw Bob looking at him as he ate a slice of his beef.

'Well, we were just about to sit down to our Sunday dinner.' Ivy looked around the kitchen directly at Sally. 'But come in, we'll not be long. I'm sure Sally will want to see you.' She opened the door wider to let Edward come in and, with his legs shaking like jelly, he walked into the warm, homely-smelling kitchen and stood next to the table with his cap in his hands, not daring to look at any of the family as they all stared up at him.

Sally could feel her heart beating fast and her face flushing, as her father sat back in his chair and regarded Edward. In a really quiet voice, Edward said hello to him.

'Well, tha's timed that badly, lad. I think Mother's just carved up the last of the beef, but you can have a pot of tea and then be on your way,' Bob said to the lad, who he knew had come to court his daughter.

'No, that's fine, Mr Fothergill. I was just passing and thought I'd say a quick hello to Sally, but I can see I'm intruding on your dinner, so I'll be on my way.' Edward looked across the table at Sally, who knew not to leave the Sunday dinner table without her father's permission.

'As you like, lad.' Bob carried on eating his dinner, as Sally looked up at Edward, and Ben sniggered and kicked his sister under the table.

'Sally love, I'll keep your dinner warm. Go and have a minute or two with Edward outside while we finish our dinners,' Ivy said and smiled at both young loves. She knew how it all started, even if Bob seemed to have forgotten. 'Don't be long, mind. I don't want it to get dried.'

Sally needed no excuse as she got up from the table, and her father glared at both her and her mother, as she and Edward walked out of the door. She heard Ben laughing, until her father gruffly told him to be quiet as she closed the kitchen door behind them both.

'I'm sorry. I didn't know what time it was. I've just had a run out on my bike down to Sedbergh, and when I passed your farm lane, all I could think about was New Year's Eve when we danced together. I've kept thinking of you, on the quiet.' Edward bowed his head.

'Yes, I've thought of you as well. I'm glad you called by,' Sally said and glanced at him, but at the same time she worried about what her father would say after he'd gone.

'Are you alright – been keeping well? I've been busy working for my father and haven't had much time to myself,' Edward said, trying to make polite conversation and feeling awkward in the cold light of day, with the realization that he had dared to knock on Bob Fothergill's door to ask to see his daughter.

'I'm grand, thank you. Busy, like yourself, and it will soon be lambing time, and then there will be no time for anything.' Sally stood near Edward and looked up into his face.

'I'd give you a kiss, but I daren't, as your father might come out and I know he's got a temper,' Edward whispered.

Sally leaned in nearer and quickly kissed him on the cheek. 'There you go, Edward Riley – that's for daring to come and see me.' She grinned and looked at the young man, who touched the place where she had kissed him.

'It will be worth getting shouted at, just for that,' Edward replied and wanted to hold her close, but stopped himself as the kitchen door opened and Sally's mother stepped outside and said, 'Father says come back to your dinner now, Sally.'

'She's coming, Mrs Fothergill. I'm on my way.' Edward winked at Sally as he picked up his bicycle and put his leg over the crossbar. 'See you again in a bit, Sally.' He pushed off down the lane, leaving her with her heart a-flutter and hoping that her father wouldn't lose his temper with her for something she couldn't control. She sat back down at the kitchen table and tried to finish her dinner without looking guilty.

'Now that was a grand bit of beef, lass. Pity it was spoilt by a visitor. I hope he'll not be bothering us again and making a habit of it, our Sally?' Bob looked sternly at his daughter as he pushed his empty plate to one side.

'No, he won't, Father. He's busy, just like us,' Sally said and put her head down. Although her head and her heart were stirring, she couldn't show it, especially to her father.

'Aye, well, you are only young. Best keep him at arm's length,' Bob replied and looked up at Ivy. 'Now, with everything done outside, I'm going to sit by that fire in the front room and enjoy my pipe. I think I deserve a bit of peace.' Bob made the most of his Sunday in winter, knowing that in a few weeks' time he would be out in the fields watching his sheep lamb, once spring was truly here. He knew all too well what the young caller was about; it had reminded him all too much of himself at Edward's age. He simply hoped the lad had more morals than he had had at that age.

106

'I'm going to make some cotton-reel tanks. Mam has given me some old wooden cotton reels and I've found some elastic bands in the kitchen drawers, to twist and thread through them and then put a stick at either end, so that when the elastic band unwinds, they move. Uncle Stanley showed me how to make them before he went home. But I'm going to carve tracks on the outside of the bobbins, and then they look more like tanks,' Ben said, taking a penknife out of his pocket. 'Did you ask Edward if I could have a ride on his bike?' he added quickly, and grinned when he saw Sally shake her head and glare at him.

'Well, mind your fingers. It's alright our Stanley giving you these ideas, but it'll be me who bandages the cuts on your hands,' Ivy said as she cleared the table with Sally.

'I'll help wash up, and then I'll do a bit more pegging of the mat we're making. I thought of walking across to see Marjorie, but it's looking like rain. And besides, I think she's still sulking with me for not telling her that I was going home with Father on New Year's Eve. She hardly gave me the time of day when I saw her outside the shop in Dent last week,' Sally said quietly as her mother passed her the wet plates to dry. 'Thanks for asking Edward in, Mam. He'd only been passing.'

'It's alright, my lass – you are allowed friends, you know. As for Marjorie, I wouldn't worry about her; she'll come round eventually. It'll be something she's been up to that she's mad about. I've never known Brian make her behave herself, so she must have been in bother. Spoilt she is, that's all; her mother's the same. Poor Brian must spend a fortune on the pair of them, as neither goes without anything.' Ivy smiled at her level-headed daughter.

'Still, she is my best friend. But I wasn't going to follow her out of the hall with that Jonathan Birbeck, as I'm not keen on him. He's big-headed and wild,' Sally said as she put the plates away and folded the tea-towel.

'Aye, and your father says that you were dancing with our Sunday caller. Now he seems a bit steadier than that Birbeck lad, and polite. You did right to stay. That Jonathan must be a good eight years older than Marjorie – he'll be up to no good, I bet.' Ivy watched a flush come into her daughter's cheeks. 'There's plenty of fish in the sea, Sally, and you are nobbut young. Don't rush into things, as there will be many lads coming your way yet.' She smiled at her bashful daughter.

'I know, Mam. Edward and I only danced, and he gave me a kiss at midnight,' Sally confessed.

'I know, your father told me. There's no harm in that. Your father wasn't happy about it, but he's happy about nowt at the moment. I don't doubt he'll have something to say about Edward calling today, when we are on our own. Just keep him as a friend until you know him better, and don't be like Marjorie – she's too easily led. Now, you get on with your rug-making, and I'm going to pull back an old cardigan of yours and reuse the wool to knit Ben a pullover. It's bright blue, but it could be worse; it could be a pink one that I'll be sending him to school in,' Ivy laughed. 'Now he would get teased something rotten if I did that.'

Sally hesitated, but while she had her mother to herself there was something she wanted to ask her. 'Mam, I know we are all covering for my father, but when I was posting a letter for you in Dent last week, I noticed that Mrs Mackreth at Holme View needed somebody to clean for her a few hours a week. Now I've left school, I could do that job and it would bring in some money for us. It's only two mornings, and I can walk in with our Ben in a morning and be back for dinner time. But it's lambing time coming up, and Father will expect me at home.'

She had been thinking for a few days about the job she had spotted and had dismissed it, knowing that she was wanted at home. However, the money would be gratefully accepted by Sally and her family, so she had decided to pick her moment and ask her mother for her thoughts. She loved helping out more on the farm, but it wasn't making her any money, and even if she could have a shilling to herself for a few personal things she would feel like a millionaire.

'Let me have a think about it. How many hours does she want someone for?' Ivy asked.

'Three hours on a Monday and Friday,' Sally said and dared to hope.

'She'll not be hard to work for, will Annie Mackreth. She'll be a good age now, as her Bert died a long time ago, and she's no family that I know of. If your father wasn't working for Pratt's, then there would be no problem, but you'll be needed here. Anyway, let me have a think. I can manage to lamb sheep, and the housework will just have to wait. Your father will just have to moan if he gets cold bacon sandwiches for his dinner, if I've no time to cook; after all, it would be all his doing.'

Ivy leaned on the kitchen chair and thought of her time in service at the Grange, before she had met Bob. It had been hard work, but it had prepared her for life.

'I might regret this, but go on – we'll manage. You go and see old Annie and tell her whose lass you are. She'll be right with you, and it will give you some money of your own.' Ivy put her arm around Sally. 'Don't say owt to your father. I'll tell him when the time is right – not that he should be bothered. Let's just have a quiet Sunday; in fact your father needn't know until he gets to find out.'

Mother and daughter looked at one another. They were both so close, and they had to be, to make the most of living with a hard-headed northern farmer as a husband and father.

'Alright, Mam, as long as you are sure? Thanks, Mam, and I hope Father isn't too mad at Edward calling,' Sally said quietly as she opened the door into the living room and made her way to the back of the room, where the wooden frame that held a hessian sack stretched tight on four planks of wood lay beside her chair. Next to it was a bag of woollen cloth strips, cut up from old coats and clothes that had seen better days, along with a dolly-peg split in two and sharpened to a point at one end. It was with this that she made two small holes in the taut hessian and pushed through both ends of the woollen rag, making a tuft on the opposite side and building up a pattern as she put in each piece. It passed many a winter's evening, and at the end there was payment for the work put into her pastime, in the form of a beautiful, durable pegged rug to be laid on whatever floor needed the warmth.

Sally put her head down and thought about what her mother had said. Not only had both her parents known that she had kissed Edward Riley, but they had both seemed to take it in their stride when he had visited her. And now her mam was letting her go and get some work. She only hoped she would not be the cause of an argument between her parents yet again.

Ivy sat back in her chair across from Bob. He'd fallen asleep and his mouth was open wide and snoring, causing Ben to keep pointing at his father and laugh. Bob would wallop him if he found Ben making fun of him, she thought, as she tugged at the already knitted wool and rewound it into a ball. She looked across at Sally and smiled. For once Sunday afternoon was peaceful; the rain was starting to lash down outside and the evening was beginning to fall. The sparse little living room felt warm and homely as the fire flickered and everyone fell quiet, full and content in the rare moment of tranquillity that Sunday afternoons brought. In the morning it would be different, as the world awoke to another week.

'It's pitch-black out there and it's pouring down. If you'd kept working for Jim Mattinson, we wouldn't have been up for another hour at least, and you'd not have so far to walk in this weather,' Ivy moaned as she sat on the bed's edge and pulled her knickers on and fastened her brassiere.

'Will you hold your whisht, woman! You needn't even get up with me. I can grab a piece of bread for my breakfast, and there's always a drink waiting for everybody when I get into work,' Bob said sharply as he pulled his braces up and put his well-worn jacket over the top of his flannelette shirt.

'And have you telling everybody that I'm too lazy to get up with you in the morning? I don't think so.' Ivy pulled her woollen jumper over her head and fastened her skirt, then stood up and looked at Bob. 'Do you not think you've made a mistake? You looked so tired yesterday.'

'No, I did not, woman. You saw how much pay I brought back the other week. It was more than Jim would have paid me for a month. Now nowt's afire outside, all the stock are fine; you've just the milking to do between you, and the foddering up. There's a list of what we need from Thompson's, if Reg Preston comes today. It's on the mantelpiece, along with his payment. It must be a month since his last visit, so he's due.'

'Money goes nowhere nowadays! The shopping gets dearer every time I go into Sedbergh or Dent,' Ivy mumbled as she went out of the bedroom door and made her way down the stairs, followed by Bob. 'That provin bill goes up every time, and all. I don't know how Thompson has the cheek to doff his hat to half of the folk in Dent.'

'Tha has got out of bed on the wrong side. Anybody would think it was you that was going to get sodden all morning, loading milk kits in and out of the wagon. Think yourself lucky you are at home with Sally, although I know it's washing day and weather's bad for that. And talking of our Sal, make sure you give that Riley lad short shift if he comes a calling; she wants nowt with him hanging around,' Bob said as he sat next to the fire and laced his strong black leather boots up; he watched his wife as she stirred the fire's embers and put the recently new electric kettle on to boil. 'Tha sees that life's got easier for you since the landlord rewired the house and gave you one plug in the kitchen. You can soon make a brew with that electric kettle instead of waiting for it to boil on the fire.'

Ivy shook her head. 'If you think an electric kettle is the answer to all my problems, Bob Fothergill, then you don't know the half of it.'

She thought back to when the house was in disarray once the electricity had finally been put into the rented property. This had been a big step in everyone's life and it had caused chaos, with electric poles being put up across the fields, and floorboards raised in every room of the house for the wires to run under. However, looking back, she should have asked for more plug sockets, especially now when there were such things as washing machines; and an electric heater wouldn't go amiss on colder days.

Ivy looked at Bob. 'I've Ben to see to, Sally to sort, all your jobs that you say have been done but haven't; and yes, the washing with that old dolly-tub and mangle, to get myself sodden to the bone.' She placed his mug of hot, steaming tea in front of him.

'Sally sorts herself, and once Ben is at school, he's out from under your feet. You've not got a bad lot, Ivy, and you know it. Now I'm off before you regret anything more that comes out of your mouth.' Bob sighed. 'I'll be back at dinner time, and tha might get a surprise. I did a bit of a deal with a fella I know in Sedbergh, and it'll make our lives easier.' Bob quickly grabbed the oilcloth coat that protected him from the worst of the weather and partly hoped that Ivy had not heard his last few words.

'What are you having us doing now? For Lord's sake!' she said as Bob made quickly for the door.

'You'll see and it will be for the best, so you needn't worry about it,' Bob shouted as he made his way out of the yard. He should have kept his mouth shut, but Ivy had been in such a bad mood that he thought he'd give her something else to think about. She had no idea of the work that went into collecting each kit full of milk from the farms up Garsdale and Dent. It was back-breaking and thankless work in this weather. However, she was right about one thing: it had been his own choice, and it was no good moaning about making the decision that he had taken. The money was good for a reason, he realized now; and aye, happen he would have been better staying working for Jim Mattinson, but he wasn't going to let Ivy win the battle. Instead he pulled up his oilcloth collar and walked the two miles in darkness to Pratt's, a wholesaler of milk, butter and cheese, getting there looking like a drenched rat.

Ivy stood in the darkness of the kitchen doorway. The sound of the rain trickling down every downpipe and gutter filled her ears as she looked out into the early morning, just making out the outline of the fellside and

114

the treeline. The smell of the cowshed and barn filled her nostrils; it was a smell that she had always been brought up with. And even though she knew townspeople couldn't understand, she found it comforting and reassuring. It was the smell of her way of life and she wouldn't change it, no matter how hard it was. The smell was even stronger that morning, with the rain intensifying the aroma of animal dung.

She'd watched Bob run down the yard into the darkness. He'd be sodden, the stupid idiot, before he got to the bottom of the lane. Jim Mattinson would have lent him his old Ford van if he'd been working there. But no, Bob had made his bed and now he would lie in it, out of stubbornness more than anything. What on earth could she expect him to bring home tonight? Ivy felt her mind drifting. Happen with Bob mentioning the washing, he might have decided to buy her a washing machine. She'd seen them in the electric shop window in Kendal, but hadn't even given them the time of day. Such machines were for the rich, and the house had not enough plug sockets, so why she was even thinking that, she didn't know. She'd looked lovingly at one in white enamel – a square box that you filled up with water and it did all the work for you by agitating the washing; no scrubbing, and there was even an electric mangle that you fed your washing through to get rid of excess water. Even Dora Harper hadn't one of them, Ivy thought, as she closed the kitchen door and shut down the dream of an easy washing day, as she went to fill the boiler in the outhouse to do her usual wash and get sodden in doing so.

Bob would never think of buying one of those washing machines. It would probably be a set of new spanners, or something to do with the farm, which he thought was going to make their lives easier. It would not benefit her or the family really, Ivy thought, as she put the water on to heat and then went to make breakfast for Sally and Ben. She regretted agreeing to Sally walking into Dent to see Annie Mackreth about a cleaning job. It meant more work to do on her own, but she had promised and she'd not let her lass down.

'Do they always pick on you like that?' Sally asked quietly as she said goodbye to Ben at the school entrance, after walking and running to Dent between the showers, which were freezing cold and heavy when they came down. Both of them were looking bedraggled, but they weren't on their own. Most children had to walk to school from as far afield as five miles, from the outlying farms and houses.

'Come on, clarty trousers. And last one in has to sit next to Thicko Fothergill,' Ben's mates shouted and grinned. They watched him talking to his sister and sniggered.

'That's not being picked on, our Sal – that's just banter. They are my mates,' Ben said and grinned. 'They are only doing it because you are here.' He put his hands in his pockets and ran towards his friends, who were standing in the shelter of the school's porchway. 'See you tonight, Sal.'

Sally watched him for a moment and then realized he was right, when they all cheered and linked arms, dragging a reluctant Ben into the school just before the headmistress came out onto the step and rang the bell to summon the last hesitant pupils to her classes. She could hear feet scrambling into the big hall for registration, and her memories of going to school there came flooding back, as she looked at the low-built schoolhouse that she had loved attending. School days had come to an end all too soon for her. She had enjoyed the smell of the paper, the excitement of learning new words and of losing herself in a book, but she'd had no option but to leave when she did; she was needed at home, and her parents weren't wealthy enough to give her further education. She smiled as she heard a chorus of voices chanting, 'Good morning, Mrs Evans. Good morning, Mrs Bentham.'

Nothing in school assembly had changed, she thought as she walked along the narrow cobbled streets, which were busy with early-morning shoppers and mothers carrying babies after leaving their other child at school. Dent village itself had not changed for hundreds of years; the sturdy stone-built houses huddled around the cobbled streets, and a smattering of much-needed businesses fitted into the main street. The ancient Norman church was the central point, as it had been for centuries, keeping local people mindful that the Lord was all-important in their lives – unless your name was Bob Fothergill, in which case you had no time for vicars or churches. Outside the church gates and standing across from the George and Dragon inn was a hard granite fountain with the name of Adam Sedgwick upon it. Dent's most famous son, he was a professor of geology and theology at

Cambridge University and a former resident that the whole village was proud of.

The long, tall cottage next to it was where Annie Mackreth lived. Sally felt her stomach churn as she picked up the courage to call. She hesitated outside the butcher's shop just down from the church entrance and stared at her reflection in the window. She looked like a drowned rat, she thought, as she pulled her knitted beret off her head and tried to tidy her long, dark hair, ready to meet Mrs Mackreth and convince her that she would be an excellent help about her house. Standing outside the front door after knocking timidly, and then more loudly, Sally waited.

'Who is it? I'll not be opening the door if you are a pedlar or hawker, so you can be on your way,' Annie Mackreth shouted through the closed door.

'I'm neither, Mrs Mackreth. It's Sally Fothergill – I've come about your job,' she shouted back, but heard no reply. 'I'm Ivy Fothergill's daughter; she used to be Ivy Sunter before she married my father, and she knows you well.' She heard the jingle of keys and the lock turning, as Annie realized who her early-morning caller was.

'Sally Fothergill, you say – Ivy's lass? Last time I saw you, you were in your pram. And now look at you: the spit of your mother at her age. Aye, you are definitely Ivy's.' Annie stood back and, unable to stand up straight, she leaned on her walking stick and squinted at Sally. 'So you are interested in working for me? Then you'd better come in and we'll talk about it over a cup of tea. I will see if you can make a proper brew. I'll start by getting my priorities right,' Annie went on, and shuffled

118

over to her chair in the corner of the main living room. 'Kettle's on the hob through there, teacups are in the cupboard, along with the teapot. Make sure you warm that first, mind – it makes all the difference.' She collapsed down into her chair with a sigh of relief and looked at Sally, who stood unsure whether to go into the unfamiliar kitchen. 'Go on then, it'll not make itself.'

'Right, Mrs Mackreth. Do you take milk and sugar?' Sally asked and hoped that she could find everything she needed in the back kitchen.

'Aye, milk is in the pantry. And you can put a bit of shortbread for us both on a plate. It's in the tin with Queen Victoria on it, bless her soul, above the fire.'

Sally looked around the kitchen, which was warm and homely. There was a drying rack hanging from the ceiling above the fire, with various garments on it drying and airing, and the Yorkshire range had a good fire going, with a blackened kettle on the edge, waiting to be put onto it. A traditional dresser was laden with pots and plates, and geranium plants stood in every window, although they looked a bit neglected and in need of watering.

'Have you found everything?' Annie shouted through, impatient for her cup of tea and biscuit, but even more so for the company the young girl would bring her.

'Yes, Mrs Mackreth. I'm just putting the kettle on to boil,' Sally shouted back as she put the kettle on the coals, and took cups and saucers from the dresser and followed instructions. She got two pieces of home-made shortbread from the battered tin that had obviously been bought on Victoria's Golden Jubilee and had never been parted with and, brewing the tea, she carefully balanced it all on a tray and walked through with it to a small table that Annie had pulled in front of her and another chair.

'No doilies? You'll find them in the drawers in the dresser, next time you bring some biscuits. I always like my plates to look a bit fancy,' Annie said as she leaned forward and took her tea. 'Now, you want to come and work for me, do you? Well, I can be a bit of a stickler, but I'll always be fair, and I'll always pay you if you do right.' She sat back and looked at the lass that she knew now. 'I remember your mother at your age and, aye, your father as well. He's a worker, is your father, but he's always got his head full of fresh ideas. I bet your mother curses him many a day. Trouble is, your heart leads your head when you are young. Like they say, youth is wasted on the young.'

Annie sighed and gazed at an ageing photo of her husband, dressed in his army uniform, and shook her head.

'You know, I miss him every day. I never thought I'd get to this age where I have all on to get myself in and out of bed every day, and not have him by my side. We were married forty-five years and never had a bad word between us. Never blessed with children, but that didn't matter as we had one another.'

'Was he in the army?' Sally asked, noticing the sadness of the old woman, who still dressed in black, apart from a red pair of woollen tartan slippers on her feet, with a pompom on them.

'Aye, he were. He went with a lot of fellas from Dent.

He was a lot older than some and a lot luckier than some. He never went and fought on the Somme. Instead he stopped in this country and was put in charge of looking after the horses that were needed up at the barracks, in the North-East. He always felt it, when he learned that one of the lads he'd joined up with never came back; he felt guilty that he had a cushy job, as he called it, and he should have been on the front with his mates.' Annie sighed. 'And now those bloody Huns are going to be at it again. You'd think they would have spilt enough blood last time.'

'Me mam is worried. She's just glad that our Ben is too young to get involved; and my father is registered as a farmer and I don't think he can be enlisted, so she says, if it does come to war.' Sally sipped her tea and wondered when she was actually going to be told what she was expected to do, if she was to get the job of cleaner.

'Aye, I bet she is. Fellas want nowt with going to war. You don't see any of the government standing on the front line, fighting, but they are willing to send our working-class men all too soon.' Annie finished her tea and biscuit and looked at Sally. 'You seem a sensible lass and I ken your family, so I can see we could get on together. Now, how about I give you two hours this morning? And then on Friday you can come and work from nine until twelve, and we will keep those hours two days a week. You can start with bottoming my bedrooms this morning. The lino on the floors needs a good clean, but don't go polishing it, else I'll slip on my backside and then you will be in trouble.'

121

'You want me to stay this morning and work for you?' Sally gasped.

'Aye, you didn't think I'd waste this much time on talking to you for nowt? Dusters are in the big kitchen cupboard, and the sweeping brush and shovel are in the scullery. And while you are upstairs, there's a big cobweb halfway up the stairs that needs knocking down, but I can't balance and do it. It's been driving me crackers, not being able to get at it – that's why I thought it was time to advertise for a cleaner.' Annie sat back in her chair and closed her eyes. 'There's some brawn for us both in a sandwich in the pantry, and Mary next door brought me gingerbread in the other day, so we'll both have a bit of that before you go home.'

Sally stood up and took the dirty cups and tray away and looked at the ageing woman, who had obviously decided to have a nap, now that she had done her business for the day. The amount of pay had not been mentioned, but she knew that would be sorted, probably at dinner time while eating the brawn sandwich – a sandwich of which Sally dreaded every mouthful. Brawn was the one thing she absolutely hated, after smelling the pig's head in the boiler every autumn, when they had killed the annual pig to get them through the winter. Still, if it was the price she had to pay for securing a job, then she'd like it and lump it and not say a word.

Ivy battled the cold February wind as she pegged the sheet that she had just washed and wrung out. It had stopped raining and the wind got up as she hung the double sheet on the washing line, which was strung between two apple trees in the orchard. It might not get dry, but at least some of the wet would be blown out of it, she thought, as the end of it flicked up in the air and splattered water in her face. Her pinny and belly were nearly as wet as the sheet itself, and she shivered with cold as she carried the empty washing basket back towards the house, stopping in her tracks when she heard the sound of a car coming up the path to the farmyard.

'Damn,' she muttered. It would be Reg Preston calling for his usual monthly provin order; and there she was, sodden and looking like a wild woman, she thought, as the black Ford van pulled up into the yard with the slogan *Thompson's for all your animals' needs*. She stood in the farmhouse doorway and pulled her fingers through her dark, wavy hairy in order to control it, then watched as the van turned in the yard. Reg Preston would delay her even more, she thought, as she painted a smile on her face and waited for the elderly man to get out of the van, with his order book under his arm. To her surprise, it wasn't the rotund figure of Reg that appeared. It was a smartly dressed man in a well-cut suit, with slicked-back black hair and the whitest teeth Ivy had ever seen, as he flashed a smile at her.

'Good morning. Mrs Fothergill of Daleside Farm, I'm hoping?' he said and walked towards her with his hand outstretched to be shaken.

'Aye, it is. I was expecting Reg when the van came into the yard. Is he alright?' Ivy asked and shook the young man's hand, smelling his cologne, which was a lot stronger than any soap that she knew of.

'I'm John – John Blades. Reg, I'm afraid, is in hospital as he had a stroke last week. They thought it was going to be touch and go for a while, but I think he's making progress now.' He shook Ivy's hand firmly and smiled and she stared at him, taken by his looks.

'Oh, that's bad luck. Reg never said he was ill. Are you replacing him for a while then? I've never seen you around here before?' Ivy looked the man up and down, with the washing basket still under her arm and feeling underdressed. The salesman stood with his order book beneath his arm and waited to be asked in to discuss the farm's needs.

'Aye, just for a while, until either Reg manages to return or they find a permanent replacement. I usually take orders from around Kendal, but I've taken lodgings at Sedbergh so that I'm nearer my round down here. So you'll be seeing me every month, or more often if needs be.' John Blades pulled his jacket around him and hoped he wasn't going to be kept on the doorstep in the bitter February wind for much longer.

'Then you'd better come in. I'll apologize for the scrow in the house. It's washing day and there's clothes drying around the fire. I'll move them and put the kettle on to make you a brew while you do your business. Reg always had a brew and a piece of courting cake; it was his favourite, he always said, and he looked forward to eating a piece every month when he called,' Ivy said and walked towards the house. 'Do you like courting cake, Mr Blades, or would you prefer a piece of gingerbread?'

'Please, it's John. And courting cake will be perfect, although I must admit I don't think I've ever tried it before, Mrs Fothergill.'

'Well, there's a first time for everything! Now if I'm to call you John, then I'm Ivy.' She felt her heart skip a beat as John flashed a smile her way and opened the kitchen door for her. She never had seen such a handsome man, and he was well-mannered, too. But she should not even think that way, she checked herself, and remembered that she was faithfully married to Bob, no matter how unloved she felt at that moment.

'Is Mr Fothergill not in today?' John asked and flashed another grin at her.

'No, he works in a morning. We only have a small farm, and he has to work elsewhere to make ends meet.' Ivy placed a cup of tea down next to John, and he put all his sales papers out in front of him and looked at her, as she carried a piece of courting cake on a plate to him and smiled back. 'He's asked me to deal with our needs, so don't worry – I can order what we want.'

'Well, I've done my homework and I see that you usually order hen pellets, Euveka flakes and sheep pellets at this time of year. Do you want to order all three this month in the same quantities as last month?' John asked, then took a bite of the courting cake and smiled. 'I can see why they call it courting cake – you could really fall in love with it,' he said, catching a crumb of the shortcake mixture as it fell from the corner of his mouth.

'Aye, it is a bit moreish. My lot never stop eating it anyway.' Ivy looked across at John as he shuffled his papers to the order page. 'No Euveka this month, as we only have the one dog. And can I halve the quantity of hen pellets, as they don't seem to be keen on those new ones that Reg said everybody else was ordering.' She sighed and flattened down her wet pinny, wishing that she looked a little more becoming for the handsome new salesman.

'I can change them back to what you used to order. We still have some of the older brand in stock,' John said and watched Ivy as she thought about it.

'Reg said you'd no longer be getting them – that's why we changed,' Ivy exclaimed.

'Perhaps he wasn't feeling quite himself. And, between me and you, the new ones were more expensive, so he'd get a bit more commission.' John winked and Ivy blushed.

'Aye, I did notice our bill was a little bit more than usual. I don't think he'd have done that on purpose, as Reg knew we watched what we spend on feed. But if I can change it back, that would be grand,' Ivy replied and took a drink of her tea. She couldn't help but keep glancing at her handsome visitor as he wrote down her needs.

'No chicken mash, pig feed or calf milk powder?' John asked, looking directly at Ivy, before pushing the order across the table for her to sign as she shook her head. His hand casually touched hers as he picked up his expensive ink pen.

'No, that's all we need and hopefully we won't be wanting sheep nuts for much longer, once spring comes and the sheep start to lamb. But then we'll have a pig to feed, so you'll not miss out on an order.' Ivy gave John his sheet of paper back and smiled.

'Surely your husband will be staying home at lambing time, Mrs Fothergill? He'll not be leaving you to it?' John said and put the order into his briefcase.

'No, I and my daughter will handle the lambing; we both know what to do. My daughter is a good hand with the stock. Although I'd rather Bob was here, but needs must,' Ivy replied quietly and felt a pang of anger that she had been taken for granted by Bob, along with Sally.

'Then your husband is a very lucky man, as not only has he an extraordinarily beautiful wife, but a clever and very adaptable one. He should count his blessings.' John stood up and finished the last dregs of tea in his teacup before he made for the door. 'It's been a pleasure meeting you, Ivy, and thank you for your order. Now if there is anything you need, let me know and I'll call in straight away. Next on my list are the Harpers next door, and I hear Mrs Harper will make me welcome there with another cup of tea.'

Ivy stood in the doorway and watched as he climbed into his Morris van. The smell of him lingered in the kitchen long after he had gone and she breathed it in. She caught her reflection in the long mirror at the bottom of the stairs and smiled to herself. 'Extraordinarily beautiful' – had he really been talking about her? He must be blind, for she was dressed like a pauper, soaked and windblown; that was a salesman's patter, she said to herself, and tried to dismiss the conversation. But all day she thought about the dashing John, and she decided that the next time he

127

called she would look a little more presentable. Just a little, because after all he had seen her at her worst and had admired her.

Then a pang of guilt washed over her. How could she ever think of dressing for any man other than her Bob? Had she no shame! Still, Bob never said anything like that to her, and it had made her feel good for the time John had been with her. A smart fella across the other side of the table once a month was going to be something to look forward to, and he had looked genuinely as if he had enjoyed her company.

Chapter 6

'I don't know where your father has got to? He said he'd be back at dinner time, but it's almost supper time, let alone dinner,' Ivy said as she brought in a bucket of coal from the coalhouse to keep the fire going through the evening and night.

'Are you going to tell him about my job with Mrs Mackreth, Mam? 'Cause I think he'll not be suited, no matter what he has actually said in the past. Now that he's working for Pratt's, he will think I should stop at home – I just know he will.' Sally looked frightened.

'We'll see what mood he's in. He can't say much, as he's always trailing off and doing something we don't approve of. He should practise what he preaches,' Ivy replied and then regretted it, not wanting to sound bitter at her husband.

'It'll bring more money in, Mam. Surely he can't moan about that, although I know he will,' Sally said. She sat down with her head in her hands, while Ben put his tongue out at her as he read his latest copy of the much-shared *Champion* comic. The kitchen went quiet, with Ivy worrying about where Bob was and Sally concerned about her breaking news, while Ben didn't care about anything except Colwyn Dane getting his comeuppance against the villain in the latest spell-binding episode.

'What's that? Sounds like a motorbike coming into the yard. It can't be your Uncle Stanley, as he'll be at work.' Ivy rushed to the door and opened it wide, only to be nearly blinded by the sharp light of a motorbike's headlight and deafened by the rev of its engine. All three of them stood in the doorway, looked out into the dusk of the yard and tried to make out who the rider was, as he turned the engine off and then shouted at them, 'Well, what do you think? This will get me to work with no bother, and you can ride pillion, Mother.'

'Oh, it's your father. What on earth are you doing with a motorbike? Have them at Pratt's let you borrow it? And why are you so late?' Ivy sighed and walked out to her husband.

'No, it's ours, lass. I've bought it with my month's wages, off Ronnie Oversby. He wanted rid of it because he's getting himself a van, and he can't run both. It's a good runner; I've been up Garsdale on it and come down over the coal road. It's a bit bumpy over the cobbles in Dent, but it'll get me to work on time, and not as wet every morning. It's a beauty.' Bob slung his leg over the back of the bike and propped it up. 'Purrs like a kitten. You'll just have to mind your leg on the exhaust, if you ride pillion, as it gets bloody hot.' He

130

patted the handlebars and dragged his fingers through his ruffled hair.

'You've bought a bike – a bloody bike – and never thought of telling me first? What happened to saving every penny? Ben could do with some new boots, and Sally could do with some new jumpers, but you said no to both, and that we had to make do and mend. Then you come home on this!' Ivy stood with her arms folded and a scowl on her face, which got worse as she watched Ben run around the bike and marvel at it.

'It's a Royal Enfield, Father. Wow! I never thought we'd have a motorbike.' Ben looked at the engine and held on to the handlebars, then ran his finger over the badge on the petrol tank.

'It's a Royal Enfield that is only visiting. You can take it back to Ronnie Oversby. Whatever possessed you to buy it, I don't know.' Ivy glowered at Bob.

'Aye, lass, you'll not say that when you see how fast I can get you to and from Dent. I'll take you on it tomorrow afternoon; you'll soon change your mind,' Bob chuckled.

'Never in a million years will I get on the back of that thing, Bob Fothergill. Just think of the scandal it would cause.' Ivy shook her head and pulled on Ben's jumper as he tried to climb upon the motorbike and sit on the seat.

'Then we'll get a sidecar, and you can nurse your shopping on your knee. Either way, it's stopping here, Ivy, because it was a real good bargain and it will save me time every day when going back and forth to work. You can moan all you like, woman, but that bike is stopping, and you'll be thanking me for buying it by the end of the week,' Bob growled. 'I'm off to do the milking. I'm late as it is, without arguing with you.'

'And whose fault is that?' Ivy spat. She folded her arms, marching back into the house, with Ben looking at every inch of the bike, and Sally standing with her head bent in the kitchen doorway, following her father to the shippon with her gaze. Why couldn't her parents agree for once? Why did they argue so much over money? Surely things were not that bad at home.

Bob walked into the shippon, feeling mad with himself. Perhaps he should have told Ivy that he was going to buy the bike. However, he had known what her reaction would be. She'd be content for him to go around with the horse and cart, or walk everywhere for the rest of his life. Times were changing; he couldn't afford a motorcar, but a bike would at least get two of them somewhere a little faster. It would prove to be a godsend for him getting to work and back – surely she could see that? Not that working at Pratt's was turning out well. He enjoyed it there, but jobs were beginning to mount up on the farm: there were some walls to be mended, and in another month or two it would be lambing time. Every lamb would bring them money in the bank, come autumn, so it was imperative that they were born alive. Would Ivy and Sally manage while he was at work or had he been pig-headed, as Ivy frequently called him, and risked his lambs' lives and his family's happiness? Ivy had become more and more upset by things of late. Could she not see that he was doing these things for the good of the family, and for their futures?

Bob sighed and pulled the bucket between his legs, then bent down and started milking Daisy, the roan shorthorn cow. 'Aye, Daisy, if only folk were as contented as you. A good feeding of hay, the warmth of the shippon in winter and a good pasture in summer: that's all you ask of me. I don't know what to do for the best, lass, when it comes to that family of mine,' Bob said and pressed his head against the side of the cow. 'I never seem to get it right, no matter what I do.' Then he smiled at the cat, which had joined him, curling his tail around Bob's boots and legs. 'And you only show me cupboard-love, so you needn't look at me with those eyes. You know all too well there's always a drop of milk left over for you.' If only his family was as faithful as his animals, he thought.

The atmosphere in the Fothergills' household that evening was awkward, to say the least. Ivy hardly spoke to Bob; Ben kept mentioning the motorcycle and asking his father how fast it could go; while his mother glared at the pair of them. Sally kept herself busy and pegged her rug, deciding not to say anything about her new job with old Mrs Mackreth. She hated it when there was tension between her parents and hoped they would soon make up with one another. They usually did, but this time she sensed that her father had pushed her mother a little too far, with both a new job and a motorcycle. Although she was quite excited about the prospect of perhaps having a ride behind her father on it, if asked.

* * *

133

Ivy lay still in bed; for once she was not going to get up with her husband and see him right for the day. It had been his choice to go to work so early, and this morning she was going to make her feelings known about his selfish ways. She'd turned her back upon him all night and had not even kissed him goodnight – something they had never failed to do in their sixteen years of marriage. She pulled the covers over her and pretended to be asleep when she heard Bob sit on the edge of the bed and relieve himself in the chamber pot, before standing up and pulling on his trousers in the darkness of the bedroom.

'Are you not getting up with me this morning, lass?' Bob asked quietly, wondering whether to shake her or not. Thinking better of it, he left Ivy still silent and made his way down the stairs to an empty kitchen, which felt cold and unloved. He looked around it and wondered whether or not to make himself some breakfast, as he pulled on and laced up his work boots. He'd never known Ivy not get up with him before; she must be really mad at him, he thought, as he decided to wait for a brew at work. And hopefully some farmer's wife would give him a piece of cake or a biscuit on his rounds, picking up the milk for the dairy. It was a hard price to pay, being ignored by the one you loved, for the sake of what he thought would be better for the family. Perhaps he should tell Ivy that evening to go into Sedbergh and buy Ben his shoes, and Sally those jumpers that she needed. Damnit, Ivy could even treat herself to a new pinny if she needed one, he thought, as he put his leg over the motorbike's tank and kick-started the engine into action.

Ivy listened to the sound of Bob leaving the yard on his beloved motorbike. She sighed and wiped the tears away from her eyes, then lay back looking up into the darkness at the ceiling. She heard her mother's words of warning many a day when she was scrimping and saving to make ends meet. Her father had said just about the same thing, thankful that he had a son who would inherit the family farm, rather than Bob Fothergill getting his hands on it after his marriage to his daughter. Why hadn't she listened? Ivy's heart had ruled her head and now she was lying in bed, crying and feeling unloved, and fed up with her lot in life.

Bob could be a hard man; he didn't show his affections easily, and a peck on the cheek at bedtime was about all she got nowadays. And he never treated her to anything, but he could buy himself a bloody motorbike, she thought, as she lay there, having only negative thoughts of her husband. Eventually she stirred. She couldn't lie in bed feeling sorry for herself, as there was a cow to milk, Ben to get to school on time and various jobs to do around the house and farm. She could sob all day, but that would get her nowhere, she thought, as she got out of bed ready to tackle the day, no matter what was thrown at her. She'd no option but to get on with life, and make do and mend.

Sally said nothing as she washed the breakfast pots up for her mother, after walking to the lane end with Ben to see him safely on his way to school with his usual friends and schoolmates. Her mother had milked the

135

cow and had been strangely quiet, which was not her way. Usually the kitchen was filled with her mother's chatter as they both did jobs about the house, but not this morning; her eyes were red and swollen and she looked tired.

'Are you alright, Mam?' Sally asked quietly, not wanting to pry too much.

'Aye, I'm alright, lass – just a bit mad at your father. We had no need for that bike, no matter how hard he tries to convince me.' Ivy gave Sally a wan smile. 'He's a law unto himself, is that father of yours, but we couldn't do without him,' she said as she put the dish of eggs that had been collected in the sink to be washed. 'The hens are back laying; spring must be on its way.'

'That'll make my father happy. More eggs to sell at Pratt's – more money coming in,' Sally replied with a lightness in her voice.

'It'll take more than a few eggs to pay for that bloody machine. And he's to fill its tank wherever he goes with petrol or whatever it runs on,' Ivy said sharply and looked out of the window, cursing under her breath. No matter how she tried, she couldn't forgive Bob for spending so much money on what she thought was a luxury.

Sally breathed in deeply. Her mother had not mentioned her work for Annie Mackreth that morning, and she felt as if she needed someone to talk to about it. She knew that when her mother was in a bad mood, only time would bring her round, and she wasn't relishing the fact that she was at home alone with Ivy all day. 'Mam, do you think I could go and see Marjorie this morning?

136

I haven't seen her for weeks,' she said and watched as her mother turned round and faced her.

'Aye, you get yourself away. I could do with a bit of time to myself. It'll give me time to calm down and try to see the reasoning in your father's purchase. Although, for the life of me, I can't see any,' Ivy sighed.

'I can, Mam. Father can get back and forth to work on it a lot faster and he can take you, like he says, on the back of it; and us two, if we get the chance. Our Ben is full of it; he loves anything mechanical – any machinery and he's there, unlike with farming,' Sally said, at the risk of getting her head bitten off.

'Happen I'm wrong, but I don't think so. Now don't let that Marjorie lead you astray, and be back for your dinner. Your father will be home by then, and he'll only moan if he knows you are over at the Harpers. Be gone with you then. Let me have some time by myself,' Ivy replied sharply and watched as Sally got her coat from behind the kitchen door. She was glad Sally had suggested a visit to her friend. She needed time to herself to sit and think things through, and perhaps shed another tear, because – like it or not – Bob had greater priorities than her, and his priorities would always come first.

'Alright, Mam. You'll be alright on your own, won't you?' Sally asked, with concern in her voice. 'I'll take a look at the sheep as I walk over to Marjorie's, so don't worry about them.'

'Of course I will. Now, go on – go and see what that Marjorie has to say for herself. I'm sure she will be full of gossip. Her mother always is.' Ivy watched as Sally couldn't get out of the kitchen fast enough. Her mood was going to have to improve before Sally and Bob returned, she thought, as she didn't like the sharp-talking Ivy when she was in a bad mood, and neither did anyone else.

Ivy sat with a mug of tea in her hands, and tears running down her cheeks. She'd sobbed and thought about Bob all morning. She loved him, but sometimes he was impossible to live with, but the scandal of leaving your husband would always be scowled upon in the Dales and was something she hardly dared think about. Her father had said, on the day of her marriage, that she'd made her own bed and must lie in it. And now, with both parents dead, she knew exactly what he had meant.

She pulled her hanky out of her pinny pocket and blew her nose. It was time to square herself up; it was a second-hand motorbike, not an extravagant motorcar or some other fancy contraption. Perhaps Sally was right and it would be a boon to them in the long run. Ivy blew her nose hard, gave herself a good talking to and then was surprised to hear the sound of a motor pulling into the yard, at first thinking it was Bob back earlier than usual on his motorbike. She wiped her eyes. It wasn't the sound of a motorbike, it was a car, and she knew that any visitor who was about to call would instantly see that she had been upset. She peered out of the kitchen window, still hoping it was Bob and that it was time to make up, only to see the salesman for Thompson's coming towards the house. He had spotted her as he waved to her through the window, so she'd have to answer the door.

'Mr Blades, now what brings you back our way this morning?' Ivy asked, trying her best to look bright and sound cheerful.

'Now then, Mrs Fothergill – it's John. None of this standing on ceremony with me. I thought that I'd made that clear yesterday,' John Blades said and touched Ivy's arm lightly, noticing that she had obviously been upset about something. 'I hope I haven't called at an inconvenient moment? It's just that yesterday I must have left my pen with one of my customers. Which I wouldn't usually worry about, but it was one that my late wife gave me just before she died,' John said quietly and looked directly into Ivy's eyes.

'Oh no, it's not inconvenient at all, John. I've just been peeling onions, which are why my eyes look red,' Ivy replied quickly and tried a smile. 'Do come in, and I'll have a look around the table. I must admit I've not noticed it when we were at breakfast.' She turned and John followed her into the farmhouse, noting the lack of smell of peeled onions as he did so.

'I've disturbed you having a drink of tea – I'm so sorry,' John said, as Ivy hunted under the latest newspaper that had been placed on the table, and gazed on the floor, without any success in finding the missing pen.

'That's no problem, perhaps you'd like to join me. I was just about to make a fresh brew and, to be honest, I could do with some company,' Ivy answered, feeling her emotions rise to the top again and fighting back the tears.

'Is there something wrong, Ivy? You look upset. Is it the latest news of the war in Europe developing? I must

139

admit it does not bode well,' John said, with care in his voice as he noticed the newspaper's headlines.

'No, no, it's not that, it's nothing really – just me being silly and getting upset over something.' Ivy sniffed while she put some tea in the teapot and set the kettle on to boil. 'I've not slept for worrying overnight and it's really over nothing, when people could be about to lose sons and husbands in another stupid war. Forgive me.' She blew her nose loudly and wiped a tear away. 'You say you are a widower. How long have you been without your wife? She can only have been young?' Ivy breathed in and composed herself, then brewed the tea and sat across the table from John and looked at him as he sipped his tea. She felt selfish, crying over a fit and healthy husband when the poor man across from her had lost his wife.

'She was – we had only been married six months. It was cancer, a terrible shock; it has taken me a long time to get over her loss. Hence my hunt for the pen, which means a lot to me, as she gave it to me on my birthday,' John replied and smiled across at Ivy. 'You make the most of each day and every second when you have lost someone dear to you.' He reached out to take Ivy's hand from around her mug. 'Now, are you going to tell me what's wrong? I promise what you say will stay with me. "A problem shared" and all that, as they say.'

'It's nothing; really, it's just me being over-sensitive. Please take no notice of me,' Ivy said, gazing across at the kind, caring face of John. If only her Bob cared as much about her feelings, she thought, and then withdrew

140

her hand from his. She enjoyed his touch and sympathetic looks too much. As she was feeling unloved and unwanted, his kind touch and voice were exactly what she felt short of, and she knew that she could easily be tempted to tell John Blades far more than she should.

'Then if you are sure, I'll be on my way. If you'd like, I could call back in next week? Just to check if you want anything, and that you are alright. It's my duty to look after my customers after all.' John pushed his chair back, leaving his cup of tea partly un-drunk, and looked at the crestfallen Ivy. 'In fact don't answer that. I will call in once a week to have a chat, and perhaps to indulge in another piece of that delicious courting cake. It can be lonely living on these farms, even if you have a family and husband. A friendly face once a week is exactly what you need.'

'Really you don't need to, but that would be nice. I'll look forward to your visit,' Ivy said and couldn't believe that she was encouraging the friendship.

'Then say no more. Until next week.' John smiled at her. 'I'll look forward to it.'

Chapter 7

Sally pulled her coat around her as she stood with her father's crook in her hand and viewed each sheep with a critical eye. Their bellies were expanding; soon the fields would be full of lambs and their dams, grazing on the sweet spring grass, but first they had to be born into the world. She only hoped that she could cope while her father was at work. And then she put her worries behind her; she'd seen many a lamb's birth, so she'd manage, come hell or high water. She had a good eye for recognizing when a ewe was in trouble. She had managed to fodder and milk the cow and see to the rest of the stock these last few weeks, and her father had not complained once to her face, so perhaps she had pleasantly surprised him.

Placing the lambing crook back against the farmhouse door, she ran off across the fields towards her best friend's house. It was time for a catch-up, she thought, as she strode out. The wind was cold, but there was the first sign of spring on its way as she made her way down the wood above the Harpers' farm. The dog's mercury was flowering and she noted that the wood sorrel was starting to appear. It wouldn't be long before the wood's floor was carpeted with bluebells and primroses and, with the warmth of spring, the fields and dales would come to life once more.

It was the time of year she enjoyed the most, but this year it would be different, as she was no longer at school with her friends. She was now at work, and once more she and her mother would be in charge of lambing the sheep, first thing of a morning. She would no longer be able to walk through the fields and visit Marjorie. Now that they had both left school, they had not seen as much of one another recently, although they were still close and always would be. She'd be needed more on the farm, especially if her father persisted in working for Pratt's, she thought, and she would have to tell Marjorie so. Marjorie could be petty over some things, so Sally hoped she wouldn't upset her with her news.

She sat on a large boulder that stuck out of the ground, left behind from the Ice Age, and looked around her, getting a perfect view of the Harpers' farm and farmyard, and a view across the other side of the dale, with Combe Scar brooding in front of her; the sides of it were dotted with small white flecks of white – sheep grazing – and the lower slopes gave way to trees and pastures. Moving on to the dividing farm walls, she stopped for a minute and placed two fallen top-stones that had been dislodged back on the limestone wall, knowing that if not replaced, they would become a larger gap and more work. It was while she was doing so that she saw a van parked up in the farmyard and could make it out to be that of the local animal-feed salesman. He must be paying the Harpers a call, as she knew he'd been at her home earlier in the week.

Sally watched as the new salesman stood close to Dora Harper; she looked twice, as she thought he had his arm around Dora's waist, then checked herself as she saw him wave and shout at Brian Harper as he appeared around the corner of the barn, and then the salesman quickly got into his van. He was probably apologizing for something or saying his goodbyes, she thought, as she looked down upon the scene, then stood up to make her way down the brant pasture to the farm that her father was so envious of. The Harpers had everything – everything that her father coveted, but knew he couldn't afford.

Even though there had been silence and arguing in the family home recently, she had felt a little sympathy for her father. He didn't spend his money so stupidly, and she could see the benefit of the motorbike, unlike her mother. She too wouldn't mind a ride upon it, if he had a mind for his daughter to do so. He was a funny stick, she thought; if Father thought it was not a woman's place in the world, he was dead against it, but if it was for his own benefit – like her being left in charge of the morning's lambing ewes – then he overlooked his prejudices.

She made her way down the pasture side and opened the gate that led into the yard of the Harpers' farm, which was called Beckside, making the two sheepdogs bark; unlike hers, they had a proper dog kennel. They pulled on their chains and barked sharply, snapping at her and making Brian Harper appear out of the barn that he had gone into, yelling at them.

'Hold your noise, dogs. It's nobbut Sally from next door.' The dogs rattled their chains and gave one more warning bark, before cowering down into their kennel. 'Now then, Sally, have you come to see our Marjorie? We were only saying she's not seen much of you of late.' Brian Harper stood with a yard brush in his hand and looked at the lass who had grown up with his daughter, although he knew the pair were like chalk and cheese in their ways.

'I thought I'd better come and see her, Mr Harper. I got a bit of a job yesterday and I'll be working two mornings a week, so I thought I'd come and tell Marjorie,' Sally explained and thought how easy it was to tell her friend's father her news, unlike her own father.

'Now that will give you some pin money. Our Marjorie could do with doing the same – it would make her value money more, if she had to work for it.' Brian sighed and looked down at his feet and then asked her, 'Where are you working at, lass? There are not many jobs around here.'

'I'm only cleaning for Mrs Mackreth, next to the fountain, just on Monday and Friday mornings. But yes, it will bring a bit of money in at home. I'm looking after father's sheep and milking some mornings as well, now he's working for Pratt's,' Sally said and smiled.

'You'll be alright there, and it will do old Annie good to have a bit of company. You are a busy lass – your father should be proud of you. Now I'm about to clean my calves out. Can you tell your father I've one for sale, if he fancies it? One of my lasses has had twin heifers, but she can only manage to feed one and I haven't the time to bucket-feed a calf. I'll sell it to him for only a little. I'll be glad to get it off my hands, if he wants it.' Brian made his way to the calf shed, nodding his head towards the house. 'They are both in, just open the kitchen door and yell. Be thankful you've just missed that bloody smarmy new salesman from Thompson's; he was only here the other day and he can't have wanted much, as Dora never yelled for me, thank the Lord. I'd rather have old Reg come a-calling.'

'I'll tell my father about the calf, thank you,' Sally shouted as she made her way to the kitchen door at the side of the stone farmhouse. She waved at Mrs Harper as she saw her washing up through the window, then reach for the towel to dry her hands as she came to the door.

'Now you are a stranger! We haven't seen you for a while, and Marjorie hasn't mentioned visiting you. You haven't fallen out, have you?' Dora smiled and saw the look on Sally's face. 'Our Marjorie can be a bit flighty, so I'd take no notice of her. She's in the front room, darning some socks for me. Although you'd think it was a terrible task, the way she has moaned about it. I'm sure she will be glad to see you – walk straight through and surprise her.' Dora Harper looked at Sally with a critical eye, noting the darned elbows on her jumper. Unlike Sally's mother, Dora was always dressed immaculately, her hair was always tidy and was jet-black, with eyebrows and eyelashes to match. Sally's mother always muttered and said under her breath that Dora was part foreign, as well as being what she called 'common'. Dora did not mix with the rest of the farmers' wives in the dale. She knew that they talked about her and looked upon her as a threat to their marriages, but quite frankly she didn't care. It was their problem, not hers, if they didn't know how to satisfy their men enough to keep them.

'Thank you. I'll go through and see her, if I may?' Sally said politely and walked through the warm kitchen with its oilcloth and rugs on the floor, unlike hers at home, which had bare stone slabs. She entered the front room, where Marjorie sat darning her father's socks next to a blazing fire.

'Oh, it's you, is it? I wondered when you'd show your face. I thought you'd have to come and say something, sometime, although I must say it has taken you long enough to do so. I've not seen you for weeks and before you say anything more it was rude, Sally Fothergill. I didn't know where you'd gone, until that gormless Edward Riley told me you'd gone home,' Marjorie said sharply.

'How could I tell you, when you were wrapped in the arms of Jonathan Birbeck up the side of the hall? Have you no shame, Marjorie? I know you like him, but outside, on your own, that's just asking for trouble,' Sally said quietly, knowing that Marjorie would think her prudish.

'Don't you start; my father nearly took his belt off on me. He found us both and was not impressed. That's why I've not been let out of this house for what seems like an age, although I have sneaked out a time or two to see Jonathan without them knowing. My father says I should be ashamed to show my face, after he found me and Jonathan at the side of the hall. It must have been only a few minutes after you had gone home, because I can remember the New Year being sung in. You could at least have shouted and then I'd have realized you had gone!'

'My father was with me and I didn't want to draw attention to you. I'd had all on to convince him that I was alright coming out with you anyway, without him seeing you lifting your skirts,' Sally hit back.

'How do you know I lifted my skirts? We just went out for a bit of fresh air – nothing more!' Marjorie said and looked down at her sewing.

'It was a bit cold, I'd imagine, getting fresh air for that long, unless Jonathan was keeping you warm.' Sally grinned at her best friend. She knew as well as Marjorie did what they had both been up to; the trouble was that half the population of the village of Dent would also, if just one person had seen them. Everyone knew everybody's business in the dale. It was how everyone got along: looking after one another's backs when times were hard or distancing themselves, if they thought fit.

'Oh, he was keeping me warm, Sally, but don't you tell anybody, do you hear? We are thinking of running away to Gretna Green to get married, but you don't say owt to anybody. It's a secret, do you hear?' Marjorie looked up slyly at Sally with a wide grin. 'I do think I truly love him – Jonathan's so handsome, and he's told me he loves me so much.' Marjorie pulled a worried face. 'I'm old enough now that I'm sixteen, and we are allowed to runaway together and, hopefully, get married without our parents' permission. I look a lot older than I am, and I'll just put my age down as twenty-one, as that's what we have both agreed to do. Because Jonathan has promised me, and never stops promising me, a happy life together. Each time we meet in secret he tells me so.'

'You can't do that. How are you both going to live? And where are you going to live?' Sally asked and stared at Marjorie. 'You were making eyes at the lads from Sedbergh before Jonathan showed his face, so how can you say you love him, after doing that? Besides, don't you think you are a bit too young even to be thinking about that?' Sally sighed. 'I want a few more years to myself before I settle down with someone.'

'I do love him – I'm sure I do. Jonathan will take care of all that's needed, he's promised. And I'm not too young, as my mother was only just seventeen when she married my father.' Marjorie looked crossly at Sally. 'Besides, I hear that I wasn't the only one getting kissed at midnight. I hear you and Edward Riley got to know each other quite well. What you see in him, I don't know,' Marjorie said and glared sullenly at Sally. 'He's got ginger hair for a start, and he dresses old-fashioned.'

'Edward is alright. I had a good night with him, so leave him alone. Anyway I've some more news. My father has bought a motorbike. My mother and he are not seeing eye-to-eye over it; in fact I'm glad to be here, out of the house, while my mother sulks about my father spending money on it.' Sally slouched down in the fabric-covered easy chair, which her mother would have loved in her front room, instead of the battered leather one that had originally belonged to her own parents.

'I don't blame your mother. What's the use of a motorbike when there are four of you? He should have bought a van at least. My father is thinking of buying a Ford car, or should I say my mother is trying to persuade him to buy a car. There's not many up Dent yet, so we'd look real swanky. I think that's why she's suddenly friends with that creepy salesman of Thompson's, as she knows that he has a car and van.' Marjorie threw down her mending onto the floor. 'Anyway, my mam and dad can do what they want, because I don't aim to be here much longer. I bet they will be glad to see the back of me, because all they do is argue, just like yours. Sometimes I think that is all parents do. And this bloody war that they say is coming – I'm fed up of hearing about it. As if Hitler is going to come stomping up the dale.'

'He might not come stomping up the dale, but he's making a good job of threatening most countries in Europe. My father and mother were talking about all the young men being enlisted like in the Great War. Mam said she was just glad that our Ben was only young and could claim to be a farmer. Your Jonathan works at home and, from what I've heard him say, hates it. I bet he'd

150

be one of the first to enlist,' Sally said and looked at Marjorie, who seemed perturbed.

'Then he'd not go – I wouldn't let him. Why should he fight a war that's of no concern for either of us? And you, Sally Fothergill, are just making me worry. I wish you'd shut up with your talk of war. You really know how to shatter a girl's dreams.' Marjorie pouted and picked up her mending, blanking Sally as she pretended to concentrate on her sewing.

'Suit yourself, but it's the truth: if war comes, all young men will be expected to fight for their country, whether they are to be married at Gretna Green or not.' Sally stood up to go. If she'd upset Marjorie she hadn't meant to, but now she knew she would be blanked or hardly talked to, if she stayed. It was time to return home and hope her mother was in a better mood, and that for once her father had returned early after his morning's work. She couldn't get the picture out of her head of the salesman with his arm around Marjorie's mother's waist; that was just not done, even if he was apologizing or something similar.

Sally walked home over the fields and was surprised to see Jim Mattinson's van parked in the yard and her father's motorbike by the side of it. Jim used to call round often, but since her father had stopped working for him, he'd not come, so it was good to see the family friend calling on them again. She opened the kitchen door and walked into the room. It was warm and homely, and the air was filled with the smell of Kendal Twist tobacco, which both men were smoking as they sat around the table and talked. They looked up at Sally, and her father was the first to speak.

'Your mother's in the front room. She's listening to the news while me and Jim do a bit of business. Go through and join her, lass, until Jim and I have settled what he's come about – that's a good'un.' Her father looked serious and nodded his head in the direction of the living-room doorway.

'It's alright, Bob. I don't mind Sally listening in. Happen she will convince you for me. After all, she isn't half growing up nowadays,' Jim said, puffing on the pipe that hung in the side of his mouth. He was a tall man with a weathered face, from always being out on the land, but had the most welcoming smile as he looked at Sally softly.

'It's alright, Mr Mattinson, I'll join my mother. You both look as if it's something important that you are talking about, so I'll leave you to it.' Sally walked through the bank of smoke that hung around the men as she made her way to the living-room door and joined her mother, listening to the news on the radio, which had entertained them and kept them informed since her Uncle Stanley had given it to them at Christmas.

'What's Jim Mattinson doing here, Mam?' Sally said, but got no reply as her mother placed her finger on her lips and said, 'Shh . . .' and listened to the latest news on the war in Europe.

'That's right; drag us into it again.' Ivy spoke angrily at the radio and the announcement by the prime minister, Neville Chamberlain, that if Germany was to

152

invade Poland, then France and Great Britain would have no option but to declare war on Germany. 'Just drag us into it, even if we want to have nowt to do with it.' She turned the radio off and sat back in her chair and sighed. 'Sorry, pet, this blinking government is as daft as brushes and intent on getting us all killed. Anyway, enough of something that might never happen – and it's nowt for you to bother your head over.' Ivy smiled. 'Aye, Jim Mattinson is here, and I have an idea he's come to ask your father to come back and work for him. I only hope Bob's not that stubborn to turn him down. He should know by now that he's better working for Jim, for less pay, than trailing to Sedbergh every morning just after dawn, no matter how much Pratt's pay him. Anyway I've left them to it, as your father can't turn round and bite my head off if I say nowt about it.'

'I hope Mr Mattinson is offering Father his old job back, because I'm a bit worried about managing, this lambing time. I don't know how we are going to cope, especially now that I'm working for Annie Mackreth,' Sally said, noticing the worry on her mother's face. Her father was always giving Ivy something to worry about, but the appearance of the motorbike had been too much.

'We'd manage, and don't tell your father any different. I'm not having him thinking we are dependent on him. He gets enough of his own way, as it is,' Ivy said sharply and then went quiet as she heard the men rise from the kitchen table, Jim cranking up his van and Bob wishing him well and sending him on his way.

'Well? What was all that about?' Ivy asked as Bob came into the front room and stood, looking pleased with himself.

'He came to ask me to come back and work for him. He's bought a lump of land above Dent station and hasn't time to do everything himself this spring. He's never taken anybody on since I left him, hoping that I'd be back after a week or two. He heard that I'd bought a motorbike and thought if he didn't act quickly, I'd never come back to him.' Bob stood and saw the relief on Ivy's face.

'What did you tell him? Are you going back to work for Jim? Please say that you are,' Ivy said, glaring at her husband, who wasn't giving anything away.

'Well, I wasn't going to look too eager – I made him sweat a bit. After all, it was Jim who came looking for me, and I worked hard enough for him last time,' Bob replied.

'Father, are you going back to work for him or not, or have you still not learned owt?' Ivy asked impatiently.

'Now then, Mother. You had all on to talk to me this morning because of that bike, but I think you owe me an apology now. Jim Mattinson has offered me more hours and more pay; in fact he's matched Pratt's wage, so what do you think I've said?' Bob grinned. 'I was getting fed up of lugging milk kits before dawn had even broken, anyway. Plus, I heard that this lass of ours has gone and got herself a job looking after Annie Mackreth, so who would have looked after my sheep in the morning?' Bob saw the colour rise in his daughter's cheeks.

154

'There's not much escapes me, lass, you should know that. Everybody in this dale talks.'

'I was going to tell you, Father, but I'd not had chance, with one thing and another,' Sally said quietly.

'I am so glad, Bob. I hoped that was what Jim had come for, and I'm glad you were back home to see him. Do you have to give notice at Pratt's?' Ivy asked, sounding relieved that her life was about to become a little easier.

'Only a week. There are plenty of young lads out there wanting a job; it will be filled within a few days. I was beginning to wonder how we were going to manage at lambing time, because you can bet your bottom dollar that my sheep lamb in the morning, when I'd not have been about. And if this one was working for Annie – however many days a week – then you would have struggled. Besides, I couldn't put up with mood you've been in. Bloody hell, it's a wonder the milk hasn't curdled, with the look on your mush of late.' Bob put his arm around Ivy. 'Never mind, old lass, everything comes right eventually. It did Jim Mattinson good to think I'm not as beholden to him as he is to me. We might be friends, but I'll not be taken advantage of.'

'No wonder my hair is turning white. All I do is worry about every one of you, and nobody ever gives me a second thought,' Ivy said and smiled. 'And the bike? Does it stay?'

'Of course, lass. Like I say, you can hop on the back behind me, and we will be in Dent in five minutes. Besides, our Ben can tinker about with it – he's far more interested in that than in farming, and happen he'll come in handy

155

that way instead. One day we will have that farm of our own and a tractor, so we will need a mechanic.' Bob stood his ground on keeping the motorbike. 'Come on, we'll have a quick spin down the lane on it.' He took hold of Ivy's arm and pulled her out of the chair, protesting.

'I'll get my skirts caught in the wheels,' Ivy said as he pulled her through the house, still complaining.

'Hold your whisht, woman, and when I lean into a bend, you do too,' Bob replied, laughing as he made Ivy climb on behind him and hold tightly to him as he turned the key and kick-started the bike into action.

Ivy held on for dear life, but laughed as the bike, with both of them on it, left the yard.

Sally sat back in her chair. She was glad her father had come to his senses, and smiled as she heard both her parents laughing over the noise of the motorbike. Now she just had to prove to her father that she was as good at farming as any lad, and that she would be there to help him in the coming years.

Chapter 8

The season was starting to warm; daisies and celandines filled the pastures around the farm and the blossom in the orchard was starting to come into bud. Spring was here, and life on the farm would get easier with the warmth of the sun's rays and the growth of grass. It was Sunday morning, and Sally walked beside her father as they made their way over to visit the Harpers to look at the calf that was in need of a home.

'It'll not be worth owt – that's why he'll be wanting to sell it to me. But then again, there's nowt spoilt if I go and look at it. Our old cow's making enough milk to feed a calf, and after next week I'll be at home more, to see to feeding it. An extra milk cow would be welcome; once it's grown, we could make butter and perhaps some cheese and sell it at the lane end,' Bob said as he walked quickly through the fields with his walking stick in his hand.

'I can feed the calf. I'll enjoy it – it's not much work and, before you know it, it will be out grazing anyway.'

Sally was having all on to keep up with her father as he strode out.

'Nay, you are working two days a week for Annie. I can't count on you on them days, but happen the others. I've ordered two piglets that'll need feeding from Tom Dixon, so that's more work. But they'll be gone by the back-end; we will be butchering them as usual,' Bob replied as he opened the gate into the farmyard, making the dogs bark their usual warning and causing Brian Harper to open the door to see who was visiting.

'Now then, Bob, she's told you about the calf then? I thought you might be interested. It'll save me taking it down to the auction mart in Sedbergh; calves are not making a good price anyway,' Brian said, coming across the yard to meet them both.

'Aye, well, I'll have a look at it. I'm not promising, but we could do with a bit more stock, now that Ben is getting up, and Sally's a good help,' Bob replied rather grudgingly and looked at his daughter.

'You are lucky – at least you've one of each. I've just my Marjorie and she's no farmer. Talking about Marjorie, do you want to pop in and see her? She's in a right mood for some reason,' Brian said to Sally in a way that she could not refuse, although she would rather have inspected the calf than have to talk to Marjorie. Her father was right: Marjorie was in a mood, and Sally had hoped not to see her until she came round, as invariably she did when she realized she needed Sally's friendship. 'She's not in the house, she's down by the beck, sitting on her tree swing, and she's been there most of the morning, whatever she's up to,' Brian explained.

'Go on, there will plenty of time to see the calf, especially if it's to come home with us,' Bob said and urged his daughter to find her friend while he and Brian did some business.

'She gets more like her bloody mother every day, does our Marjorie. Feisty and bloody moody. I don't know what I've done to deserve the pair of them,' Sally heard Brian say as he walked across the yard with her father, and her father replied saying something that she could not catch. She wandered behind the farmhouse past the hen hut, with the hens calling loudly inside it as they laid their daily egg. She felt the warming breeze on her face and went past the blackthorn, which in another week or two would be covered with its snowy covering of white blossom. She bowed under the branch of an aged oak and spied Marjorie sitting on the rope swing made by her father, next to the small beck that gave the farm its name.

'Marje, your father said I'd to come and find you. He told me you were here,' Sally said, going over to her friend as she held on to the ropes on either side of the swing and balanced on the wooden plank that acted as the seat. Her head was lowered and, as Sally approached, she heard sobbing coming from her best friend.

'Just go away. I don't want to talk to anybody. He shouldn't have told you where I was – I wanted to be alone.' Marjorie sniffed, with tears rolling down her face, which was all crumpled from crying for most of the morning.

'What's up? What are you crying for? I thought you and Jonathan were running off to be married and all was perfect in your world.' Sally put her arm around her friend's shoulders in sympathy, as Marjorie never ever cried; she lost her temper frequently, but she never, ever cried. Something must be wrong.

'I'm not talking about him ever again. My mother said that old bag Preston said she'd seen Jonathan going to the new picture house in Sedbergh with Alison Redman, of all people. Alison Redman! She's so ugly, and last week Jonathan promised me that we were to marry. I really thought he loved me. I did things I really shouldn't have done, just to keep him. Now he'll be doing the same with her. I hate him; I hope he drops down dead.' Marjorie sobbed while Sally looked at her and tried to offer some comfort.

'He might just have been keeping her company. You don't know that he was courting her,' she said and tried to calm her friend as she sobbed in despair.

'What, with his arm around her and Alison gazing up at him? Old bag Preston said she was shocked to see such goings-on in broad daylight as she came back with her shopping. Jonathan's courting her, I know he is – he's never been near me this last week. Ever since I told him I was late . . .' Marjorie started wailing again. 'He's abandoned me, and so will my parents if I tell them what bother I think I'm in.'

'Late? You don't mean what I think you do? You don't think you're having his baby, do you?' Sally whispered quietly with a look of dread on her face. This was

160

what happened to bad girls; her mother had always warned her, and now her best friend was exactly in that situation. 'You can't be – you are not old enough,' she protested and stared at Marjorie, partly with disgust and partly in sympathy.

'Don't be daft. Of course I'm old enough, but I don't want it!' Marjorie gasped. 'I don't want to live, at this moment in time, because everything is wrong and I've nobody to turn to. By the look on your face, even you are disgusted with me. I thought he loved me, Sally. I'd have done anything for him,' Marjorie wailed and hung on to the rope swing as she sobbed, with snot running down her face.

'I'm not disgusted – just shocked. It could happen to anyone. And I didn't mean you are not old enough to be having his baby. I meant you are not old enough to be a mother. Anyway you might be imagining it; you might be crying and getting upset over nothing.' Sally stared at the roots of the giant oak tree to which the swing was attached. At the base of the tree were some shelves of flatbed rock from the river, which the girls had made when they were younger. On the roughly-made shelves were broken pieces of pottery, saucers with cracks, and cups with chips in them that their mothers and grand-mothers had given them. They had called it their pot-house and had spent many a happy hour playing there, making pretend teas for their pretend families. But now Marjorie, at the tender age of sixteen, was perhaps all too soon going to be a mother. Sally didn't know what to say.

'I'm not imagining it – I know I'm not. I'm having

Jonathan's baby, but I'll not say anything to anyone until I really have to, and even then I'm not saying that he's the father. If I'd been another month younger, he would have been going to jail for what he has done to me. He's been waiting until I got to be sixteen, I know he has.' Marjorie sniffed in hard and wiped her tears away. 'And you, Sally Fothergill, are not to say anything to anybody. In fact you needn't come and visit me anymore, in case you blab. It's my secret and I'm going to keep it that way, and you had better not say a word to anyone.'

Marjorie jumped down from her swing and kicked at one of the pieces of pottery that she had been so happy playing with when she was a child, smashing it into a million pieces. She glared at Sally and stood with her hands on her hips.

'I'll have to win my Jonathan back and then he'll stand by me, I know he will. And we can still run away to Gretna Green. Alison Redman can't have him – I need him.'

Sally hung her head as she watched Marjorie stomp off across the fields, full of fury and fear. If Marjorie was honest with herself, she would realize that Jonathan Birbeck would not want her back; she'd been used, and she knew it and was now in a right pickle – a disgrace to her family, and soon to be the talk of the dale. Poor Marjorie, she didn't yet know it, but she needed Sally as a friend more than ever, she thought as she turned her back on her safe childhood place and walked back to see if her father had bought the calf they had come for.

She'd not say a word to anybody about Marjorie; after all, nature would soon tell of her situation, as her stomach would grow and that would be when it became obvious, no matter what Marjorie did. Sally only hoped that Marjorie would want her back soon, because she was a true friend to her, and Marjorie would need her over the coming weeks, despite her thinking to the contrary. Her thoughts turned to Edward then. He was not at all like Jonathan; he was a gentleman, who had asked her to do nothing she felt uncomfortable with. Lately, the more she thought of him, the more she realized there was something between them, or so she hoped.

'She's a bonny one, Father. I'm glad that we are taking her back home.' Sally looked at the young calf, with both pairs of its legs tied together at the hoof, hoisted over her father's head. Bob carried the young heifer upon his back, as she mooed and protested about the indignity of being lifted so high and having to leave her mother.

'Aye, she'll be alright. And I'll give Brian his due: he didn't charge me a lot for her. I couldn't have bought her that cheap at the auction. Sometimes I get the man wrong,' Bob said as he waited for Sally to open the last gate onto their land. 'But I'm not wrong about his lass. You could do with a better mate than Marjorie – she's a madam; even her father thinks she is. I don't doubt I'd be taking my belt off to her, if I was him,' Bob said, slightly out of puff as he held tightly to the young animal when it decided it wanted to escape.

'You always threaten to take your belt off to us, but you never do.' Sally grinned and rubbed the head of the little roan-and-cream calf. 'I'll not be going to see Marjorie for a while, so you don't have to worry. I haven't the time, now I'm working, plus she made it quite obvious that she's not bothered about my company at the moment,' Sally replied casually and hoped that her father didn't notice the upset in her voice.

'That's because she's too busy with the lads, but there's time enough for that yet. It'll get her in bother, you mark my words.' Bob noticed his daughter blushing. She knew what he meant and he'd say no more, but unlike Marjorie, his lass had her head screwed on right. Hopefully she'd not get a name for herself. But he'd not say too much, as you never knew what your children were going to do in life.

Once back home, Bob lifted the wriggling calf from his back, untied the string from its legs and let it stand, looking confused and lost, in a corner of the barn where he had made a pen from some old gates and had put bedding down for it to sleep on. 'Tell your mother to warm a pint or two of milk and to put it in a bucket. We'll have to learn the calf to drink from us now, not her mother.'

Bob watched as Sally ran into the farmhouse and soon returned with a metal bucket full of semi-warm milk.

'Now look, dip your hand into the milk and then put your hand in the calf's mouth. She'll not like it at first, but she'll soon realize that if she sucks your hand, there's milk on it, and then you gently put her nose and mouth in the milk.' Bob dipped his hand in the milk and then offered it to the calf for her to lick, forcefully at first; and then she realized that there was milk for the taking, as she sucked with her rough tongue on his hand while he gently introduced her mouth into the bucket, until it realized how to drink. A time or two the calf blew bubbles in the milk as she dipped her head too deeply into the bucket and covered her nostrils, but then she resumed drinking, and soon the pint or two of milk had disappeared and the calf looked content as she went to a corner of the barn to sleep.

'Aye, I reckon I've got a good buy with that'un, lass. We'll keep her fed between us. She'll be a good milk cow in another year,' Bob said, satisfied with his latest purchase.

'I'll feed her tonight, Father – it can be my job of an evening,' Sally offered and remembered the feel of the calf's nose and the smell of her newness.

'Alright, she can be your ward of an evening. Now what are we going to call her? She'll have to have a name.' Bob closed the barn door and walked across the yard, then put the bucket down outside the kitchen door.

'I think she should be called Snowdrop, as she must have been born when they were in full flower.' Sally opened the kitchen door.

'Then Snowdrop it is. Aye, we'll always remember how old she is then. That's a good do, lass.' He smiled; his lass was not as simple as next door's and he was thankful for that small mercy, as he sat down in his usual corner and watched his family sitting around him on a quiet Sunday morning. Peace had returned to his life; just a

165

little longer working at Pratt's and then things would be back to normal. That job had opened his eyes to a different way of life, but trailing out at all hours of the day to hoist milk kits about was not his style. He'd stick to being content working for a good friend, and looking after his farm and family. Ivy had been right all along, but he'd never tell her that, else he'd never hear the last of it. As for the motorbike, well, she had enjoyed every minute of her ride behind him, so now it was definitely staying.

Chapter 9

It was Friday morning and the house was empty. Everyone was at work or school, except Ivy, and she was waiting for John Blades to arrive, as promised. Although Bob had been nothing but kind for the last day or two, she had found herself thinking quite often of the dashing salesman and his promise to visit her in the hope of building a friendship. She had even put on one of her more decent skirts and a cardigan for his visit, and stupidly felt her heart missing a beat as she heard his van pull up in the yard at exactly eleven o'clock. She only hoped Bob would not return early, before she had offered John a slice of his favourite cake and he'd looked across at her with the brown eyes she had noticed on his very first visit.

She gave herself a strict talking to as she crossed the kitchen floor, and calmed herself down and tried to stop feeling like a love-struck teenager. John was calling as a friend, after seeing her distressed the previous week –

nothing more. However, she did feel her heart missing a beat as she opened the door and watched him walking towards her in his sharp suit, and with a smile on his face.

'Ivy, see, I did promise I'd return. Now how are you? Feeling a bit brighter, I hope.' John touched her gently on the arm and smiled as she opened the kitchen door to him.

'Yes, I'm sorry if I made a fool of myself. I was, as you said, feeling a little bit lonely. I'm sure I'm not the only one who feels that way occasionally.' Ivy smiled. 'Really, there was no need to return and check up on me. I'm fine now.' She stood next to him and looked at the man who was the exact opposite of her Bob, in both looks and ways.

'Indeed, I didn't think you were a fool at all. I some-times feel like that, since I lost my dear wife. I miss her soft touch and the smell of her perfume, and I must admit when I first saw you, you reminded me of her so much. The same caring look in your eyes and the same dark, bobbed hair.' John looked straight into Ivy's eyes, making her turn quickly away from his gaze.

'I'll put the kettle on. And I've made you some of that courting cake that you enjoyed, last time you visited,' Ivy said quickly and caught her breath. She had to busy herself or she'd find herself doing or saying something she might regret. John Blades was a forward-talking man and she wished she hadn't encouraged his attentions, but at the same time she found him flattering, and the way he looked at her made her feel special. She had been angry with Bob when he had visited last time, but now she felt more settled with her lot in life. She turned when she realized that he was standing behind her as she reached for two mugs from the pot cupboard.

'Ivy, you are very attractive, do you know that?' John said. He put his hand on her free arm and leaned in to her so closely that she could feel his breath on her face.

'I'm not at all. And you are forgetting that I'm a married woman,' she replied. She put both mugs down sharply and gazed at him as he drew her close.

'A married woman who's unhappy and unloved. Just like I'm unhappy and unloved. Ivy, we could be there for one another. Here, let me kiss you?' John said and tried to hold her in his arms.

'I might be lonely some days, but I'm definitely not unloved. I think you have misread the situation, John. I think you had better be on your way, before you say anymore. My husband will be back at any time, and it doesn't take much for him to lose his temper.' Ivy pushed John's arms away and glared at him. 'How dare you take advantage! I'm not that sort of woman, so get in your van and be on your way, before we both do something we regret.' Ivy felt herself shaking as she watched John's eyes flash as he stepped back. She'd been foolish; she had invited this man to visit her, and she hardly knew him. He could do anything to her, and nobody would be there to help. She was outraged that he compared her to his dead wife, who must have been more than precious to him, by the way he talked about her.

'I thought you were up for my visits. You encouraged me – I saw the way you looked at me – and you even offered me courting cake. What else could a man think, when you open your heart to him and ask him back to comfort you,' John replied with a shocked look on his face. But he did not come any closer, once he realized he was unwelcome with his advances.

'I'm sorry, you have read me all wrong. I was just having a bad day. Now I think, if you don't mind, I'd like you to be on your way.' Ivy stood her ground as John stared at her.

'It's your loss, Ivy. We could have had a nice understanding between us. Nobody would have known. A visit from the farm-feed supplier – nobody would have said or suspected a thing. We could both have had satisfaction without anyone knowing.' John reached for his hat, which he had laid on the table. 'You are not my kind anyway – a bit rough, if you ask me. Just another stupid farmer's wife who knows nothing.' He grinned and put his hat on his head, then turned to go.

'You needn't come back. We'll change our supplier. Your prices are too dear for us to pay, so don't show your face again,' Ivy shouted as he walked across to his van without a backward glance, leaving her shaking and feeling stupid indeed. A bit rough – was she really a bit rough? She'd kept her figure, and so far there were not many wrinkles on her face. Clothes-wise, yes, she was not that posh, but which housewife up the Dales was, on an ordinary working day?

John Blades was a chancer and a bastard, she thought as she slumped at the kitchen table and saw the two mugs and slices of courting cake on a plate, which had been waiting for him. Perhaps she had encouraged him; and she had found him attractive, but not to the point of whatever he was suggesting. Bob must never know; he'd kill John if he ever found out, and at least the salesman would not come back for at least another month, and Bob would deal with him then. That is, if she did not do what she had threatened and changed supplier. If he was to return, she'd make sure she was not in when he called, as she never wanted to see the debonair John Blades ever again.

Sally was starting to realize it was more the company that she had been employed for, with Annie Mackreth. No sooner had she done the washing up and tidied the kitchen than Annie would say, 'Put the kettle on, lass' and that would mean a half-hour natter about the goings-on in Dent.

'Now then, tell me what's going on at home. It's not far off lambing time – it's the time of year that I love the best. The dale comes alive with the sound of their bleating, the blossom is out, the sun is starting to gain its warmth again and the winter is behind us. But it'll be busy at your place, I bet. How big a flock does your father have? He'll not have that much land, will he?' Annie asked as she sipped her tea and enjoyed her ginger biscuit.

'We've fewer than fifty lambing ewes – just enough work for my father, he says, although we all help.' Sally looked at the old woman and smiled. 'You'll have to take a walk down and visit us. My mam would make you welcome.'

'Nay, lass, these old legs will not get me that far, but

I might have a wander to the Mill Beck fields on Easter Monday. I like to watch the young ones rolling their pace-eggs down the grass banking – it makes me chuckle. I remember when I used to do it as a lass. The last egg to be un-cracked always won, and there were some fancy painted and decorated ones, I can tell you. My mother used to boil ours in onion skins, with some ferns from the garden bound inside them, so that they left a pattern; and sometimes she'd boil them in cochineal, which made them bright red.' Annie smiled and sat back in her chair, remembering her youth.

'Yes, my brother Ben is wanting to go. In fact all of us usually go; it's a nice gathering every year – as you say, the start of spring.' Sally rose from her seat to go and tidy the bedrooms.

'Aye, and of course I'll have to go to church on Sunday. I've no excuse, seeing as my pantry window looks out onto the churchyard. Besides, that's what you do if you have Christian bones in your body.' Annie put her cup on the table as her eyes began to feel sleepy.

Sally didn't reply to that, as her family were not big churchgoers. Christmas, weddings, christenings and funerals – that was about their lot. But her grandmother had been a real stickler, and Sally could just remember being dragged along to services when she stayed with her, and hating every moment. 'I'll go and clean your bedroom now, Mrs Mackreth, and then I'll pop out and get whatever shopping you want, and something tasty for your dinner.'

'Aye. Alright, lass, I think I'll just rest my eyes for five minutes. I've come over all tired,' Annie said as she made

172

herself comfortable in her battered chair. 'You do what you want – you are a good lass.'

Sally smiled and pulled the woman's woollen blanket up around her knees. She liked Annie; she was going to enjoy working for her, especially now that her father would be back at home the following week and would be keeping an eye on his flock.

With the bedrooms cleaned, Sally looked at the shopping list that she had compiled: bread, sugar, tea and a packet of ginger biscuits, which Dinsdale's made and didn't seem to last five minutes as they were Annie's secret indulgence. She'd also visit the butcher and buy Annie some potted meat for a sandwich at dinner time, and some scrag-end of mutton to stew with an onion and some potatoes – that would be her supper for two or three days, once cooked. Although she had only just started working for Mrs Mackreth, Sally knew that she was set in her ways. There was nothing extravagant in the kitchen; indeed there was nothing extravagant in the whole house. Annie lived a simple, frugal life.

Sally picked up her basket and checked on her slumbering employer. Annie was snoring under her breath, and Sally quietly closed the front door behind her, stepping onto the cobbled streets and making her way across to the main grocery shop in Dent village. Outside the shop there were various horses and carts waiting for their owners, and the doctor's car from The Gate was making a noise, as the engine had been kept running. He must be in a hurry, Sally thought, as she walked past the car, which was still a novelty to Dales folk, so they waved at it and knew exactly who was driving it. She nearly bumped into the tweed-suited doctor as he came quickly out of the shop. He doffed his hat to her and then quickly jumped into his car, as Sally stood in the doorway with the shop's bell tinkling over her head.

'There's a baby coming at Milthrope. Alice Banks, she's having twins and is in bother,' Phyllis Richmond said as she noticed Sally turn and look at the scurrying doctor.

'I hope she will be alright. It doesn't seem long since she had the last one. And you say it's twins this time? She's going to have her hands full.' Sally put her basket on the counter and looked at Phyllis, who was a few years older than her, and passed her Annie's order.

'Aye, she should learn to keep her legs together, and her fella out of the pub. You'll not get me shelling babies out like she does, if I can help it. My man will have to wait – unlike some I could mention,' Phyllis said and watched as Sally blushed. 'That mate of yours is a forward hussy, from what I hear, although I haven't seen her about for a while.'

'I don't know who you mean,' Sally said as she watched Phyllis getting the items on the list, then lowered her eyes so as not to look at Phyllis as she stood with both hands on her hips.

'Yes, you do. I mean Marjorie Harper, and I bet she's in a bit of a state, because I hear that Jonathan Birbeck is walking out with somebody else now. Silly cow; you should never give a fella an inch, else he'll take a mile.

That's what my mam always says and she's right.' Phyllis smirked. 'Anything else?'

'No, that's it, thank you.' Sally took the money that was owed out of the little leather purse that belonged to Annie, and paid Phyllis. 'Last I heard, both Marjorie and Jonathan were truly happy, so perhaps you shouldn't listen to gossip,' she said sharply as she picked up her basket and walked out of the shop. Marjorie could be a silly cow, but she was her best friend and, no matter what Phyllis said, she would stick up for her.

'By, thou looks in a bad mood,' Edward Riley said as he caught sight of Sally making her way to the butcher's while he watered his horse at the fountain outside Annie's house.

'Oh, Edward, I never saw you there. Are you alright? I haven't seen you since your visit, although I have thought of you often.' Sally looked up from her path to the butcher's and changed her expression to a smile, as she saw Edward pat his horse while it drank thirstily at the fresh-water fountain.

'Aye, I'm alright. I've kept meaning to come down and see you again, but I don't think your father was right suited last time I did. How are things with you?' Edward asked and then added, 'I right enjoyed our dances and time together.'

'I'm grand, thank you. I have started working for Mrs Mackreth, who lives just here. I'm doing her shopping and then I'm going home.' Sally nodded towards Annie's house and smiled at Edward. 'I enjoyed the dance too, and your company. It would be good to see you more often, no matter what my father says. My mam will talk him round, if he moans at us seeing one another.'

'It's a pity there hasn't been another dance, else I'd risk coming a-calling and asking you to accompany me, then I'd prove to your father that I am to be trusted with his lovely daughter. We made a good pair, I think.' Edward held on to his horse's harness as it lifted its head from drinking.

'That would be grand. There should be one soon after Lent, there usually is, and I'd love to join you again. My father's bark is worse than his bite, and he'd have to get used to you calling.' Sally looked coyly at him.

'Did you say you were going home? It's just that I'm on my way to Sedbergh. I could walk with you to your lane end. I don't mind waiting until you've done the shopping and made everything right with Mrs Mackreth?' Edward said, gazing at the lass that had taken his eye.

'I'd like that. Are you sure you can wait? I won't be more than ten minutes, if the butcher isn't busy.' Sally felt her heart flutter slightly as Edward looked her up and down.

'Right then, I'll sit here with Clover and wait for you; neither of us is in any hurry. Take your time at the butcher's, and make sure Annie Mackreth is alright. I'll sit out here and wait for you, so don't fret.' Edward sat down on the edge of the granite fountain and held tightly to his horse's reins, then watched as Sally nearly ran to the butcher's, greeting the Landlord of The Sun inn as he swept his step. Then she disappeared around the corner of the street to the butcher's. He was glad he had come across her; he'd kept thinking of Sally, wanting to visit her again, but fearing her father, as he knew the man wouldn't make him welcome, so he had bided his time. Now he knew where she worked, he'd make a point of being there on the days when Sally was at Annie Mackreth's. That was, if his new job let him, because he was soon to be working for the coalyard down in Sedbergh instead of for his father.

Sally had been served straight away at the butcher's and she walked quickly back to the house and grinned like a cat that had got the milk when she saw Edward still sitting, waiting for her. 'I'll not be long. I've just a sandwich to make for Mrs Mackreth, and to put this meat in a stew pot to cook in the side-oven, and then I'll be with you,' Sally said. Then she noticed the lace curtains twitching, as Annie Mackreth looked out of her front-room window and spotted her talking to Edward. 'I'll have to go,' she added and quickly went into the house.

'I've been for your shopping, Mrs Mackreth. I've got you some nice potted meat for a sandwich, and I've already buttered you a scone. I've got all that you asked for on your list.' Sally walked into the front room and looked at Annie, who was now wide awake.

'You are a good lass. Now is that lad outside with the horse waiting for you? I'll not be coming between two lovebirds. I remember those days all too well, and they go too fast for anybody to spoil.' Annie smiled. 'I can soon make my own dinner.'

177

'That's Edward, and we are just friends. He's waiting for me, but he's in no hurry, so I'll finish making your dinner and put this meat in to cook in the side-oven,' Sally replied and went into the kitchen to put the kettle on to boil, and to prepare both the meat and the sandwich. Her mind was on Edward and she smiled, remembering the look on his face as he glanced up and saw her.

'That's how it starts, my lass. You become friends, and then it grows into much more. If he's a good lad, don't keep him waiting. Is he local – should I know him?' Annie shouted through to the kitchen as she heard her dinner being made, and smelt the onion for her stew being chopped.

Sally wiped her hands after putting the scrag-end of lamb into the side-oven and making the sandwich and a cup of tea, which she placed in front of Annie, who looked up at her, wanting to know more about Edward. 'He's from up the dale, up Cowgill. His father, Thomas Riley, farms at Rayside. Edward danced with me on New Year's Eve, that's all,' Sally said quietly.

'Aye, that's how it begins. I met my old man at a dance – so light on his feet he was, I felt I was dancing on air.' Annie smiled. 'Those were the days,' she whispered. 'Now go on. My house is as spotless as a new pin, and I've got my dinner and my supper is cooking, so don't let him be waiting any longer. You just enjoy every minute of your youth, because believe me, you are old before you realize it.' Annie patted Sally's hand. 'Go on, I'm right as rain. Get yourself walking with him,

178

and tell him to behave himself.' Annie winked and watched as Sally blushed, as she pulled her shawl around her shoulders.

'You're sure there is nothing else you want me to do?' Sally asked.

'No, go on – enjoy your walk. I'll see you again on Monday, if you haven't run away with that bonny lad of yours.' Annie sat back with her sandwich in her hand and wished it was her, walking down a spring lane with a young man and his horse. Time was cruel, she thought, as she heard the young couple laughing together outside, before making their way along the cobbled street. It went past in the blink of an eye, and you didn't realize how precious every minute was until it was too late.

Sally watched as Edward pulled on his horse's bridle and joined her, leading it beside her. 'You can ride her if you want, I don't mind,' Sally said, smiling at the lad, who she quite liked but was uncertain of her feelings for.

'Nay, I'd rather walk beside you until your lane end. I'll get on her and ride the rest of the way then. I'm in no hurry to get where I'm going anyway. I'd rather be going home, but needs must,' Edward said and glanced at Sally.

'Is there something wrong at home?' Sally asked in concern.

'Nay, nothing's up. It's just that we are struggling on the bit of land we own, and my father has told me it's time for me to go and work for somebody else. He's lined me up with a job at Dawson's coalyard next to the station; that's where I'm going now, to see what hours

179

Ray Dawson wants me to work.' Edward sighed. 'I don't want to work there; it's a mucky job, filling sacks with coal all day, and back-breaking, but we need the money.'

'Yes, I'd rather be at home too, but we are the same. It's a struggle to make a living on the few acres everybody owns or rents in this dale. If we're lucky enough to have a good lambing time, we should survive another year, when it comes to selling the lambs this back-end,' Sally explained as she walked by Edward's side.

'Aye, if Hitler lets us. Every day it seems to get worse. That's another reason why I wanted to stop on the farm. I'm not one for obeying orders. If it comes to conscription, them in the army can fight their own war, as I'm stopping right here where I belong.'

'I hope it doesn't come to that. I wouldn't want you to go fighting, and you don't think it will, do you?' Sally asked.

'I don't know, but if it does come to a war again, there will be lives lost – and all for nothing,' Edward replied quietly. 'Now, let's change the subject and not look on the dark side of life. I see your father's gone and got himself a motorbike. He nearly ran into me and Clover on the bend near the monument. He was on the wrong side of the road and going like a bat out of hell. Is he fit to ride it?' Edward laughed.

'I don't know. He got it to go back and forth to his work at Pratt's, but now he's about to leave and return to working for Jim Mattinson. He should never have left in the first place, but who am I to say that? It's like my mam says: we don't really count sometimes,' Sally said and looked at Edward.

'Aye, I know what you mean. My father is a stickler, expects me to work all hours for nowt and then, in the next breath, he's sending me to work for Dawson's, so he'll expect some of my wage and still the same work that I've been doing at home. It's us farming families: we work ten times harder than those in offices or shops.'

Sally lifted her face up to the early spring sunshine and admired the primroses that were starting to bloom along the hedges of the road; spring was finally here, she thought as Edward regarded her.

'Do you fancy sitting for a while? We are nearly at your home and I'm right enjoying your company,' Edward said bashfully as they approached the stone milk-kit stand for the nearby farm at the edge of the road. 'I really don't want to go to Dawson's coalyard today, but I know there will be hell at home if I don't.' He sighed.

'Yes, I'll sit with you a while. My mother will expect me back soon, but I'll tell her I stayed a little longer with Mrs Mackreth. She'll not know any different, and anyway we are not doing any harm sitting together,' Sally replied. She pushed herself up onto the kit stand and swung her legs, as Edward sat next to her while his horse grazed the grass verge.

'No, we'll not get up to stuff like your mate Marjorie and Jonathan Birbeck – all the Dales talking about them. I bet her parents don't know, though. My father said it was the subject of conversation by the domino players at the Cow Dubb; you'd think they'd have something better to talk about. He asked me if I had anything to

181

do with them, and I was glad to say I'd nothing to do with either of them. I never mentioned you,' Edward went on. 'To be honest, your mate Marjorie frightens me to death, she is that forward; and Jonathan is nothing but a bully – always has been since he was little.'

'Aye, I don't like Jonathan, and I think it's all going to end in tears if they are not careful. He's courting someone else, I think. And Marjorie, well, she's broken-hearted and worried. I told her that Jonathan wasn't up to much, but she knew best.' Sally smiled and looked down at her feet as Edward reached for her hand and squeezed it.

'I'd never be like him, Sally; I'll always be a gentleman. Marjorie will be worried if he's two-timing. My girl will only get respect.' Edward looked at Sally with love in his eyes. 'Saying that, may I kiss you, just the once? I enjoyed it so much on New Year's Eve and I haven't forgotten how it felt, but I could do with remembering again.' Edward leaned forward and hoped he was not asking too much of Sally – a kiss in broad daylight – even though the road to Dent was relatively quiet.

'I don't know, Edward. Somebody will see us,' Sally said, but squeezed his hand tightly and hoped that he would.

'No, they won't. Look, nothing is coming either way; you can see a good distance, and the road is clear.' Edward leaned further forward and gazed at Sally. He'd never noticed how bonny she was before New Year's Eve, and now all he could do was lie in bed and think about her. He put his hand tenderly around her face and took his chance as he puckered his lips, and she closed her eyes as he kissed her, softly and gently, and then smiled. 'There, you see, no harm done – nobody's seen us.'

Sally blushed. 'No; no harm done and I enjoyed it.' She leaned towards him again and returned his kiss, this time opening her eyes and looking at him. 'There, we've sealed our pact, Edward Riley. I think we should see more of one another, if we can.'

'Aye, I'm in agreement with that. Are you going to the Easter celebrations at Mill Beck? I can meet you there,' Edward said and looked at the lass that he was starting to have feelings for.

'I am, but my mother and father will be there, as well as our Ben.' Sally was worried that her parents would not approve.

'There's no harm in enjoying our day together. There will be other folk there, and they'll not be watching us every minute,' Edward replied. 'I'll see you there. It's always a good day, apart from the singing of hymns, but you can't get out of that, seeing as it is Easter we're celebrating.' He looked to either side of them and risked another kiss, before they both climbed down from the milk-kit stand. 'We'd better be on our way, else I'm going to be late, and your mother will wonder where you are.'

'Yes, I'll meet you there. We can sit together when we have the outside picnic – by accident, of course.' Sally grinned.

'Of course, and I can show your Ben the best way to make his pace-egg last the longest.' Edward reached for his horse's reins as they started walking the few yards left to the end of Sally's farm lane, before climbing on his horse's back. 'I'll see you then. We will both have a grand day, as long as it's not raining.' He looked down at Sally and then, in the distance, saw and heard her father coming on his motorbike. 'Your father's on his way home, so I'd better be on my way, else he'll have something to say. See you Monday – it'll be grand,' Edward shouted as he urged his horse on and left Sally watching him for a brief second before she hurried up the lane, out of view of her father, who was speeding up the road to get home.

Sally smiled and felt like her feet were walking on clouds as she entered the yard just in front of her father. She had to hide her excitement, as Bob made the dust fly when he entered the yard and turned his motorbike's engine off.

'That bloody Riley lad that danced with you on New Year's Eve is nothing but a nuisance, with his old horse that's about ready for the knacker's yard. I've nearly run into him twice now, as he gallops down this road like the devil's on his back. Did you not see him?' Bob asked and glared at his daughter.

'No, I must have been walking up the lane when he was on the road. I never saw him, Father,' Sally lied. She knew she would only get the third degree in questioning if she admitted to walking with Edward.

'Aye, well, if I see him again, I'll tell him he's not fit to be out on that horse. His father would have something to say – riding the farm horse like he does,' Bob growled and then strode in front of Sally into the house, leaving her smiling. Edward had said just about the same thing about her father, so who was right? However, it didn't matter; she had Edward's kisses to think about.

The field at Mill Beck Farm was busy with people gathered to celebrate Easter Monday, after attending church over Easter weekend and Holy Week. Families from up and down the dale gathered for a picnic tea, and to watch as their children threw pace-eggs down the steep bank of the field, cheering and smiling as the eggs either survived another roll or smashed into pieces, to be eaten quickly by the owner.

Ivy stood next to Beatrice Caruthers and smiled as she watched Ben prepare to throw his egg, with so much concentration on his face and his tongue stuck out between his lips, as he gently rolled it down the hill and cheered at the bottom when it remained whole, then running back up the hill, where Sally stood watching the fun. Ivy smiled as she noticed that Edward Riley stood next to her and they kept looking at one another. Her little girl was growing up, whether Bob liked it or not, and it seemed as if she already had a suitor who was showing an interest in her.

'Is that your Sally standing next to the Riley lad? They look as if they are good friends,' Beatrice commented while she ate her slice of Victoria sandwich cake, made by the expert bakers of Dent Women's Institute.

'It is. I think they are just friends, but you never know – she's at that age when she doesn't say a lot.' Ivy smiled as she saw Edward place his arm around Sally.

185

'She'll be up and married before you know it. My lass is to marry next year; that is, if her fella doesn't end up fighting abroad. He's in the army up at Catterick Garrison, and what he says doesn't bode well for the country. Worrying times, Ivy, that's what it is.'

'It is indeed. I'm glad my lad is not old enough to go fighting. I can just remember when half the men of the dale went for the last war; there was enough broken hearts then.' Ivy shook her head. 'We all lost somebody.'

'Aye, we did, but I never thought it would happen again. I thought it was the war to end all wars, or so one of our politicians said. So much for listening to them,' Beatrice said drily. 'Anyway, let's lighten our conversation. Have you had that new salesman call from Thompson's? My Alfred dealt with him, when he came to us. I must say he's a good-looker, although I've heard all sorts about him. He's a bit of a ladies' man, from what I can gather, and a liar.'

'Yes, we've had him at ours – he's not your usual salesman,' Ivy replied and remembered her liaison with him. 'I wasn't keen on him. Bob can deal with him in the future, now he'll be back home.

'Alf Thompson says he doesn't know what to make of John Blades. All the farmers are complaining that he's too forward with their wives, so I don't think he'll be working for Alf much longer. Hopefully, if Reg gets over his stroke, he'll be back soon.' Beatrice leaned closer to Ivy and whispered, 'John was a tad too friendly with me the other day. His hand lingered just a little bit too long on the top of mine, when I passed him his tea. Not that

I'm complaining – I was quite flattered, but my old man would bloody flatten him if he did anything more.'

'He's missing his wife; she's only just died of cancer, that's what he told me.' Ivy looked at Beatrice, who she knew as a friend, but Beatrice was not the sexiest woman in the dale.

'That's what he's telling everybody, but Alf Thompson says his wife has left him and is living in Blackpool, as she was fed up of him having affairs. Anyway, whatever or whoever he is, John Blades is keeping our other halves on their toes, and a bit of opposition never goes amiss,' Beatrice chuckled.

'That he is.' Ivy felt angry that she had been lied to and used. Bob could certainly deal with John Blades in the future. She'd not have the time of day for him ever again.

She grinned as she looked up at Sally and Edward at the coconut stall, laughing and enjoying one another's company. They made a good couple, but were a little too young yet to get serious, and she only hoped that they would be careful.

Chapter 10

Sally sat with her father behind the weathered limestone wall and watched the ewe that was about to give birth to her first lamb at any second. It was the middle of May and very warm. Down below, around the farmyard, the swallows and swifts had just arrived and were busy ducking and diving and calling in their shrill voices, finding nesting places in the barns and outbuildings. Overhead the skylark sang, and the smell of wild mountain thyme was in the air.

'It's a grand time of year is this, lass, but it can be hard and all. You have to watch each ewe with a good eye; they can soon lose their lamb if they get into bother. This lass has never lambed before, so I thought we would sit together, right quiet, and see how she manages.'

Bob leaned against the wall and puffed on his pipe, filling the air with the smell of Kendal Twist. It was the smell of her father, Sally thought, as she sat close to him and felt his tweed jacket next to her skin.

'Your mother keeps at me to let you do more, so you might as well join me shepherding. Besides, if this ewe gets into trouble, you've smaller hands than me. The lamb might come out backwards or twisted, and then I'll have to show you how to put your hand inside her and pull it out right for her.' Bob watched as the lambing sheep pushed as another contraction came over her.

Sally looked at the sheep; she hoped she would lamb on her own, but at the same time she wanted to learn how to help a ewe in trouble.

'Hey up, she's alright; here's the front feet and head, and she's doing just grand. Stand up, our lass, and help her. Now, you pull when she pushes and that'll help her a little.' Bob remained sitting as Sally went and talked gently to the sheep as she lay panting and pushing, giving birth.

'That's it – it's coming now; pull it clear and clean its nose out. There might be another yet.' Bob watched his daughter, who Ivy had convinced him to take under his wing and stop putting all his hopes on Ben, who showed no signs of becoming a farmer.

Sally looked down at the newly born lamb covered in its birth sack, coloured yellow and acting doddery on the grass next to its mother. It raised its head straight away and answered its mother quietly, as she automatically bleated a welcome to the world to her lamb and looked around at her newborn.

'Now, come and sit back down here. Let's just see if she's got another one in her, and let her clean and look after the one that's come into the world.' Bob ushered his daughter to his side. 'Don't touch the lamb

189

too much, else she'll not take to it,' he warned as Sally sat back down.

Sally watched as the mother ewe got up onto her feet and lost the birthing bed, as she turned to clean and lick her newborn, pushing and nuzzling it with her nose, while bleating gently.

'Looks like it's just a single, Father. A gimmer, I think,' Sally said and smiled. 'I don't think there's anything as bonny as watching that.' She watched the newly born lamb struggle to stand on its feet, and its mother urging it to drink from her udder.

'Tha could be right lass. It's always a wonder. Mind, we have the perfect lambing-time weather. You wouldn't be saying that if it was pouring down with rain and bitter cold and the old lass was having bother. You've got to take the rough with the smooth and admit that nature is your boss.' Bob puffed on his pipe contentedly. 'Your mother says you are growing up and I should learn you more, whether you're a lass or not. It doesn't fit well with me. I always thought of a lad being the farmer, but Ben is not showing any inclination, although he might do yet.' He puffed again and looked at his daughter. 'She also told me that she saw you with that Riley lad, laughing and larking about the other day. Remember that you're nobbut young yet, and there will be plenty of lads come your way. Besides, his father only rents his farm, just like us. Try and find yourself a fella that owns his own farm and then you'll want for nowt.'

Sally blushed. 'We are only friends, Father. I'm not going to run off with Edward and marry him just yet.

He's not even a farmer anymore; he's working for Dawson's at the coalyard.'

'Less of your cheek, young lady. I said I wasn't ever going to get married, and then six months later I was walking down the aisle with your mother by my side – not that I've regretted it for one minute. I'm only saying you don't know what's in store for you in your life, so just be careful. It's a bad do that Edward has to work for Dawson's, but Rayside will barely make his family a living, as it's got even less than here.'

Bob gazed out over the dale. Times were changing and all the farmers' lads were having to find work elsewhere, as there was no money to be made in smallholdings.

'And tell him that my bike at least has good brakes, better than his old horse. I swear if I meet him again on that road, one of us will go a-pearler.' Bob grinned at Sally. 'Behave yourself and you can carry on seeing him. I might be getting old, but I'm not that daft. I'd rather you courted openly than sneak about, like that friend of yours.'

Sally bowed her head. Her father had known she and Edward had seen one another the other day, on the lane; she didn't know how, but he did. 'Thank you, Father. You know Edward's alright, he's steady.'

'Aye, I know, else I'd be kicking his arse by now. Just behave yourselves, that's all I ask. Now, let's away and see what your brother is up to. He was looking at my bike and wondering if he dared ask to have a ride with me. He's not as tough as you, but he'll make something of himself. After all, he's my lad and I've noticed he's always hatching a plan of some sort, a bit like his old father.' Bob strode off down the field with his shepherd's crook in his hand, giving the newly lambed ewe a backward glance as the lamb helped itself to its mother's milk and its tail wriggled. You had to look after your young'uns, no matter what, and only hope they came out less battered in life than you, he thought as his lass tried to keep up with him.

Ben lifted his head as his father and sister entered the farmyard. He was sitting down on his haunches, trying to figure out how his father's bike worked, looking at the engine and the various parts that he could see, without unscrewing anything or touching anything that he shouldn't.

'I've not touched it, Father. I was just looking. I want to know how it all works,' Ben said quickly, thinking that he was in bother.

'It's alright, lad. Now I've a bit more time, how about you jump on the back as pillion and we will go and see to Jim Mattinson's sheep for him up at Dent station? They have already lambed, so we just have to make sure they are all there. You can help me count them. And hold on for dear life, as we climb up that steep hill to the station.' Bob looked at the doubt on his son's face. 'It'll be alright. I'll go slowly and then I can tell you how a bike works, seeing as you are so interested.' He walked over to the open kitchen door to leave his crook in the usual place.

Sally grinned at her brother. 'Go on then. It's a grand evening and you've wanted to go on the back of the bike for weeks. Father's in a good mood tonight. He's back doing what he likes and is still making good money.' Sally winked as she saw both her mother and father come to the kitchen door.

'If you go with your father, hold on tight to him. Don't fool about, and mind your legs on the exhaust,' Ivy shouted as Bob scuffed Ben's head and put his leg over the bike, helping his son climb on and cling to him, once he had kick-started the bike into action.

'Are you alright? Don't let go and you'll be right,' Bob shouted above the noise.

'Yes, I'm right, Father,' Ben replied and gripped more tightly to his father than he had ever done in his life before. He felt sick with excitement as he closed his eyes and felt his father balance both bike and his passenger as they went down the lane and onto the main road. He was travelling faster than he had ever gone in his life before, and he loved every minute as gradually he got used to the motion, and his balance. For once he and his father had something in common: the love of the motorbike. Now he just had to find out how it worked, he thought, as he crossed Barth bridge, holding on for dear life while his father waved at Richard Milburn with his horse and cart.

It was warm in the kitchen, and Sally was enjoying time alone with her mother. Ivy sat down and looked at her daughter. 'I've not said anything so far, but now your father and Ben are out of the house, I thought I'd have a word with you.'

Sally felt her stomach churn. If her mother had mentioned once the price of boys having their own way, she had told her a hundred times, and now she was going to get another lecture. 'Mother, I know what you are going to say. And yes, I know not to raise my skirts for anyone.' She pulled a face; she had enjoyed a lovely time with her father, and now her mother was going to spoil it.

'I know you do, but your friend at Beckside hasn't been heeding the same warning. Brian, Marjorie's father, was swearing like a good'un, your father said, this morning at the bottom of the lane. He told your father that Marjorie is expecting and that she's at least five months pregnant,' Ivy said quietly. 'She's only just sixteen, the silly lass; she had all her life in front of her.' She shook her head and sighed.

'So she's told them then, has she? I've known for nearly a month, but Marjorie made me swear not to say anything and she didn't want me near her. That's why I've not visited her of late and I've been busy working for Annie.' Sally bowed her head.

'Why didn't you tell me? If the Harpers had known earlier, they might have been able to do something about it. As it is, now Marjorie's going to live with her aunty in Liverpool until the baby is born. She's ruined her life. She won't even say who the father is, although your father says he's got a good idea who's to blame.

'What do you mean: they could perhaps have done something about it?' Sally asked innocently and looked, wide-eyed, at her mother.

194

'There's some women that can get rid of babies, if you are not too far gone. But Marjorie's begun to show, and that's how they know she's at least five months gone,' Ivy replied, noticing the confusion on Sally's face. 'You don't need to know how, and I pray to God you are never in the situation that Marjorie is in. She might say she doesn't want to see you, but I bet she could do with a good friend at this moment in time. She'll be frightened and lonely.' Ivy stood up and put her arm around her daughter.

'She'll need you, no matter what folk think of her. Her father's packing her off on the early-morning train on Saturday, so you have only this week to see Marjorie. I'll not tell your father that you are going to see her; she's just gone and done what everybody thought she would. Father's never thought a lot of her.' Ivy paused. 'Has she said if Jonathan Birbeck is the father? Rumour has it that he is – not that he'll stand by her, as men like that never do. In fact I hear he's courting Alison Redman.'

'She didn't say, Mam, but she's always gone about with Jonathan.' Sally didn't want to name names, but she guessed her mother would put two and two together.

'Like you do, with that Edward Riley. I saw you both at Mill Beck together, although he doesn't seem a bad lad, from what I saw of him.' Ivy gave Sally a knowing look.

'Mam, don't start. I'm not like Marjorie, and Edward is definitely nothing like Jonathan Birbeck.' Sally held her head in her hands. 'What do I say to her? All Marjorie wanted was to get married, and now she's going to lose everything.'

195

'Well, it's too late to tell her to keep her legs together, as the damage is done. Just give her your support – that will be enough. It could happen to any lass, as we are all susceptible to a man's charms, believe me.' Ivy thought about the other slander that Bob had heard on The Sun's grapevine while playing dominoes on Friday night. Now that would shake the Harpers' happy home, if it was right, and she hoped it was only malicious gossip.

Sally stood on the doorstep of Beckside and waited for the door to be opened. The back door of all the local farms was usually open to the world in the spring and summer months, but the Harpers were obviously keeping their lives private, she thought, as she heard someone coming to answer her knock.

Dora Harper came to the door. 'Have you come to gloat or to show Marjorie sympathy? Whichever it is, I wish she had behaved herself, like you do. Lord knows, I've talked to her until I'm blue in the face, and she's still been stupid enough to end up the way she has,' Dora said sharply and glared at Sally.

'I can hear, you know. I do still live here,' Marjorie yelled, appearing behind her mother.

'Not for much longer, you don't. You are in disgrace, and you are lucky your Aunty Theresa is willing to take you in hand, else you'd be out on the streets, my girl, if it was up to me,' Dora snapped and left both girls looking at one another as she went about her business.

'Come on, we will go down to the beck – it's no good talking in here,' Marjorie said and slammed the kitchen door behind her. 'You'd think I'd bloody killed someone. It's a baby I'm having; it's not the end of the world,' she grunted and strode across the yard, following the back of the barn to the field that ran down to the river, and to her own and Sally's favourite place.

'You are in a bit of a pickle and causing quite a scandal. But like you say, it's only a baby, even though you are quite young to be having it,' Sally replied, as Marjorie jumped on the rope swing and sat with her head hanging down, while Sally sat on the large beck-stone boulder, like she always did.

'Some friend you are! You sound as condescending as the rest of them. It could just as well be you who is pregnant, and not me, and then how would you feel?' Marjorie spat.

Sally didn't reply. She couldn't be in Marjorie's shoes, as she'd never let a lad go that far until there was a ring on her finger, no matter how much she loved him. Marjorie must have really loved Jonathan or been too easy with him, to let him get her pregnant, she decided, but thought better of saying so in case she looked stupid.

'I'm sorry; I bet you are having it hard at home. Your mother is definitely mad with you, but how's your father?' Sally asked as she noticed tears running down her friend's face.

'He's not talking to me. It's as if I'm not here anymore, and I hear my mam and father arguing all the time and it must be about me.' Marjorie lifted her head and wiped away a tear from her red eyes, which looked as if they had been crying every day for weeks. 'They both hate me!'

197

'They don't hate you; they just don't know how to help you. Have you told them who the baby's father is yet? That would help, if you did. He's responsible as well: it takes two to tango, as my mother says.'

'No, I have not. How can I, when Jonathan's just announced to the world his engagement to that Alison Redman? I wonder if she's expecting too, as he's not courted her that long. Lord, I hate this baby that's growing inside me. How could I have been so stupid?' Marjorie wailed and burst back into tears.

Sally stood up and shuffled her body onto the swing next to Marjorie, putting her arm around her and squeezing her tightly. 'Hey, it's not that bad. Your mother and father will think differently when they see their grandchild in your arms.'

'Do you think so? I don't. They are sending me to my aunty in Liverpool – my bloody Aunt Theresa, who has pictures of the Sacred Heart everywhere on her walls and is constantly mumbling something over a rosary. She's the religious one of the family; talks thick Irish, unlike my mam. First thing she did was to have elocution lessons when they left Dublin, as she didn't want to be known as a Paddy.' Marjorie gasped and tried to control her breathing. 'That's where my aunty is sending me, when it's my time. She's sending me to the bloody nuns in Ireland. A mother-and-baby home, where you have to work in their laundry to earn your keep.'

'Oh Lord, Marjorie. I didn't know your mam was Irish. I knew she wasn't English, but I'd never have guessed Irish. And when you have given birth, do you get to keep your baby?' Sally asked, remembering what her mother had told her.

'I think so – that's what my auntie has told me. But she doesn't speak of it, because sex is dirty and the baby is going to be born out of lust, so she doesn't even want to look at it once it's born. That is why I'm going to Dublin. Hidden away, a disgrace to the family – all because of one quick fumble,' Marjorie sobbed and Sally tried to comfort her.

It took more than one quick fumble to get her in the state she was in now, Sally thought as she hugged her friend. But no matter how many times she and Jonathan Birbeck had been together, it was always going to end up in disgrace. Both were headstrong and selfish, and now regretting ever seeing one another, and they were the talk of the dale.

It was early on Saturday morning when the horse and cart with Marjorie and her father pulled into the yard at Daleside. Brian Harper sat, saying nothing, in the driving seat as Marjorie lowered herself down and walked over to the open doorway with a parcel in her hands and a brave smile on her face, as she approached Ivy and Sally.

'I've just come to say goodbye. I don't know when I'll be back or, indeed, if my mother and father will have me back, after this one.' Marjorie patted her stomach. 'And you might not want to remain friends with me, for all I know.'

'Don't be silly. We will always be friends. I'll write to you at least once a week and will give you all the gossip,' Sally said and hugged her dearest friend close.

'I've brought you these, because they are no good to me at the moment and my mother says I'll have to act my age, if not older, when I'm with my aunt. There's one or two dresses in there that I know you like, and some cardigans and jumpers.' Marjorie shoved the brown-paper parcel into Sally's arms and wiped back a tear. 'Just don't flirt too much in them, because look where it gets you.'

'Oh, Marge, don't – you'll start me crying.' Sally sniffed in hard as she hugged her friend even harder and took the bundle of much-needed clothes.

'It'll pass, love, and then you'll be back with us sooner than you know it. You'll just have to be brave,' Ivy said and looked at the lass she remembered bouncing on her knee when she had been a baby. 'It's not pleasant having a baby, but us women keep doing it, so it can't be that bad.' She stepped forward and kissed Marjorie lightly on the forehead.

'Thank you, Mrs Fothergill. You've always been good to me, and I appreciate it. I'll have to go now, as the train comes at ten-thirty. I'll miss you, Sally,' Marjorie cried as they hugged one more time, before leaving one another's arms.

'I'll miss you too, Marjorie. You'll write, won't you?' Sally yelled as Marjorie climbed up again beside her silent father.

'Yes, of course I will. Just try and stop me.'

Sally watched her friend disappear down the track in the quiet, still heat of the morning.

Chapter 11

May was a busy month on the farm; it brought life back to the land. Bob covered the ground with manure from his horse cart, making the two meadows that he farmed come to life with daises, buttercups, blue bugle and yellow penny rattle. Hopefully by the end of summer the meadow grass would have grown long enough to be mown and harvested, for feed for his stock in the coming winter.

When he wasn't doing this, Bob was making sure that his lambs and those of Jim Mattinson were delivered safely and were going to thrive. There was new life stirring in the farmyard too, as a hen had been clucking and hatching in the barn, unbeknown to anyone, until she proudly paraded her family of chicks one morning, to everyone's surprise. Tom Dixon had come up to the farm in his battered truck and had unloaded two young piglets, much to Sally's distaste. She loved to see them arrive all pink and cuddly, but she knew all too well that, come autumn, they would be slaughtered, for the family to have bacon and ham throughout the winter, along with black pudding, savoury ducks, made from minced pork and pig's liver, brawn and anything else that her mother could make of their carcasses. The noise of the young piglets as they screeched and grunted for their mother, at being made to go into the pig hull, had filled the yard, and Sally had been near to tears as she watched them hide in the corner of the hull, underneath the clean straw bedding, and comfort one another.

'Don't forget to put all the waste from those potatoes and cabbage that you are peeling into the pigs' swill bucket – they'll eat just about anything, will a pig,' Ivy said as she watched her daughter peeling potatoes for their main meal. She then started to roll out the pastry for the lid of the mince-and-onion pie that was to accompany the vegetables. Deftly she laid it on top of the enamel dish, running a sharp knife around the edge before washing it with an egg glaze and putting it into the oven to bake. 'I'm surprised you haven't had a letter from Marjorie yet. I thought she'd write to you as soon as she could, once she'd settled in Liverpool.

'Mam, it's only been a fortnight. And she said her aunty was strict, so perhaps she hasn't let her write. I think she is quite the opposite of Marjorie's mother – she's a strict Catholic.' Sally placed the potatoes and cabbage on the stove to boil.

'I don't know what went wrong with Marjorie and her mother then, if they come from that sort of background. Because neither of them have any morals,' Ivy said sharply and then regretted it, as she sounded just like the gossips that she tried not to listen to. 'Sorry, Sally. I just cannot understand Brian Harper putting up with the comings and goings at his house. Your father would certainly have something to say if you had carried on like Marjorie, besides everything else.'

'Everything else, Mam? What do you mean? Is there something wrong at Beckside?' Sally asked and looked at her mother, expecting to hear what was on her mind.

'Nay, nothing. I just mean if he'd kept an eye on things, Brian wouldn't have all the bother he has at the moment. I'll give your father his due: he keeps both his eyes and ears open and knows everything that anybody gets up to. He'd soon have been giving you a good tongue-lashing if you'd been carrying on like Marjorie. Although I understand he's given his blessing to you seeing that Edward Riley, despite him not having much brass to his name. He's always hoped you'd catch the eye of somebody of wealth – although where you're supposed to find someone like that around here, I don't know.' Ivy smiled and glanced out of the window as she heard the sound of Bob's motorbike pulling into the yard. 'Talk of the devil, here he is, so it must be dinner time.' Now that her husband had returned from working for Jim Mattinson, she started setting the dinner table.

Bob entered the kitchen and made straight for the sink, then ran himself a quick drink of water in a mug, standing next to Sally as he gulped it back in one. 'You alright, lass? Helping your mother, are you? By, I was thirsty. I stopped for ten minutes at Green Cottage on my way back and had a talk with Dick Jackson. I thought he was never going to shut up, and it's such a warm day.' Bob gave a worried look to Ivy and then turned to Sally. 'Can you just go and check those pigs? They were making a funny noise when I came into the yard.'

'Yes, of course I will,' Sally said. Something was afoot; she'd seen that look between her parents before, and there was something they were going to discuss without her being present, she thought as she walked across the yard on a job that she knew didn't exist.

Bob sat down and shook his head, while Ivy sat herself opposite him. 'What's up, Bob? You look worried.' She looked across at her husband.

'Aye, I am. Like I say, I've been talking to Dick, and by God he is worried,' Bob replied. 'I don't doubt there's war coming to us, whether we like it or not.' He shook his head again and looked at Ivy. 'Bob's lad and all his squadron have been put on alert, and he can't have any leave. So Dick is worried to death about him, although he doesn't know the half of it because everything is top-secret. But he showed me the paper's headlines for today – he was reading it in his front garden when I passed. Our Sally will be upset. That's why I sent her out.'

'Go on, what did they say? She'll be back shortly.' Ivy leaned towards Bob over the table.

'The government's going to be conscripting all men aged twenty to twenty-two for six months' military training. That means her fella that she seems to be sweet on, that I do know, along with quite a few others in the dale. It's a pity Edward went to work for Dawson's at the coalyard; he might have been alright if he'd said that he was farming with his father.

'Oh Lord, that will just be the start of it. There's going to be some broken hearts again in this country – not least our lass's, if she thinks more of Edward than she's letting on. Not that she's seen much of him, but she has already lost Marjorie.' Ivy put her head in her hands. 'All those lads – thank heavens a lot of them farm with their fathers around here.' She sat back. 'That'll not include Jonathan Birbeck, thank heavens he'll still be able to get married with him being a bit older than some. That will be a relief to Alison.'

'Aye, that was one bit of news: the lad's having to get married. He's gone and got Alison in the family way, but the Redmans have made him marry her. He needs a knot tying in it, I'd say, so perhaps the army will do that one good.' Bob leaned forward in his chair. 'As for the other news that I mentioned: aye, it is still carrying on; John Blades was seen coming down the lane late last night. He's another bugger that wants gelding.'

'As if that Dora Harper hasn't got enough trouble in her house! You know I might not like her that much, but I never did listen to half the gossip I heard about her. But this time I think it might be true, because he's just her sort,' Ivy said bitterly.

'Aye, well, leave her to it. We can only be here for Brian when he needs us. I owe him a thank-you or two, because his young calf that he sold us is thriving and looks to be making a good heifer. As long as me and mine are all alright, that's the main thing. But you'd better tell our lass about her fella facing conscription, as we don't want her falling for a lad that she might never see again, if he goes to war. God help us, as we lost enough the first time around without it happening all over again.'

Sally had written a letter to Edward asking him to meet her at the monument on the roadside where they had kissed earlier. It was Sunday morning, and since the moment her mother had told her, she could not think of anything else but of Edward perhaps going off to war. They had both hardly had time to see one another, with their work and the farms, but they both knew there was something special between them.

Sally sat at the edge of the road and listened to the church bells echoing down the dale, carried by the wind. She knew that prayers would be being said for all the young men who were being conscripted, and for peace to be kept in the country. Although she hadn't even been born at the end of the Great War, she knew what it had done to many a family, and she knew what Uncle Stanley went through on the nights when he was still fighting the Hun in his nightmares. She sat patiently and looked down the bankside at the River Dee that flowed alongside the road; its banks were shady and the last of the blue-bells were still flowering as she leaned over the railings and watched them nod their heads in the slight breeze.

'Penny for them,' Edward said as he sneaked up on her while she was deep in thought and put his hands over her eyes, laughing as she jumped.

'Oh, Edward, you took me by surprise!' Sally turned

and looked at the lad she had feelings for. Then she put her arms around him as he squeezed her tightly.

'Meeting on a Sunday, in broad daylight – it must be serious. My mother had a fit when she took the letter from the postie and realized that it was a woman writing to me for the first time in my life,' Edward said as he held Sally in his arms and gazed at her.

'I just needed to see you. I've done nothing but worry since my father heard they were conscripting men of your age. Have you heard anything yet?' Sally asked when he let go of her as she sighed.

'No, not yet, but I know it'll be coming. And I know I'll have no option but to go, when they do call me. There's going to be a war, Sal, and no matter where we live, we're all going to be caught up in it, one way or another.' Edward linked his arm in Sally's and they started to walk in the direction of the bridge that spanned the clear-water river and formed the main road into the village of Dent. 'Perhaps we should not get too involved with one another – you might be courting heartbreak?' he suggested as they stopped in the middle of the bridge and leaned over, looking at the water below.

'If you think I could be that shallow, Edward, you can think again. Anyway, even if you do get called up, you'll not be going anywhere except Catterick Garrison, as we have nothing to do with it all yet,' Sally said, trying to sound cheerful and positive.

'You know, and I know, that our government would not be enlisting without consent if we weren't planning to go to war. Italy's vowed to fight on the side of Hitler.

Mussolini and he signed a pact together last week: two men with egos who want to run the world at all costs – that's what everybody is saying. They have to be stopped!' Edward sighed. 'So far I've heard nothing, so perhaps they still think I'm working for my father, with a bit of luck. But Dawson's stamp my card every week, so they will pick up on me through that.'

'You should have kept working for your father, until this had passed. Farm labourers and farmers are exempt, my father was saying.' Sally stood and looked at Edward. 'Even my father and mother know that I'm meeting you here today, and they have not said a word against it. My mam said to tell you to take care, as she's worried for you.'

'By, we must be serious, if your mother and father know about me! I haven't seen much of your father on that bike of his of late, since he stopped working for Pratt's. One less danger for me. If the Nazis aren't going to get me, your father was going to have a bloody good go at it.' Edward grinned and shook his head.

'Funny, he says that same about you: he says you're not fit on the road with a horse and cart.' Sally laughed and looked up at Edward as he leaned down and kissed her gently. 'You will take care, won't you?'

'Of course I will. I'm not going anywhere yet, unlike Jonathan Birbeck,' Edward replied and held Sally tightly. 'He's joined up of his own accord – went last week and left poor Alison Redman in a right state. The wedding was all planned and everything, with there being a baby on the way. I think her father will shoot him long before any Nazi does, if he shows his face around here again.'

'Oh Lord, I don't know what everybody sees in Jonathan. He's no morals, that's for sure. Did you read in my letter that Marjorie's gone to Liverpool to have her baby? You do know it's his, don't you?' Sally gazed innocently at Edward.

'You don't say! I think half of Dent and Cowgill know who the baby's father is – all, that is, except Marjorie's father and mother. Anyway, there's nowt they can do about it now, because he's gone to serve God and kingdom, and Jonathan knows that he is well out of it.'

'It's the poor lasses he's left behind that I feel sorry for. We could all be tempted, if we wanted to be,' Sally said and then blushed.

'Not before I'm married, lass. That's what I believe, so you are alright with me. Plenty of kisses, though. But tha does look right bonny today, I must say, and it wouldn't take much to get me carried away in my thoughts.'

'Perhaps I shouldn't have worn this skirt and cardigan. Marjorie gave them to me before she went away; she knew I'd always liked them, and they don't fit her anymore.' Sally looked down at the shorter-than-usual skirt and the lacy cardigan. 'There were one or two pieces that she gave me that I daren't wear – they're far too revealing!'

'Nay, you look just fine. Nowt wrong with that, and there will be nowt wrong with the other stuff. It was the lass wearing them that caused all the upset. I know you are not as forward as Marjorie, and never will be.' Edward held her tightly. 'We'll be alright, Sally; no matter what happens, we will be alright. Marjorie must take after her mother, from what I hear.'

'What do you mean, Edward?' Sally asked.

'Nay, I'm not for saying. But there's a bit of gossip in the dale about her and all.' Edward regretted saying it straight away. 'It's not for us to worry about, my lass.'

It was the following Tuesday, and Ivy busied herself in the kitchen as she saw John Blades entering the yard in his van. She didn't even look up and give him any recognition when he waved to her, once out of his van, and walked towards the house. She sighed and cursed under her breath; he must still be the replacement salesman for Thompson's. She thought they would have got wise to his ways by now.

'Now then, fella, have you come to get our latest order for the month,' Bob yelled from out of the barn and quickly caught John up. 'I don't think we want much; in fact I'll go so far as to say we want nowt off you.' Bob stared at the smarmy, confident fella who had all the dale talking.

'Are you sure? I usually have a steady order here each month. Not even some dog food?' John stopped in his tracks and looked at Bob, who he had found a lot harder to deal with than his wife.

'Aye, I'm sure. I picked up what I needed from the mill myself the other day, seeing as I was passing. So you can be on your way.' Bob stood his ground, leaning against the van and hinting for Blades to get back into it.

'I'll just pop my head around the door and say hello to Mrs Fothergill,' John insisted and started to head for the house.

'She's busy. Now I've not got time to be blathering to you, so tha's best on your way,' Bob said and opened John's van door. John said nothing, but walked back to his van. It wasn't the first time he'd not been given the time of day that week, and he knew that his secret was out and about in the community, so it was perhaps time to move on again.

'Sally, there's Edward Riley coming up the lane. I saw him from my bedroom window. Has he come a-kissing and canoodling?' Ben grinned at his big sister, who he'd heard his parents say was courting.

'No, he hasn't. Now shut up, our Ben – he's just come a-visiting,' Sally replied, with as much surprise as she saw on her mother's face. She hadn't expected Edward to come visiting quite yet. And then she looked worried, realizing that he must be arriving with bad news, else he wouldn't be coming anywhere near.

'Oh Lord, are we tidy? Did he not tell you he were coming, Sally? I'd have made a cake and have got my best china out. I don't want him to think that we have nowt.' Ivy quickly tidied the kitchen, as Sally went to the door and opened it, to find her father talking to Edward and taking his horse's reins as he led the animal to the barn to rest, after being ridden down the dale at speed.

'Edward, I didn't expect you. Are you alright?' Sally asked as she walked towards him.

'Aye, I am, but I had to come and tell you: my papers came today. They've conscripted me, and I've got to go to Dent village hall and attend a medical to say I'm fit and well, and then I've to go to Catterick for my training.' Edward looked close to tears as he told Sally, but then composed himself. 'It'll only be for six months at most – don't worry.'

Sally felt her own tears welling up inside her as she stood looking at him, wanting to hug and comfort him, but holding herself back, because her parents were watching them both; not to mention Ben, who was listening to every word.

'My mother and father are beside themselves with worry, and my father is blaming himself for making me go and work in the coalyard. I'm their only one; my mam is broken-hearted at me having to leave.' Edward hung his head.

'It hasn't happened yet, lad. Perhaps they'll find something wrong with you, especially if you play on something like a bad back. Those army surgeons will not be that particular. Tell them you have bother walking and fake a limp.' Bob patted Edward on the back as he came and joined his daughter and sweetheart.

'Nay, I can't do that. If I'm asked to fight for my King and country, then that's what I'll have to do, regardless of who I leave behind.' Edward squeezed Sally's hand.

'You've not got a bad lad there, Sally. Many would do anything to get out of going, for the sake of themselves,' Bob said and then shouted, 'Mother, put the kettle on – we have a visitor.'

'I know,' Ivy replied, coming over to them. 'The kettle is already on, so there was no need to shout, Father. It's lovely to meet you again, Edward. I only wish you were here with better news.' Ivy put her arm around Sally and gave her a brief hug. 'Now come in and have a bite to eat and tell us more.'

'I will in a little bit, but may I talk to Sally on my own for a short while? There's things I need to say,' Edward said quietly.

'Aye, of course, lad.' Bob looked at Sally and smiled. 'Mind what you are doing.'

Edward took Sally's arm and walked down the lane, only to hear Bob shout, 'Here come back, thee – they don't want you listening in' at Ben, as he followed them. Bob knew that what the couple were going to say was private, and even though his daughter was young she should be able to talk to her man without her brother eavesdropping. And after all, young Edward seemed a decent lad who was about to be caught up in something that was none of his doing.

Ben came back with his head down and looked up at his father.

'You are too young to be with them, lad, so leave them be. Lord knows, every second will be precious to them.'

Chapter 12

'Aye, lass, you seem at sixes and sevens with yourself today. What on earth is up?' Annie asked Sally as she placed her dinner in front of her, but forgot to bring Annie the tea. 'Did I hear you crying upstairs as well? Tell me what's to-do.' Mrs Mackreth reached for Sally's hand and took it, with a kind look of age and wisdom in her eyes. She'd a good idea what was wrong in Sally's world, but didn't want to upset her.

'I'm sorry, I didn't mean to bring my worries with me, but I can't stop thinking about them. And I promised to join Edward this afternoon when he goes to Dent village hall to meet the conscription officers,' Sally replied and wiped a tear away from her eye.

'You mean the lad that was outside with his horse and cart? The one you are only friends with. Or have things grown between you of late, as they usually do?' Annie asked with a smile on her face, and patted Sally's hand.

'Aye, he's that age when the government says he's to

go and give six months' service, along with one or two other lads that don't farm with their fathers. But we all know, with the news as it is, that it's more than that. They are taking him to fight and I'll be lucky if he ever comes back to me again, if he goes,' Sally sobbed.

'Aye, lass, I've been here before. And the hearts that had been broken last time were nobody's business. We all thought it would never happen again, but sadly it looks as if it is going to, no matter what this country tries to do. Those bloody Germans – you'd think they'd have learned better last time, but it only takes one madman in power and all reason leaves folk. As for those bloody Eyeties, their country is bankrupt, that's what, and we have a lot of them already in this country. But none of that is helping you or your lad, no matter how I rant. You'll just have to let him go, and hope that he keeps his bonny head down and comes back to you, if this country does get involved,' Annie said and felt her heart break for the lass who was in tears in front of her. 'It's not the first time and it won't be the last. He'll be alright; it might all be huff and puff by this Hitler fella. Britain isn't in this war yet.'

Annie shook her head. She knew that she was giving false hope to the young lass. Most of Europe was either up in arms already or getting ready to do so, and the country needed lads like Edward: young, fit and ready to fight as soon as he was called. He'd be off to the front as soon as he'd had his training, if not before, and there was nowt poor Sally could do about it.

* * *

Edward stood nervously outside Dent village hall. By his side stood Sally, whom he had put in charge of his horse, as he tried to calm his nerves and accept whatever the outcome of the next few minutes was.

'I'll be alright, pet, don't worry. I don't think I'll be leaving you today. They surely can't make me do that. My mother was peeling potatoes for my supper tonight, so they'd better not upset her.' Edward was trying to make light of the nerves they both felt, as they looked at two soldiers dressed in the uniform of the Royal Northumberland Fusiliers guarding each side of the main entrance.

'Riley, Edward James – this way,' the staff sergeant yelled and frogmarched Edward in, without a word said between them.

Sally felt sick to the bottom of her stomach. She might not actually know yet if she loved Edward, but she did have feelings for him, and the last thing she wanted was for him to join up and be parted from her.

'Has Edward been called up? I have, too, and I don't want to be. What's this war with the Jerries got to do with us? It's thousands of miles away,' Tim Hartley said as he waited his turn and looked as pale as a ghost. His nerves were getting the better of him as he turned and retched into the street.

'Are you alright, Tim?' Sally looked at the lad who worked at the blacksmith's and thought he looked far too young to be fighting any wars. 'I believe everybody thinks like that, but there's not much we can do about it,' Sally said; she could have done the same as him, if she hadn't kept swallowing and taking in air. She held on to the horse's reins as it reared its head at the smell of Tim's stomach contents.

He wiped his mouth on the sleeve of his jacket and said to Sally, 'Are you two courting, then? That is one good thing – I'm not walking out with anybody, so I can't break a lass's heart. Not like that Jonathan Birbeck; now he's been a bastard. I thought the army only wanted real men, and he's definitely not a man; he's more of a rat. Leaving my cousin expecting, and looking forward to their wedding.'

'Yes, he's definitely no gentleman. I'm so sorry for your cousin Alison. Perhaps Jonathan will come back and make things right with her on his next leave.' Sally really didn't want to take part in a conversation about Jonathan and Tim's cousin. She was too worried about Edward to care about anybody else.

'Oh shit, Edward's back, and I know I'm next,' Tim said and felt his stomach churn as he saw Edward standing next to the window.

'Hartley, Timothy Robert,' the sergeant bellowed, and Tim, on shaking legs, walked over and into the hall, leaving Sally wondering where Edward had gone. But it wasn't long before he emerged carrying a folded uniform, a cap and a pair of regulation army boots.

'Well, it seems I'm in the army now. Your father's idea of pretending that I had a bad back didn't work. As long as I could bend over, that was enough. All they did was measure my height, my weight and test my reflexes, and ask what infections I'd had when I was younger. I think they would have taken me on even if I had two

217

broken legs.' Edward put his arm around Sally, who looked subdued on seeing the uniform.

'Oh no, Edward. I was hoping they would find something wrong with you and then they would reject you – nothing serious, of course. What happens now? When and where do you go?' Sally hung on Edward's free arm and gazed up at him.

'Tomorrow they are sending a wagon to pick up everybody from Sedbergh and Garsdale, so at least we will all know one another – happen it will not be so bad. They pick me up at the bottom of our lane at one, and then carry on to Sedbergh. We are only training at Catterick; it's not a million miles away. We can write to one another.' Edward could see the tears in Sally's eyes. 'I'll be alright. I'm not on my own. And if poor Tim Hartley, who could never fight his way out of a paper bag, has to go, then so should I.'

'I just don't want you to go; we have only begun to know one another. With you going tomorrow, it doesn't even give us time to say goodbye properly. You need to go home and spend what time you have left with your family. Your mam will be worried, and she must come first.' Sally looked up into Edward's eyes.

'I'll be back, and you'll be the first person I visit on my arrival home. I'll not forget you, Sal, if that's what you are worried about. And, like you say, I'll write. Besides, what do they say: "absence makes the heart grow fonder"? Although I must admit I'm already fond enough of you, Sally Fothergill.'

Edward pulled her to him and kissed her slowly, in

218

front of some of the locals out shopping. Both of them felt no embarrassment, knowing it was their parting kiss.

'Now go home, as your parents will wonder where you are at. And I'll have to break the news at home, and that's going to be hard. You take care, my Sally, and you write to me. I'll send you details when I know them.'

Sally lingered, holding his hand for as long as she could, and then knew he had to make things right at home, before he left his family behind. 'And I'll write to you. You take care,' she said. She stopped herself from saying, 'I love you', as she didn't know if it was love that she was feeling for Edward or not. But she knew she had never felt this way before and that there was an ache in her heart, which made her shed tears all the way home.

She'd lost Marjorie and now she was losing Edward, and her world seemed suddenly smaller and more dangerous to live in, she thought, as she walked down the road on a beautiful early summer's day. But the weather did not matter to her; the war was taking Edward away and that's all she could think about.

The following day Sally stood at the bottom of her farm lane, waiting for the army truck that was to take her Edward to Catterick Garrison. She'd sobbed all night, feeling sorry for herself more than anything, for losing a good friend and the boy she now thought she loved. It would be the last time she'd see Edward for at least six months, so she wasn't going to miss out on waving at him as the wagon drove past.

Her mother and father had looked at her, but had not said a lot, knowing that no matter what they said, it could not mend the situation, which nobody could do anything about. Many a lass had been broken-hearted in the Great War – Stanley's girlfriend being one of them, hearing that he had been lost in action. Then, after no word from him for six months, she had married the lad next door, which broke Stanley's heart on his return and only added to his condition. War and the run-up to war were cruel; they had no time for people's feelings, or for such a frivolous thing as love.

Sally heard the sound of a wagon changing gear as it made its way around the corner, and of men singing. She could hear, 'It's a long way to Tipperary; it's a long way to go' being sung at the top of the conscripts' voices as the khaki-coloured wagon with its tarpaulin over the back drove nearer.

She stood at the side of the road and watched as it passed, with the driver honking its horn at her and the new recruits leaning out of the back. In the middle of the group was Edward, hanging on to a hand-strap and looking down at her as the wagon sped past.

'I'll be back. I'll write,' Edward yelled and blew her a kiss, as all the other lads around him whooped and hollered at him, and tried to pull him back within the confines of the wagon.

Sally stood and waved at him until the vehicle was out of sight and then, under her breath, she whispered, 'I think I love you, Edward Riley – just you keep your bonny head down,' before walking slowly back home with tears in her eyes. He might only have gone to Catterick training camp, but to her it might as well be the other side of the world, until he came back to Dentdale and her.

'What does the letter say, Father?' Ivy asked as they sat around the table, with the postman enjoying his usual cuppa with them.

'I can tell you, without you opening it: every farm's got one this morning. It's from the ministry – the War Ag – saying they are coming to visit. They want to see how productive your farm is. Bill Mason showed me his letter as soon as I delivered it,' the postman said, as he dunked a biscuit into his tea. 'They need to know the far end of a fart and where it's gone to, according to Bill.'

'I don't want them nosing around my land or telling me what to farm, but by the looks of it, I've no option,' Bob said as he read the letter. 'They say I can expect a visit next Monday at one o'clock.'

'Aye, that will be about right, because they said they were visiting Dillicar an hour before you,' the postman replied as he finished his tea and rose from the table.

'You might just as well have opened all our letters and read them to us, Graham. Tha seems always to know what's in them,' Bob said and grinned.

'Nay, I only remember what I hear, and it's been nowt but bad news for everybody of late. It's no joy being a postman at the moment. I'd much rather deliver birthday cards and postcards – although I see your lass has got a

221

letter from Liverpool this morning. That will no doubt be from that Harper lass, sent in disgrace to her aunty's.' Graham looked at the letter placed on the mantelpiece ready for Sally to read at her leisure.

Bob shook his head. There was nowt that came in the post that missed Graham's scrutiny. No wonder he liked postcards, as he could read everybody's business on the back of them. 'Aye, it could well be. She'll be opening it when she comes in, and in privacy.'

'Well, I'll be on my way. The Jacksons at Green Cottage look to have a letter from their son – they'll be anxious to hear news of him, I'm sure. See you tomorrow, if you have some post.'

'Aye, no doubt. You take care, Graham,' Bob said. He looked across at Ivy, who opened the door for him, glad for the postman to be on his way.

'That fella knows everybody's business. He'd either be a godsend to the government or a nightmare, if he was a spy.' Ivy laughed and watched Bob, who was scowling as he reread the letter from the War Ag.

'These buggers will expect us to do all sorts, I know, and will never leave us alone. As Graham says, it is all bad news that he's delivering at the moment.'

'It'll be alright, Father. Whatever they say, we'll just have to make the best of it. At least our Sally has got a letter from Marjorie, which might brighten her day up, because she's been a bit down in the dumps of late.'

'Aye, she must be worried about both Marjorie and that lad of hers. Although he'll be alright as long as war isn't declared. But it's heading that way, else fellas like this one from the War Ag wouldn't be checking on what the farmers can supply, and what they can squeeze out of us. As for Marjorie, well, once she's had that baby of hers, she'll have to make her mind up what she's doing with her life.'

Bob got up from the table. He was going to check his sheep, to give himself some time to himself and to think about affairs. He might be getting paid more by Jim Mattinson, and his lass was working now, but his worries were growing; and a man visiting from the ministry was yet another one to add to his pile. Owning his own farm was merely a dream at the moment, no matter how hard he saved.

Sally sat on the edge of her bed, reading the letter Marjorie had written to her. It was full of hurt and despair:

22 Chester Street, Liverpool

1st June

Dear Sally,

I've finally got round to writing to you and have persuaded my aunt to post this letter to you. I'm hating every minute here – it's like being in prison. My aunt does not let me go out, because she is so ashamed of me in my condition. She thinks all the neighbours will talk. She also makes me pray for forgiveness every morning and night. No wonder my mother has little to do with her!

She tells me that in another month or two she's booked me into a mother-and-baby home in Dublin, like I suspected. When I'm there, they don't let me have any outside communication – a true prison. I don't want to go, and I'm frightened. What if I can't give birth to this baby? I might even die. But then again, nobody will care, will they? I'm so lonely. I don't think I will ever see my home again.

Is there any news of home? Have you seen Jonathan, and has he asked after me?

Please write soon.

All my love,

Marjorie

Sally felt so much sympathy for Marjorie, as it could so easily be her in the same position, if her love for Edward was a bit deeper. But she didn't fear the wrath of her parents, if she was found in the same position, as any girl could be. She'd write back to poor Marjorie and tell her what news she had; she'd even tell her that Jonathan Birbeck had joined the army, along with Edward, and had not got married. At least that would give Marjorie a little hope that one day he might yet be hers; and she needed anything to cling on to, by the sound of it. They were both without their man, and it hurt.

Bob stood in his hobnailed boots, with his worn trousers held up by his thick leather belt and wearing his cotton shirt, leaning over the farm gate and watching the man from the ministry walk around his main meadow.

The man, bespectacled and dressed in a sombre grey suit, looked around him. 'None of your land is extremely fertile; it's like all these upland farms – barely able to offer anybody a decent living. None of these Dales farms are suitable for growing wheat or barley, but you could grow potatoes, kale or turnips, if you were to plough your fields.'

'And why would I want to do that? These meadows are to generate hay for winter foddering for my sheep and cows, not tatties. We have them in the garden around the side of the house.' Bob sighed. The fella had no idea how his farm worked.

'Yes, I see that you have your own supply of vegetables. But if war comes upon us, we will look to our farmers to supply the nation once again. Perhaps the paddock the young calf is in could give a good yield, if planted?' the ministry man said and made a note in his book, which contained every farm's details within its pages. 'You have pigs and poultry, and how many sheep at the moment?'

'Near enough a hundred, if you count this year's lambs. But they'll be sold in the autumn, to raise our income for the year. Or will you be commandeering them, like you have the young lads of this dale?' Bob asked angrily and glared at the pompous little man.

'Now, Mr Fothergill, that is not the attitude to have. We are just ensuring the country and its farmers can sustain the people of this nation, if it comes to war. On behalf of the government, we are visiting every farm and will report back with our findings. And then, if need be, we will return with some suggestions to make your farm – and others – more profitable for all of us.'

225

The man folded his notebook.

'This may even benefit you Dales farmers. Indeed, I've hardly seen a farm this way with a tractor in use. I can tell you now that the government is negotiating a deal with our American colleagues for the Fordson Tractor Company to supply us with tractors, if war does come to our shores. They will be offered to farmers who think they will benefit from them, so I would say you need to plant potatoes in the small field and let the government pay you for your trouble – that is, if war does come.'

'You know damn well that war is on its way, else you wouldn't be doing this, as well as all the rest that's going on. Neville Chamberlain can talk to Hitler until he's blue in the face, but he and Mussolini will do what they want, not to mention the Japs. You'll be back too soon for my liking,' Bob replied and watched as his visitor walked towards his spotless car, with a chauffeur driving it. His farm, and that of others in the dale, was about to change, whether he wanted it to or not.

In Catterick Garrison, Edward lay on his bunk bed. He'd marched, saluted and obeyed orders until he had nearly dropped. Every bone in his body ached, and his head was spinning with the orders and instructions shouted at him every day, since he had arrived in what he called hell. Army life was not for him, but most of all he missed Sally and his home. Although the camp was no more than thirty miles from Dentdale, this was a different life and, to make matters even worse, he had no privacy. And Jonathan Birbeck was in his battalion and was acting like the cock of the north. How he longed for home and his Sally.

'You alright, Edward?' Tim whispered.

'Aye, I'm alright, but I'm knackered and homesick.' Edward sighed.

'Aye, me too,' Tim replied and rolled over in his bunk.

'We didn't realize quite how lucky we were, did we?' Edward said, but got no reply from Tim.

Chapter 13

The summer months were flying by, and every day the papers reported Hitler invading more and more innocent people's lives, and causing chaos, havoc and death. The people of Britain watched and listened, and waited to see how far it would go before their country got involved. There was an unspoken unease, as people listened to the radio and spoke to one another in huddled groups.

Annie Mackreth sat outside her house on the edge of the granite fountain and watched people go back and forth along the cobbled street

While Sally cleaned her house and made her dinner, Annie was making the most of the warm weather. Come winter, the days would be cold and miserable, so a bit of summer sunshine on her face was more than welcome, as well as the company of the local shoppers, who all stood and talked to her, shared their concerns and told her the news.

'Have you not finished yet, lass? You do too fine a

job of cleaning for me. Although I do appreciate your care and attention,' Annie shouted into the house as she saw Sally pass her open doorway, then place her lunch on the table next to Annie's chair, as usual, before leaving for home.

'I have just finished. It's taken me longer today because there was a bit more ironing to do,' Sally replied and sat down next to Annie on the rough seat of the sandstone fountain.

'That'll be my cotton dresses and skirts. They all needed ironing, and I've been waiting until now to wear them. Like my mother always used to say, "Don't cast a clout till May is out."'

'But it's nearly July, Mrs Mackreth; summer won't be with us much longer.' Sally smiled and looked at the old woman enjoying the sunshine.

'Aye, but it's just right, now. Hopefully the weather will keep like this until the end of September, and then my old bones will start hurting again, with this blasted arthritis. You enjoy your life while you can, because old age is nowt, I can tell you.'

'Well, I can't say I'll be enjoying tomorrow, if it's this hot. Ben and I are helping my father gather the sheep and lambs from up the fell; it's time for them to be sheared. Running about like extra sheepdogs, with my father yelling at us, is not exactly what Ben and I wanted to do this Saturday, but it has to be done. The sheep need their summer wardrobe as well.'

'Mrs Bentham has said her husband and her lads are clipping. She's just been to the shop for an extra loaf of bread, as she'd run out, from feeding them all. She's got four lads of course, and she was worried to death that one or two of them would be getting papers for them to sign up, but they have a lot more land than some of 'em around here. Talking about getting signed up, have you heard owt from that lad of yours lately?' Annie asked and looked at Sally.

'Yes, he's written, just a few lines. He says he's well, but missing home, and being trained hard. He's expecting to have to go and fight. However, he doesn't say a lot more than that, because I think his letters might be censored, even though he's only up at Catterick.' Sally hung her head, but tried to smile.

'They will be, lass. The army likes to keep itself to itself, and it was like that last time. As long as he's writing, that's the main thing, and safe.'

Both of them raised their heads as they saw Alison Redman walking into Dent past the cottages outside the churchyard, and past the shop and Deepdale Road end, with her head down, looking tired and with the baby within her now visible to everyone.

'Aye, the poor lass, look at her – carrying a baby that its father didn't want, and leaving her standing just about at the aisle. She must be feeling it, poor lass. It's a good job her family are standing by her. Unlike your friend's family. Shipped off to Liverpool just because she's expecting. A baby is a blessing, whether it's wanted or not. Me and my old man would have done anything for a child.' Annie shook her head and watched as Alison made her way past The Sun inn. 'She must be in need of a friend at the moment, poor lass,' she went on, as she stood up with the aid of Sally's arm.

'She must. Maybe I should go and walk home with her – show her some sympathy,' Sally said and helped her charge to her chair.

'Aye, do that, lass. Although this is a grand spot to live, it can be a lonely one when you are feeling down.'

'Are you sure you are alright until Monday? Is there anything else you need doing?' Sally asked, glancing around her.

'No, I'm right. My house is tidy, my cupboards are filled and my clothes ironed, so I want for nowt. Get gone and catch Alison up, as she'll welcome a friendly face.'

Sally quickly said goodbye and ran along the cobbled street past the village hall and the school where Ben was having his lessons. She finally caught Alison up as she made her way down the road to Sedbergh.

'Alison, wait. I'll walk with you,' Sally shouted and ran down the road to catch her.

'What do you want to do that for? Are you only going to walk with me to gloat, like everybody else?' Alison carried on her way, not waiting for a breathless Sally.

'No, not at all. And I'm sure nobody is gloating at you. After all, it isn't your fault you are in this situation,' Sally said, trying to smooth things over.

'No, it bloody well isn't – it's that Jonathan Birbeck's. First, he leads me on and then promises to marry me, only to join the army to get out of doing so. Am I really such a bad prospect to marry?' Alison stood defiantly in the centre of Barth Bridge and glared at Sally.

231

'No, you are not at all, Alison. It's Jonathan – I'd like to say what I really think of him, but the air would be blue,' Sally replied. 'I just want to make sure you are alright, and tell you that if you want somebody to talk to, I'd listen.'

Alison calmed down and wiped a tear away from her cheek. 'Is it right what they are saying: that Marjorie Harper is having Jonathan's baby as well? He'd finished with her, and that I was next? Or it could even have been going on behind my back when he was courting me?' Alison quizzed Sally.

'I don't know who the father of Marjorie's baby is.' Sally tried not to make eye contact, knowing that Alison would realize she was lying.

'He is, isn't he? You needn't tell me; you know he is. You are Marjorie's best friend, and she'd tell you anything. Poor cow, she's been sent to her aunt's in disgrace, I hear! At least my family are standing by me and the baby will be kept. Now whether I can bear to love it, I don't know. But I did love Jonathan, you know – he's just a bad lad with charm,' Alison said softly.

'Yes, Marjorie's in Liverpool, but she's about to go to a mother-and-baby home in Dublin, run by nuns. I never knew her family were Catholic until this happened. She's lonely too.' Sally walked to the end of the bridge with Alison.

'She's in a worse spot than me, poor devil. As for Jonathan Birbeck, sometimes I hope he gets his head blown off by the Nazis, and the next day I wish he was here by my side. You can't help loving the wrong man, can you? You must be missing your fella; I hear he's up at Catterick Garrison. It was so unfair that he had to go.'

'Yes, he is. He's alright, though, but I do worry,' Sally said and smiled, at having Edward called her fella.

'Well, I hope he stays safe, as he's one of the decent ones. Now I'm heading up here on the back lane. I just thought I'd have a walk and stop my mother forever looking at me, worried to death. I'm sure she thinks I'm going to take my own life, but I'd never do that and give that sod Jonathan such satisfaction. If he does come back, he can be held responsible for his ways – or be shot by my father.' Alison smiled. 'Give my best wishes to Marjorie, and let's see whose baby comes first. Poor li'l things; they can't help having the same father.'

'No, they can't. You take care as well, and you know where I live, if you ever want to talk.' Sally watched as Alison walked up the back lane behind Dent towards her home.

'You, too, as we have to stick together,' Alison yelled back as she turned the bend out of sight, leaving Sally feeling relieved that she wasn't in the same position as both Alison and Marjorie.

Chapter 14

It was Saturday morning and the summer sun was shining through the window. It was the day at Daleside that was always welcome when it was over. Sally knew that her mother was already busy in the kitchen, despite it being only five in the morning, and she could hear the low voice of her Uncle Stanley talking to her father outside.

As she got dressed she heard Jim Mattinson's van drive into the yard. Even her father's employer helped out on a day like today, to get the task done for another year. Shearing the sheep – or 'clipping day', as it was known locally – was one of the hardest days of the year, and all farmers and friends helped one another get their part of the fell clear of sheep and lambs, take them down to the pens built specially to hold them, and then clip the older sheep free of their fleece. However, first they had to be gathered; and that was a job for the dogs and the young ones of the family, chasing the stragglers and making sure the flock came down in an orderly way. Most of the sheep did, but you could guarantee that there would be one with a mind of its own.

Sally watched her mother, busy handing out bacon sandwiches to the men who were standing outside, leaning on their walking sticks and looking up at the steep-sided fell, which they were going to climb before the heat of the day set in. She picked up the tray filled with mugs of tea and passed it around, saying good morning to her uncle and Jim Mattinson.

'I don't know where Brian from next door has got to. He's usually the first one here,' Bob said to Stan and Jim.

'Perhaps he's forgotten, or got a cow calving or something,' Stan replied and sipped his tea.

'Nay, he'll not have forgotten, but there must be something amiss, else he'd have been here. It doesn't matter, as we will manage without him, but he's a good hand at clipping.' Bob was puzzled.

'Are you going to be helping us, Sally? You are a lot more lish than any of us,' Jim Mattinson said as he bit into his bacon sandwich and winked at Ivy as a thank-you.

'Yes, I will. I know everybody dreads the gather, but I quite like it. I always like being up the top of the fell, and the heather is not far off coming out in bloom, which makes it all the better.'

'If you'd gathered these fells as long as we have, you'd not be saying that; or if your knees ached as bad as ours. You can tell that you are young.' Stanley grinned and then emptied the tea leaves that were left in the bottom of his mug out onto the dry earth of the farmyard. 'Your father's gather is not a bad one, but this fella is aright

235

pain in the arse, with being up the side of Great Coombe.'
Stanley patted Jim on the shoulder.

'You get paid for mine, so what are you moaning about?' Jim grinned.

'Aye, in mutton, and happen a bit of bacon come back-end – never cash.' Stanley grinned back.

'I tell you, in another month or two you'll be glad of that payment. I feel sorry for all the poor devils in the towns, if war does come. They went hungry last time, and it will be worse this time,' Jim Mattinson said and leaned on his stick.

'Aye, whisht for just one day all this talk of war. Let's get this fell gathered, and then we can get on with clipping. I'll go up the right side; Stan, you do the middle, and, Jim, do you think you can do the left-hand side? Sally, if you are coming, do the same as last year and run after the stragglers.' Bob looked at Ivy as she collected the mugs. 'And when that lad of ours gets out of bed, can you and he open the gates down into the yard for us and drive the sheep into the pens?'

Ivy nodded, and Sally heard her mother shouting upstairs for her brother to get out of bed, as she walked through the yard to the top field and then up towards the rough grassland of the fell. Bob and Jim's sheepdogs ran in front of the group with their tongues hanging out, excited that they were going to be put through their paces and show who was boss of the stupid sheep.

'Away, Spot; away, Rex!' Her father and Jim shouted at the dogs when they were halfway up the fell, and both dogs shot like bullets from their owners and disappeared out of sight, then ran over the fell top to gather what sheep they could find.

Sally walked as fast as she could up the fellside, catching her breath and stopping to look at her home, way down at the bottom. As she climbed higher and higher, she could hear her father and Jim whistle directions to their dogs, while Stan flapped his arms and guided the sheep already gathered together, and then they were easier to manage. Sally ran to the far edges of their land and followed the drystone walls, looking for sheep that the dogs and men might have overlooked, and finally finding one and her two lambs grazing near a sinkhole. She flapped her arms and then made a noise, scaring them down her father's side of the fell.

The mother of the twins turned to look at her in defiance as she bleated to her offspring, and then thought better of arguing, once she heard the two dogs yapping at the rest of the flock. She ran down the wall side – at least in the right direction, Sally thought as she strode out over the sphagnum moss and heather at the top of the fell and watched the flock being herded by the three men and the dogs, in a line down the fellside. She could see her mother and Ben at each farm gate, eagerly waiting for the flock to pass by them, so that they could close it behind them.

She heard the lambs bleating, not knowing what was going on in their lives, while the older sheep that had been hefted on the land knew their way all too well and were not about to argue with either man or dog. Sally was hot and her long, dark hair felt sticky at the back of her neck, and she knew her cheeks were ablaze. Still, there was no better place that she knew of, and she loved the smell of the fell, and the dale that lay in front of her. She loved the sight of her father herding the sheep with his friends and relations. There would be a nice feel about the farm all day, as the men clipped the sheep, and she and her mother kept them fed and rolled the fleeces into balls, for collection for the mills in Bradford.

This was a perfect Dales summer, she thought as she walked down the fellside, picking her mother a bunch of the bluest harebells to be put into a vase in the kitchen. How could Hitler even think of invading an inch of her country, without somebody putting up a fight for it? She was proud of her Edward; he'd gone to Catterick without any qualms, and she only hoped he would keep his head down and stay safe, Sally thought as she followed the trail of sheep wool and lamb droppings across to the sheep pens. The men had already started sorting the lambs from the sheep, by the deft closing of a gate that separated mothers from their offspring, making the bleating in the yard almost deafening.

'Shush now. You'll be back with your mother before you know it – she's only gone to the hairdresser's. But in another few weeks, you'll have to do without your mam. She needs a rest before she has another of you, and then you will have to find a new home.'

'You are crackers, our Sally! They don't know what you are saying to them. Everyone knows sheep are thick and they just follow one another,' Ben said as he leaned over the top of the railings of the lambs' pen.

'I know they don't, but I can't stand their cries, and the look of being lost after being separated from their mothers. I'm just soft.' Sally watched as Ben climbed down from the railings. 'Come on, we'll go and help them wrap the wool – you are old enough now. If I can do it, you can.'

Sally pulled her brother across the yard to where the men were starting to shear the sheep. Each animal was seated on its bottom, as its wool was clipped off with a sharp pair of shears; it was cut as a whole fleece, so the men started around the stomach and then sheared the rest, taking care around the head, and clearing the bottom of the sheep of any dirt or infestation of fly-eggs. Then, once clipped, the sheep were daubed with ruddle, an oily mixture that identified the sheep with the individual mark of the farmer. Bob's mark was three straight lines on the sheep's shoulder. The sheep were then released back into a pen, and Ivy took the wool to be wrapped and put in a pile, ready to be taken by a wagon that came from the woollen mills in Bradford.

'Look, watch me,' Sally said as Stan passed her a full fleece, before pulling the argumentative ewe back to its pen. 'You fold it out and then you put where the legs were into the centre, then you roll the whole lot up and tie it off, with this bit that used to be the tail. Simple,' she said and watched Ben's face. She'd learned the task a few years back, but Ben had never done it before. She watched as he took hold of a fleece that his father had shorn.

'Mind what you are doing with it – don't go tearing

239

it, else it will hardly be worth anything. We don't get a lot of brass anyhow; it's hardly worth all this work. But my lasses need to keep cool in this weather,' Bob said, then wiped his brow clear of the sweat that was running down his face.

Ben looked at the fleece; it was full of lanolin and it smelt. But, encouraged by Sally, he followed her instructions and managed to do one in three times the time it usually took her. But he didn't tear it, merely struggling to fasten the fleece off as deftly as his mother and sister.

'That's it, you've got it,' Sally said as Ben took his fleece to the growing pile. He looked flushed in the face with the heat and the pride that, for once, he had actually done something right, and his father had given him a nod of approval.

'You've got a farmer there, Bob. He'll do you proud yet,' Jim Mattinson said as he looked across at the man who worked long hours for his family, and hoped that one day he'd own a larger farm for them to inherit.

'Aye, happen if he can stick at it.' Bob winked at Ben as he threw him the next fleece and bent down to tackle another sheep, with the sound of the hand-shears clicking, and the ewe protesting about its predicament as it struggled in Bob's strong hands.

'Aye, and your Sally – she's not frightened to get her hands mucky. Grand lass, is your Sally.' Jim smiled across at her, while she got on with the job in hand.

'Ben will stick at it and he'll get faster. He's just like I was, the other year when I was learning,' Sally said

240

and smiled at her brother. At last there was something that he was showing an interest in, and getting her father's approval.

By the end of the day all the sheep were clipped, and Jim had returned home to his own farm. The following week he would be doing the same at his farm, with the help of Bob and neighbouring farmers, but he had four times as many sheep as Bob and it was going to be a long, hard job.

Stanley swept the clippings and dirt out of the pens, and Bob opened the gates to the fell, with Sally and Ben helping both sheep and lambs back up to the pastures they preferred. The sheep were looking clean and white, with their shorn coats, and the lambs were glad to be back with their mothers as they made a well-ordered line back to their summer eating.

Ivy shouted to Stan, 'Are you stopping for supper, Stan? I've a beef casserole in the oven, along with a milk pudding, and there's enough for you.'

'Aye, that'll be grand. I appreciate a good meal, and you get fed up of cooking for yourself. I've brought a fir tree to be planted in the beckside wood; Ben can help me plant it before I go home. I've had it growing in a plant pot for over twenty years, but it's got too big for any pot now, so I thought here was a good home for it,' Stan said as he brushed his boots down and then went and swilled his hands under the yard tap. 'I've grown it from some seeds that I brought back with me from Germany when I was a POW there. The camp was next

241

to a forest, and one day this big fir cone landed in the camp. I'd never seen one as big, so I took the thin paper-like seeds out of it and kept them safe until I returned to Blighty, and then I planted them. Lord knows why, because I never want to be reminded of that hellhole.' Stan sighed and joined Ivy standing outside the farm-house, and watched as the rest of the family walked towards them with Bob.

'Anyway, it needs a home, and I thought Ben might like to see how fast it grows. The tree it came from must have been all of twenty foot, so it will eventually tower over everything else. It's a good job Jim picked me up, else I would never have got it here myself.' Stan pointed to the fir tree, which had been placed outside the barn. 'I thought that if it was planted here, perhaps it would never be touched and would be left to grow. A reminder of me, when I'm gone.'

'You're not going anywhere yet, Stan, so you can forget that! But you can plant it up the gill edge; it will not look out of place there.'

'There will be another lot of soldiers going to foreign fields and bringing back memories they don't necessarily want soon, I reckon.'

'Aye, I think there will. You know our Sally's friend has been conscripted – he's up at Catterick Garrison? He's only young, and his father could have done with him at home.' Ivy sighed.

'Aye, it was the same last time. The world never learns. Let's hope that he returns, or that this Hitler sees sense.' Stan smiled at Sally as she walked into the house with her father. 'He'll be alright, lass, don't you fret,' he whispered in Sally's ear, but he knew he was lying. The boy would be going through hell at the camp, and even worse if he was sent abroad to fight.

Chapter 15

'What's Brian doing here first thing on a Sunday morning? He's just walked into the yard and he's standing there, looking lost,' Ivy said as she looked out of the window and spotted their next-door neighbour.

'He'll have come to apologize for not showing his face yesterday. But it was alright, we managed without him.' Bob puffed on his pipe and was enjoying his quiet Sunday morning, after milking the cow and checking that all was as it should be in his world.

'No, there's something wrong. He's sitting on the oil barrel outside the barn now, and he looks as if he's thinking twice about coming across to see us. I'll give him a yell.'

Ivy wiped her hands on her apron and stood in the doorway.

'Brian! Brian, are you alright? Is there something wrong? Bob expected you yesterday, not today,' she shouted across the yard and looked at the man with his head in his hands, who did not reply. 'He's not right, Bob. Are you going to him or should I?' she said.

'There'll be nowt wrong with him. You go and see what's up. Like I say, he'll be thinking of how to account for missing yesterday.' Bob picked up the Sunday newspaper that the paperboy had delivered and then put it straight down again, as he saw the horrific picture of the atrocities taking place in Germany.

'No, I'll go and see what's up.' Ivy set her tea-towel aside. 'Happen he's not well.' She headed out of the house into the warming farmyard, which was full of the noise of hens clucking and laying the day's eggs and of the summer insects flying around her, while the smell of crushed chickweed under her feet filled her senses. It was a perfect Sunday, but for Brian.

'Brian, are you alright? You don't look it,' Ivy said gently, as she could see that their neighbour seemed in despair as he lifted his head.

'She's gone, Ivy. She's gone and left me. I've nobody, nor nowt worth owt, now I've lost her and my lass Marjorie.' Brian gulped and looked up at her with reddened eyes.

'What do you mean? Marjorie went a while ago – has it only just hit you?' Ivy asked and put her arm around the quaking man.

'No, it's Dora – she's gone, packed her bags and left me a note telling me not to try and find her. She's left me high and dry.' Brian stood up shakily. 'She's buggered off with that bloody salesman from Thompson's. I thought he had been calling a lot of late. I came back from

Sedbergh the other day and his van was just going up the road. She said he hadn't called, but I knew he had, as I could smell that bloody stinking stuff he puts on himself. And she was too happy – Dora's never usually that happy. Especially since, you know, our lass got that way,' Brian said bitterly and turned to Ivy.

'Eh, Brian, I don't know what to say. Come in and sit down with Bob and talk to him. We are here to listen and help, if we can,' Ivy replied as they both walked across the yard. 'You are sure now? Happen Dora's gone to Liverpool to see Marjorie, because she must be worrying about her.' She shook her head at Bob as they entered the kitchen.

'Nay, she'll not be doing that. Dora said she wanted nowt more to do with her, as she took the news of Marjorie expecting worse than me. It's one of the biggest sins going, if you are Catholic, and although Dora doesn't practise anymore, she still has her principles. No, she's gone. Here, I'll show you her letter.' Brian pulled a crumpled, screwed-up piece of paper out of his pocket and gave it to Ivy, as he sat down next to Bob and regarded the man he envied. Bob hadn't a lot, but he had a wife who was faithful, and children who respected his words as head of the household.

'I'm sorry to hear all this, Brian,' Bob said, once he'd heard the news. 'I thought better of Dora. Tha's given her everything she could ever wish for, and she was a lucky woman, if she did but know it. My lass has often said you have everything at your house. Now are you alright? I don't know what to say, lad.' Bob looked at his heartbroken neighbour.

246

'Dora doesn't hold back with her words, does she?' Ivy said, after reading her letter. 'There is no need to have put all that, about you not having the time of day for her. She was always treated better than any woman in the dale, from what I could see. She was always dressed well, and I know she visited Sedbergh every week. Lord, I wish Bob would buy me and Sally the clothes that you bought for the pair of them,' Ivy went on with disdain. 'She'll be back, Brian. That salesman John Blades is only a fly-by-night; he's a smooth talker who chances his luck. All the women of the dale are on about him – he tries it on wherever he can.'

Brian shook his head. 'I don't want her back. I don't want either of them back, ever. Marjorie takes after her mother: she's a flighty madam, and look where that's got her. I spoilt them both rotten, and look what they have done to me.'

'Now you are only saying that because you are hurt. You can't want never to see your lass Marjorie again, or her baby. You are its grandfather, it could be a lad, and it could turn out to be a farmer. You've a lot to look forward to, when she comes home with the baby,' Bob said and watched Brian's hard face.

'It'll not be coming home. Sally has probably told you that Marjorie is to be sent to Dublin to have her baby, in a mother-and-baby home. When she's in there, the baby will be taken off her and adopted. She's too young to look after it, and I can't be doing with the shame of her being unmarried with a baby, under my roof. She's only herself to blame,' Brian responded quietly.

247

'Oh, Brian, she'll be broken-hearted, poor lass.' Ivy slumped down into her chair. 'You can't do that to Marjorie.'

'Aye, I can. Her mother was ashamed of her, and I'm not having any bastards in my family.' He turned to Bob. 'We know damn well it's Jonathan Birbeck's baby, although Marjorie has never said as much; and anyway he's already left that poor lass at the top of the dale unmarried and carrying. I don't want his offspring in my house. I hope the bastard gets shot, if we go to war.'

'Brian, watch what you say. I've never heard you speak this way before.' Ivy shook her head.

'Come and have a walk with me, Brian. You are upset; we'll talk man-to-man, out of earshot of our Ivy and my lass. You are angry and I don't blame you for being so, but some words are better held back.' Bob stood up and ushered his neighbour and friend out of the house and hoped that he could calm Brian down and help him to vent his anger. It would seem that Brian Harper had everything, but at the same time he had nothing, Bob thought as he turned round and looked at Ivy, and noticed Sally standing at the bottom of the stairs. She had heard everything that Brian had said and she looked upset.

Sally waited until her father and Brian had left the house and then went to her mother.

'Did you hear any of that?' Ivy asked, seeing the shock on her daughter's face.

'Yes, I heard everything. I feel sorry for him, but it will break Marjorie's heart, of that I'm sure, if she doesn't

248

keep the baby. Even though she said she didn't want the baby before she went, I'm sure she will feel differently once it's born. I would, if it was mine,' Sally replied quietly. 'I can't understand why Mrs Harper has left her husband – she had everything that we don't have.'

'Everything perhaps but love and understanding, by the sound of it. I didn't know Brian Harper could be as hard and cold as that. Although I do feel sorry for him at the moment. Is he right? Is it Jonathan Birbeck's baby Marjorie is having? Everybody has been saying it is, and I know that you know, although you are not for telling.' Ivy looked at Sally.

'It is, Mam. Jonathan promised to run away to Gretna Green with Marjorie and to marry her. Then the next thing she found out was that he was courting Alison and wanted nothing to do with her. She was beside herself with grief and anger at him, but she never gave his name to her parents. I bet she wishes she had done now.' Sally sighed. 'As for Mrs Harper, I think the salesman has been seeing her for some time. I saw him with his arm around her waist when I went to visit Marjorie in the spring. But I thought nothing of it.'

'Aye, well, he's best gone out of the dale. I think he's been trying it on with various women, but Dora has fallen for his charms. He's not worth the time of day. She'll regret what she's done and all.' Ivy sighed, thinking of the time she might have had the chance to have a fling with John Blades. 'As for Marjorie, don't say a word of what you have heard. It's none of our business; it's up to her father and mother to see she's done right by.

Although by the way Brian is talking, he'll not be doing owt. I wouldn't be sending my daughter to a mother-and-baby home run by nuns. I've heard of them – they are called Magdalene Laundries, and they're run by bitter nuns who have had no life of their own and want to punish young girls who have seen a bit too much of life. Poor, poor Marjorie; her life will be hell, and she's nowt to come home to now.' Ivy shook her head and went to peel some potatoes for Sunday dinner.

'Mam, I should tell Marjorie. She's my friend – happen she could get out of going to Dublin. Please let me write to her,' Sally pleaded.

'No, Sally, it's nothing to do with us. Besides, the baby is probably better being adopted. The way Brian was talking, it will never be welcomed with open arms now. And don't say a word about her mother, do you hear? Folk will gossip enough when they hear the news.' Ivy shook her head. Dora had fallen for the sleazy, lying salesman when she would have been better putting up with Brian; she'd had no financial problems with him, but she would now. What a carry-on at the Harpers', she thought as she prepared Sunday dinner, although she couldn't help sympathize with how Dora had fallen for Blades' charms; she herself could have done the same quite easily, if Bob had not come to his senses.

Sally went back upstairs to her room, where she had been writing to Edward until she had heard Brian Harper's voice in the kitchen. She would finish her letter to Edward and would include a picture of herself and

Marjorie that had been taken last summer with Stanley's Box Brownie. And then, despite what her mother said, she would write to Marjorie.

Marjorie was her closest friend, so she had to warn her what they were going to do with her baby, once born, although she would not mention Marjorie's mother leaving home, as that would only upset her more. She looked out of her bedroom window and watched as her father patted Brian Harper on the back. She had always thought that her father was hard, but now she knew he was nothing like Mr Harper. Her father would never turn his back on her if she got in trouble, she thought; and her mother would definitely not run off with another man. They might not be wealthy, but they were a tight family, she decided, as she wrote the last line in Edward's letter, signing off with: *I miss you and am counting the days till your return. All my love, Sally.*

She was missing him so much in fact that she had to stop herself from saying more in her letter to him; she didn't want to seem too forward – that only got you into trouble, from what she had seen so far in life. For now, she'd keep Edward as a very close friend and see how things developed over the coming months, if their love was allowed to develop at all.

She picked up her pen, after sealing the letter to Edward, and wrote to Marjorie. Her mother would never know, and hopefully it would help her friend – one way or another – if only to prepare herself for being parted from her baby, which nobody seemed to want. Poor

Marjorie, she was always so sure of herself, and now her family and her life were in tatters, Sally thought, as she carefully chose what words to write.

'Are you coming in for some dinner? There's always enough for one more on a Sunday, and the company will do you good,' Bob said to Brian and waited for a reply. His next-door neighbour was more than upset; his language and his actions had been terrible while he had been telling Bob what he'd do, both to John Blades and to Jonathan Birbeck. But now Bob hoped that Brian had calmed down enough to join his family for dinner.

'Nay, I'll not do that. I'm not right good company, and I'll have upset your Ivy, but I don't know what to do with myself.' Brian ran his hands through his hair. 'The bloody woman – she decides to leave me at the busiest time of year, and with us on the edge of war as well. I just don't know what I'll do. And I loved her, Bob. I love our Marjorie as well, but I could murder the pair of them right at this moment in time.' Brian shook his head and his eyes nearly filled with tears, but he fought them back, as northern farmers never cried.

'I know, it's a bugger. But don't blame your Dora; that John Blades has been sniffing around everybody's wives, from what I've heard. It's a wonder he hasn't chatted my Ivy up.' Bob smiled and patted his neighbour's shoulder.

'Your Ivy would have more sense – like your Sally has with the fellas. You are lucky, Bob. Cherish your family, because I've lost mine in a blink of an eye.' Brian shook his head again.

'You needn't have done. Bring your Marjorie back home; she won't be the first lass to have a baby out of wedlock, and I always thought you two were close,' Bob suggested.

'No, she's too much like her mother – flighty and wants everything. And I couldn't even look at that baby of hers. It's best Marjorie stops where she's at. Besides, I'm going to be too busy. I've yet to clip my sheep and then it will be haytime. There's a good crop on the fields this year; you look to have a good crop too.' Brian went back into farming mode to hide his grief.

'Aye, it's grown well this year, but I don't know if it will next year. The man from the War Ag seemed to think I should plough all my fields up for root crops. I think he was talking out of his arse. How he thought we were going to survive on tatties and turnips, I don't know.' Bob smiled at Brian.

'Aye, he told me the same. They are going to make us grow some, though. I suppose they will be needing that if we go to war, as the boats won't get through with imports. Happen it was that which made Dora think of leaving me, as I can't see her wanting to bend down and pick tatties up from out of the field.'

'Aye, happen. I can't see her doing that, either. Try not to dwell on it, mate, as there's nothing you can do about it, and she might come back with her tail between her legs yet. Now do you want a hand with clipping? I can help the week after next. I can't this week, because I'm at Jim's for most of the week, clipping there.'

'No, you are alright. My brother's coming up to stay next week for a month to help clip, and with the hay.

He might not want to come now, though, if he knows we have to fend for ourselves. Not that Dora was much of a baker, but it was better than nowt.'

'My Ivy will make you a bit of something, I'm sure, so you'll not go hungry,' Bob replied as he smelt the Sunday dinner cooking.

'Aye, well, I'll come and mow you your two hay meadows. It's easier with the tractor and cutter bar than with the horse or by hand-scythe, and its not out of my way. You've been here for me many a time, not least this morning. I was beside myself when I came into your yard.' Brian looked down at his feet.

'I know, lad. Don't you get down. Your Dora will land back, and so will your lass.'

'I don't think I want either back, Bob. I'm tired of wasting money, and my voice, on both of them. I'm better off without them. After all, Dora was from the backstreets of Liverpool, and she was never meant to be a farmer's wife. I was just taken by the way she dressed, but my father did warn me.'

'There, all the more reason for you to go soft on that lass of yours and bring her home. She takes after her father and thinks she knows better. Bring her back home, Brian, where she belongs. Marjorie can run the house for you until she finds herself another man; and the baby can't help the way it's going to be born into the world.'

'I'll see. Week after next to mow your meadows, is that alright?' Brian asked as he started to walk out of the yard, determined not to take up the offer of Sunday dinner.

'Aye, that will be right. Give our love to Marjorie, and bury your pride for once – get her back home.'

But Brian didn't reply; he simply waved his arm in the air as he trudged home with his broken heart.

Chapter 16

Edward lay in his bunk bed and looked at the photograph Sally had sent him and read the words of affection that she wrote. In the top bunk above his head lay Tim Hartley; he too couldn't rest comfortably, and at one time Edward thought he could hear him sobbing. This was a different world from the one both lads had been brought up in. This was one of being belittled by rules and having to take orders, whether you wanted to or not. The uniform itched, the shoes rubbed, and the gun he was made to carry everyday was heavy. He'd have done anything to be back home in the dale he loved, with Sally by his side and his mother's dinner on the table, he thought, as he smiled at the photograph and kissed it gently, before wedging it between the boards of the hut behind his bedhead.

'What's that you got there, Riley? Don't tell me you have a woman back at home. You are not the kind, and surely nobody will look at you twice?' Jonathan Birbeck walked over and leaned down towards the picture that he'd noticed Edward looking at all evening.

'It's nowt to do with you if I have or I haven't. And at least I'm not like you, leaving women all over the dale in the family way, and hiding here out of the way,' Edward replied, meaning to hurt Jonathan, who was turning into the camp bully.

'You can shut your bloody mouth. You don't know what you're on about. Here, let's have a look at the lass that's daft enough to see something in you.' Jonathan reached over the top of Edward's head and grabbed the photograph out of his grasp. He stood and stared at it, and Edward could see the shock on his face as he recognized Marjorie as one of the lasses he had forsaken.

'Ugly bloody pair! I wouldn't want either of them looking down at me in my bed; or, coming to that, in bed with me. You want nowt with this.' Jonathan grinned. 'Here, I'll help you get rid of it,' he said with a cruel smirk and began to tear the photograph into small pieces, as Edward jumped out of his bunk bed and stood his ground with the far larger lad who nobody particularly liked. All the other resting recruits turned on their sides and watched the two men square up to one another, and one or two of them stood at the bottom of their beds and waited for the first punch.

'You shouldn't have done or said that. You know very well who they both are. Marjorie couldn't have been that ugly, as she's carrying your baby, you bastard.' Edward stared at Jonathan, while there was deadly hush in the barracks.

257

'You telltale rat – you take that back.' Jonathan grabbed Edward's shirt collar and held him close to his face.

'Go on hit me, but I'll bloody well hit you back. You are nowt but a bully, and you are certainly no gentleman. If you thump me, it will be the guardhouse for you, mate; or worse, if I lose my temper. It's a wonder the army has even let you in, with that yellow streak down your back when it comes to facing your responsibilities.' Edward waited for the punch, as Tim Hartley hid his head under the bedcovers and didn't dare to look.

'Birbeck! You put Riley down and get back to your quarters. That is, unless you want to answer to me as well,' the sergeant shouted in a voice that boomed around the room. 'You can do plenty of that when you are fighting the Hun.' He marched over to the two of them, with his swagger stick under his arm, and stepped in between them. 'Whatever it is that's going on between you two, keep it for out there in the field, as every one of you will need to watch one another's backs. Now, leave it, get this tidied up and return to your billets. Unless you do want to end up in the guardhouse,' the sergeant yelled.

He watched as Jonathan let go of Edward's lapels and snarled at him.

'That's it, lad, go back to your bunk and calm down. You might think you are a big fish in a little pool but, believe me, you are only a tiddler, and I can soon squash tiddlers.' The sergeant smirked as Jonathan walked back to his bunk at the far end of the barracks. 'Lights off, lads. Tomorrow you have a ten-mile run with all your kit on. Sweet dreams, my lovelies.' He had a chuckle in his voice as he turned and left Edward picking up the pieces of his photographs.

'I thought he was going to bloody kill you,' Tim Hartley said and pulled his bedcovers up.

'He could have tried, but Jonathan's all mouth. He's nowt, is that lad; all he thinks about is saving his own neck. I wouldn't want to rely on him to cover my back.' Edward looked at the torn photograph in his hand; it was the one thing that he had to remind him of Sally and now it was beyond repair. Jonathan Birbeck would live to regret that, and he had done himself no favours in full view of the sergeant and the rest of his colleagues. Nobody said anything bad about a fella's sweetheart, or picked a fight for no reason. The company had to be strong and have no rogues within it, if they were all to survive. Jonathan was going to be the one who let them down, at the end of the day.

'This came in the post today, madam.' Ivy held out the letter to Sally that had been returned to sender, when she got home from working at Annie Mackreth's. 'I thought I told you not to write and tell Marjorie what was going to happen to her baby?' Ivy was feeling quite vexed that her daughter had written to her friend behind her back. 'Somebody – I presume her aunt – has opened it and then resealed it, and has written on our address and added, "No such person at this address".' She shook her head. 'It's just as well, with what you put in your letter. I told you: it is none of our business.'

Sally's face became flushed. 'I'm sorry, but I thought Marjorie had a right to know. After all, it's her baby that she's carrying; it's not anybody else's to make a decision about.'

'Sometimes your parents have to make a decision. Marjorie's too young to take responsibility for a baby. And besides, she has no mother now – wherever she's at with her fancy man. It's a pity Brian hasn't got it in his heart to forgive her; he's still saying she's not welcome to return home, especially with the baby with her.' Ivy sighed. If it had been Sally in the same position, then no matter who the father had been, she'd not have been an outcast. Family was family, and you stood by them through good times and bad.

'It'll break Marjorie's heart, and you know it. I couldn't part with a baby, no matter what.' Sally looked at her mother. 'I feel so bad for her; she's about to have to give her baby away, her father doesn't want her home, and her mother obviously doesn't give a damn about her. I used always to think the Harpers were a perfect family, but it seems it was all a sham,' Sally went on. 'Marjorie must already have gone to Ireland, if her aunt is returning her letters. I hope she will be alright over there. I can't help but worry.'

'Her mother was always all fur coat and no knickers, although I shouldn't say so. Brian was far too good for her. It doesn't surprise me that poor Marjorie is in trouble. I only hope the nuns look after her, and that if she does return home, her father makes her welcome. The poor man doesn't know whether he is coming or going, and

260

Dora's left him at one of the busiest times of the year. But then again, it never is quiet on a farm, it's always hard work.' Ivy picked up the newly pegged rug and took it to the doorway, to shake it free of hayseeds and straw that Bob had brought in on his boots. 'If the weather holds, your father is going to start haytime next week.' She came back into the kitchen and laid the rug on the floor.

'Yes, there's already a field or two mown, and I heard two men talking in the shop this morning who sounded Irish. The hiring fairs must be doing business in Settle and Kendal, for them to be finding work for a few weeks up here in the Dales.'

'Well, your father won't be needing Irish workers. Brian has offered to mow the two meadows for him with his tractor, and he'll do it in no time, compared to your father mowing it by hand. Although he's out behind the house, sharpening his scythe with a whetstone and complaining that tractors and their mowing blades leave half the grass behind in the corners of the field – he's never happy, is your father.' Ivy sighed.

'He's not talked about buying his own farm for a while, or at least I've not heard him going on about it,' Sally said.

'Oh, don't you worry, he's still got that going round in his head. The extra hours' pay that Jim gives him all goes into the savings pot, and I'm not allowed to touch a penny unless I'm desperate. Dora Harper didn't know quite how lucky she was. She should have been married to your father, and then she would have had something to complain about.'

'Mother, you wouldn't have anybody else, and you know it.' Sally looked with disdain at her mother.

'Do you need me for anything this afternoon?' Sally asked Ivy and hoped she said no, as she wanted some time to herself. She was worried about Edward and Marjorie. And, besides, Annie Mackreth had not been that well that morning, and she had been hesitant to leave her.

'No, you do what you want to do, my lass. You'll earn your keep next week when we have to help your father turn the hay.' Ivy smiled at her daughter; she wanted Sally to enjoy her life before a husband and children took it over; and that would come all too soon, now that she was courting.

Sally was thankful she was not wanted at home as she climbed the steep fellside and sat down on a large stone that had been left protruding out of the ground, as a reminder of when the Earth had been covered with glaciers and was still forming. It was her favourite perch and she sat down, feeling the warm stone beneath her, as she looked down over the dale.

The smell of the fell filled her senses: a smell of sphagnum moss, wild thyme and the clean, pure air that made her life in the Dales so special. She listened to a lamb bleat, looking for its mother as it had strayed too far from the safety of its dam; and to the crickets that noisily rubbed their legs together, enjoying the summer's sunshine and filling the air with a soothing hum. The fellsides were about to turn purple with the oncoming autumn's show of heather and ling; soon the dale would be ablaze with autumn colours, but not before the farmers had gathered in their crops to keep their stock fed over the winter.

In the distance she could see that a farm down in the dale had already mown its meadows; they were making the most of the good weather. She looked down into her family's farmyard: her father's scythe glinted in the sunshine as he sharpened the blade in readiness for the coming work. She watched as Ben wandered home up the lane from school, going into the house and coming out again as soon as he'd left his school books behind. He'd better things to do in his life at this time of year, she thought, as she watched him go across to the barn and pick up some rabbit snares. There would be rabbit stew for the next night or two, if he managed to catch some poor innocent creature that found itself tangled in the cruel noose of his wire snare. She couldn't help but think of the fluffy animal that had wandered the fields and fells until caught in Ben's trap, whenever she had rabbit served in front of her. Still, it was tasty with onions and carrots and herbs from the garden, and it made a change from the usual mutton or bacon.

Feeling lazy in the warmth of the sun, Sally moved and lay back down onto the dry, stubby grass of the fell and looked up at the sun through squinting eyes. She thought about Edward being at Catterick army camp; she also thought about her best friend in Ireland, without friends or family, feeling alone and vulnerable, although Marjorie would never let anybody know that.

People were complicated, there was no doubt about it, she thought as she closed her eyes and relaxed.

She suddenly awoke to the sound of a distant droning in the air. It was a noise hardly ever heard in the Dales, and she sat up and looked into the sky. A group of six aeroplanes were flying over Winder Fell and she wondered whether to seek cover and hide, in case they were German and war had been declared on England without her knowledge; but she stood her ground and sat up on the rock again and watched them fly in her direction.

Her heart beat fast as they came closer and closer and then, with relief, she recognized the green-and-brown camouflage and the shape of the Lancaster – the model plane that Ben had been given at Christmas. They were English, so she was in no danger, she thought, as they came nearer and nearer. The emblem of the RAF was clear on their sides and wings as they flew directly overhead – so close that she could see the pilots within the cockpits, and one of them actually waved at her. She wondered if he might be the son of Mr and Mrs Jackson at Green Cottage and that was why he had waved. No matter who it was, they were brave, just like her Edward. Everyone was talking about the war, which nobody was in any doubt was going to come and change everyone's lives. She smiled as she waved back. It was only a matter of when the war started, thought Sally, as she watched the formation of Lancasters flying over the dale back to their airbase and to safety, she hoped.

* * *

'Did you see them? Did you see them, our Sal? Lancasters exactly like mine. I was picking up a rabbit that I'd snared, and they flew right over the wood and made the trees sway,' Ben shouted excitedly as his sister came into the yard.

'Yes, I saw them. One of the pilots actually waved; I swear I could nearly have touched them,' Sally replied to her young brother. He wasn't worried about the threat of war; he was more interested in the new planes, tanks and other mechanical things that were being developed for war against other human beings.

'I want to do that. I want to be a pilot, or at least learn to fly like them. Just think of being up in the clouds without a care in the world.' Ben smiled.

'Tha'll not be doing that, my lad – or it will be over my dead body. I'll not have one of mine fighting a war that's none of our doing,' Bob said as he walked across to his two children. 'There will too many tears, I reckon, before this year's out, the way things are going. You stick to catching rabbits; it's a lot safer.' Bob patted his daughter's shoulder. He could tell what she was thinking and knew there was nothing he could do to stop the oncoming heartache.

Chapter 17

'Aye, the barometer is set high – it's going to be a good week to start on the hay.'

Bob sat at the breakfast table after milking his cow, and before going to work for Jim Mattinson for the rest of the morning. His trusty barometer, which he had knocked slightly on its glass face, had not moved and the pressure-arm was set firmly on high, predicting good weather in the coming days. The barometer he trusted far more than the weather forecast given out on the Home Service on the wireless, because how did they know what the weather was going to be like up Dentdale? It was better to trust in the things you knew to be right, Bob thought, as he downed his porridge and looked across at Ivy.

'You'll be alright with Brian, on your own? He knows the two meadows to mow, so you can leave him to it, but you could maybe take him some drinking at eleven and some dinner; I should be back by two. Jim has hired two Irish men to help him get his hay in. I'm to do some walling above the station this morning – suits me better than turning hay, as I'll have enough of my own to do.' Bob pushed his chair back and looked as Ivy put a gooseberry pasty into the oven, then cracked some eggs into a bacon-and-egg pie to feed them all while they were in the hay field.

'Aye, Bob, we only have two meadows. Brian can't miss them now, can he? I'll keep him fed, don't worry; and I'll listen to him if he needs to bend my ear. He still seems in a right old way with himself.' Ivy placed the shortcrust-pie crust on top of the eggs and bacon, then deftly trimmed the excess pastry off, before glazing it and placing the dish in the top of the oven to bake. 'I just wish he'd bring that lass of his back home. He shouldn't be that ashamed of her. After all, it's that lad Jonathan Birbeck's fault and he sounds a right one, leaving two lasses expecting and not giving a damn.'

'Aye, well, he'll be regretting going where he's at now. He'll be wishing he'd never enlisted in such a hurry, as things are looking bad, lass. I don't doubt war is coming to all of us.' Bob put his jacket on and drank the last sip of tea.

'I know – those aeroplanes told us everything the other day. The military are getting ready, so it must be bad.' Ivy was worried. 'Now you get on your way. I'll see to Brian.'

'Right, lass, see you this afternoon.' Bob headed outside and started up the motorbike that had proved to be a godsend since he had bought it hastily. It had got him the full length of the dale, had carried Ivy into Dent for

267

shopping and had balanced many an object for the farm upon it. The bike had been a good buy, although Ivy would never admit it, he thought, as he drove down the farm track to his walling job, high on the fell above the railway station. There curlews and lapwings dived and called, and the world was at peace.

Sally knocked again on Annie Mackreth's door, but there was still no answer. Locals were looking at her as she knocked even louder, disturbing Mrs Dodd who lived next door.

'What's to do, lass? Can't you make Annie hear? If you give us a minute, I've a spare key hanging up at the backdoor for emergencies. Wait here and I'll get it.'

Sally peered worriedly in through the window, but couldn't see anything amiss. She'd not been in Dent over the weekend, else she might have called in to see Annie, after she had said she felt unwell on the Friday as Sally left for home.

'There we go – it's a good job she's left one with me. I'm sure she's alright, as I saw her sitting on the edge of the fountain, on her usual perch, on Saturday afternoon. But when I think about it, I didn't hear her yesterday, although I was at chapel most of the day.' Dorothy Dodd chattered as she put the big key in the heavy lock and turned to look at Sally. 'Happen she's gone to the shop, but I'll let you go in first and call for her, because she never ventures out that far.' She stepped back and let Sally enter the living room, which was crammed with mementoes and memories of a past life.

268

'Hello, Annie! Annie, where are you?' Sally shouted and went through to the kitchen, with its evidence in the sink that Annie had eaten either that morning or the previous evening, because dirty plates were piled up there, ready for Sally to wash.

'She's not up the back or in the wash-house, or I'd have seen her. Besides, the back door is bolted.' Dorothy paused. 'We'd better go upstairs to check the bedrooms.' She was clearly hoping Sally would lead the way again.

'I'll go,' Sally said and led the way. 'Annie? Mrs Mackreth, are you there?' she shouted and, with her heart pounding, opened the shut bedroom door.

'Oh Lord, no! Mrs Mackreth! Mrs Mackreth, we are here – wake up, wake up,' Sally went to the old woman's side, but as soon as her hand touched Annie's skin, she knew she was dead. Quickly she stood back, staring at the old woman, who lay at peace in her bed. She'd never seen a dead person before and didn't quite know what to think. The body was there exactly the same, but there was no life, and the colour had drained from the old woman's face, which was usually quite ruddy.

'Aye, Lord, she must have died in her sleep. She looks peaceful enough. Poor old lass, at least she'll be back with her husband. She mentioned him nearly every day, and I have often seen her kiss his photograph downstairs, next to her chair. Saying that, look here: she's put him next to her on her bedside cabinet. Happen she knew how badly she was, before she got into bed.' Dorothy smiled at Annie as she lay asleep in another world and then turned to Sally. 'Aye, lass, you look ashen. Is this your first time?'

'Yes, I've never seen anyone dead before.' Sally wiped an escaping tear from her cheek.

'Well, she's not going to hurt you – not that she would have done, even when she was alive. She was a good woman, was Annie, and I know she was enjoying your company of late.' Dorothy touched Sally's hand lightly. 'Now, can I ask you to go for the doctor, just to confirm her death. And then I'll start to lay her out, ready for the undertakers, once he's been. We had an arrangement that I should do that, in case this ever happened. She's been my neighbour for the last thirty years, and I'm going to miss her.'

Dorothy sighed as Sally went to the doorway and gave Annie a long last glance.

'Once you've told the doctor to come, you go home, lass. It will have upset you something rotten. I remember seeing my first dead body, and it upset me terribly. At least Annie has died peacefully in her sleep. I've seen and witnessed some terrible deaths in my time,' Dorothy continued and looked down at her neighbour.

Sally nodded her head and said nothing in reply. She didn't want to hear about the painful deaths that Dorothy obviously wanted to tell her about. She wanted to go home and cry. Happen if she had walked into Dent over the weekend she might have seen the old lady and realized she was ill, and could have got her the doctor before it was too late. She blamed herself for Annie's death, even though Annie had told her to stop fussing when she had left her on the Friday lunchtime.

She was going to miss her two mornings a week with

270

the kind old lady, as she had grown quite close to her and felt a sadness at her passing. After telling the doctor of Annie's death, she walked home and shed tears as she remembered the time they had spent together. It might not have been for long, but she'd never forget Annie Mackreth, of that she was sure.

'You are home early, our Sally,' Ivy said as she passed Graham, the postman, his usual morning cuppa and saw her daughter come into the kitchen.

'Oh, mam, it's been an awful morning. I knew Mrs Mackreth was poorly, but I hadn't realized quite how poorly she was. Her next-door neighbour had to open up her house and let me in, and together we found her in bed, dead. It was terrible – I've never seen anybody dead before.' Sally sat down at the table next to Graham and sobbed, feeling awkward as her mother put her arms around her and the postman offered his condolences.

'Another old stalwart of the Dales gone. She'd be a good age, though; she's lived at the cottage next to the fountain for as long as I can remember,' Graham said and shook his head.

'Are you alright, Sally? It's always a shock to see somebody dead, but at least you weren't that close to her. It's always worse if it's somebody you love.' Ivy squeezed her daughter, then filled her a cup of strong tea and urged her to put plenty of sugar in it.

'I had grown fond of her, though – she was a lovely woman,' Sally sniffed.

'Aye, she was a grand woman, was Annie. Always the same, always talked; in fact at times she talked too much.'

271

Graham finished his cup of tea, looking at the time on the clock. 'Saying that, I'll have to be on my way as I've the rest of the dale to deliver to. There's some important letters this morning, and folk will be waiting for word from some of their sons. It looks like you have been written to and all, Sally.' Graham smiled. 'I hope it's good news, as you could do with it this morning.' He placed his postbag over his shoulder and thanked Ivy for his drink, before going about his business.

'I've a letter! Is it from Edward?' Sally rubbed her eyes and felt her heart miss a beat.

'Aye, it looks like it. I recognize his handwriting – it's like a spider crawling across the page, just like your father's. Good job they use their hands for work and are not behind a desk. It's up there on the mantelpiece.'

Sally rose from her chair and picked up her letter, then looked at it in her hand.

'Go on. There's only me here – you can read it,' her mother said and took the dirty teacups to be washed at the sink, while her daughter stopped her tears and quickly opened her letter with shaking hands, then read it to herself and smiled as she told her mother the contents.

'Edward is coming home; he's coming back on leave, just for two days. All his regiment are, at the end of this month. They have completed their training and now are allowed home to see their loved ones,' Sally said in an excited voice. Her day had gone from one of sorrow to one of rejoicing and she felt tears rolling down her cheeks, both in joy and in sorrow, as she looked at her mother.

'That's good, my love. You'll be relieved to see him,' Ivy replied, but felt her stomach churn. She knew that Edward was probably coming home on leave before he was sent overseas to fight. The tears for Annie dying were going to be the start of many in the coming months, the way the world was, and she wished she could shelter her daughter from the heartache she was going to endure.

Brian sat on his tractor seat and went back and forth across Bob Fothergill's two meadows in straight lines, with his mower slashing down the long grasses and flowers of his fields. The air was filled with the smell of newly mown grass and herbs, and the sun shone down on him as he kept glancing back at his mower to make sure it was doing the job it was intended to do. The sleeves of his shirt were rolled up, and his skin was tanned by all the hours spent outside, checking his stock and walking his fields.

To any outsider watching him, they would not have had a clue as to the pain he was feeling over losing his wife to another man and the heartbreak that Marjorie had given him. He looked up from his tractor and saw Ivy walking through the hay field's gate with a basket on her arm, and waving at him as he assessed the last few yards that he had left to mow. He turned his tractor's engine off, then lifted his leg over the gearstick and jumped down from his seat and went over to Ivy.

'Nearly finished. Just that odd strip left, and then you are done and it's your turn for the hard work,' Brian said as Ivy sat down behind the limestone wall and started to unpack the haytime hamper with her baking inside, and two flasks of hot tea, and he joined her. 'Lord, it's a hot day. At least your Bob will have a bit of fresh air, walling his gaps up above Dent station.'

'He should be back anytime – he's usually home by dinner. He'll know where to find us, and anyway Sally has come home early, bringing bad news with her.' Ivy uncovered all that was in her basket and laid it out in front of Brian, then poured him a drink of tea in a mug and watched as he drank thirstily.

'There's nowt better than a drink of haytime tea. It must be the smell of the grass and the odd hayseed that gets into it,' he said. 'What's the bad news that Sally's brought back from Dent?' he asked and waited for a reply.

'Annie Mackreth has died. Sally found her dead in her bed, and it was quite a shock for her,' Ivy said and looked out over the hay field.

'She'd be a good age, though, and had seen a good bit of life, although I don't think she will ever have been out of the dale, as folk like that are content with little. Unlike the one I married.' Brian spat a hayseed out of his tea into the field.

'Aye, Brian, no matter what I say, I can't make it any better. Have you heard from your Marjorie? The baby will be nearly due.'

'No. And don't start, because I'm not having her back, no matter what you say. She's made her bed and now she must lie on it,' he replied firmly and reached for a piece of bacon-and-egg pie. Then he looked towards the

274

road as both of them heard the noise of Bob returning on his motorbike.

'He said he'd be back for his dinner. He can join us both here – I brought an extra cup.' Ivy watched Bob pull into the farmyard and then walk their way.

'By God, thou wastes no time rolling about in the hay field with my wife.' Bob grinned at Brian and saw Ivy frown at him, for teasing his friend.

'I should have been rolling about in a hay field with someone like Ivy, instead of trailing after something a bit different all those years ago. That's where I went wrong.' Brian caught a crumb that he had dropped and put it back into his mouth.

'Your Dora has only had her head turned by that smooth talker – she'll be back. Pass us the tea, Mother, and a slice of the pie. All that walling has made me hungry,' Bob said as he sat down next to his wife. 'I see our lass is back. I heard the news in Dent as I was passing through. The undertaker was parked outside Annie's house, so I heard that Sally found her, along with Dorothy. Is she alright?'

'She is now – now she's heard from that Edward. He's coming home on leave for two days at the end of the month. All them from around here that got enlisted are.'

'I bet that bloody Jonathan Birbeck doesn't come home, as he'll not find a welcome on the hillside here. I'd happily shoot the bastard, and I bet the Redmans would help me do it.' Brian scowled and jumped to his feet. 'He only joined up to get out of his commitments to the lasses.'

275

'Now, Brian, don't be going and getting yourself in bother – the lad's not worth it. Besides, if he's in the army now, he'll be one of the first to get shipped out to fight. He'll be shot at soon enough,' Bob said, noticing the anger on his friend's face.

'Father, think of what you are saying! Edward will be off as well, and we don't want anything to happen to him, so watch what you are saying – especially in front of our Sal,' Ivy said sharply.

'Aye, but they'd be doing me a favour if them Nazis put a bullet through that bloody Jonathan's head. Couldn't happen to a better person.' Brian set off towards his tractor, shouting back at Bob, 'I'll finish your meadow off and then I'll away home. I'm going to mow my own fields tomorrow, although how I'll get it in dry and in the barn on my own, I don't know. My brother was supposed to stay and help, but he soon decided better of it.'

'You are not on your own, Brian, we'll all help. My two are handy with the rake, and even our Ben can pitchfork hay nowadays. I'm beginning to think he's shaping up a bit better than I'd realized lately.' Bob looked at Ivy as she glanced with concern at her neighbour.

'You've just to say, Brian, and we'll be around to help you,' Ivy shouted after him, as he put his hand up in recognition and climbed up onto his tractor, after turning the starting handle into action before finishing the job in hand.

* * *

Bob leaned on his scythe and looked around the newly mown field. It was a good crop this year, he thought, as he took the scythe in his hands and gently rocked back and forth in a smooth action, cutting through the grass that the tractor and mower could not get to. Every mouthful of hay would be needed through the winter months if he was to keep his stock fed, so every blade that he moved was precious.

Tomorrow, once the grass had died down a bit, he'd get all the family out with the rakes and would scale the grass, to get air and sun in it, to dry it out. Once it was dry and crisp, and weather permitting, they would drag it back into rows and then pull it into haycocks, called 'billycocks', before loading it onto the sledge to be pulled to the barn and kept dry in the haymew. It was hard work for everyone involved, and he could understand Brian worrying about having to cope on his own, but he was sure the neighbouring farmers would help him, knowing his predicament.

Bob concentrated on the job in hand, sharpening his scythe as it cut swathes of grass, making it sharp and accurate as he worked up the side of the field, gathering grass from under the wall. Suddenly he was stopped in his tracks as he felt the scythe hit something under the grass. He swore and bent down, as a pain shot into his leg and he saw blood seeping through his trouser. The sharp edge had hit a stone that had fallen from the wall top, and had made the scythe deviate from its path and it had cut into his leg. With blood soaking his corduroy trousers, Bob quickly made the decision that he needed his wound to be seen to, propping the offending weapon against the wall side as he hobbled across the meadow, with blood seeping into his boots.

'Oh Lord, Bob, what have you done?' Ivy said as she looked at her husband leaving a trail of blood across the kitchen floor.

'Bloody scythe bounced and I cut my leg.' He was white with shock as he sat in the kitchen chair, then watched as Ivy took off his boot to look at his wound as she pulled up his trousers. 'It's not good, is it, lass?' He sighed, feeling faint.

'No, it isn't.' Ivy padded around the wound with clean tea-towels to stop the flow. 'You need the doctor. It's going to need stitches – and you are going to need him fast.'

'The bike, get me to the bike. I'll show you how to drive it, and I'll sit on behind you. Dr Batty will be in his surgery, and he'll soon stitch me up and stop it from bleeding. But we will have to be quick, as my head is going dizzy.'

'Oh Lord, I can't do that – I'll kill us both,' Ivy replied, fighting between her fear of driving the bike and saving her husband's life.

'You'll have to do it, lass, else I'm not going to make it.' Bob hoisted himself up and made for the kitchen table. 'Come on, you'll manage the two miles to Dent, even if we go in the same gear all the way.

'But I'm in my pinny!' Ivy protested as she put her arm around Bob and, with a fast-beating heart, helped him out of the house across the yard and to the motorbike, which she had been so against when it had first arrived.

'Get yourself on and then I'll climb on behind you. Don't worry – you can do it.'

Ivy lifted her skirts and put her leg over the machine, realizing quite how heavy it was as Bob climbed on the back.

'Now stand up and kick-start it. You've seen me do it many a time. Just push down really hard and then, after a time or two, it'll start. I'll keep the bike as steady as I can while you get the engine going.' Bob prayed that Ivy had the strength to get his bike started and convey them safely to Dent.

Ivy had tears running down her cheeks as she pushed and kicked down with her leg on the starter pedal. She couldn't do it, she simply couldn't do it; and then, on the last attempt, the engine sprang into life.

'Now, clutch out gently and we are away,' Bob said and sighed, as he could feel Ivy shaking as she took control of his bike. He pressed his head into her back and prayed that they would get safely to the doctor's without incident. He didn't dare to watch as the trees and hedges flew past.

Ivy trembled with every move the bike made, and she fought with the weight of Bob on the back, as they made their way into the village of Dent. The sight of the white-washed houses and cobbled streets was never so welcome, as she followed Bob's instructions and went straight to the doctor's surgery door. Leaving the bike on its side, she put her arm around her husband and helped him into the surgery, where waiting patients gasped as she helped Bob into the consulting room, bursting in to find Dr Batty with another patient.

'Oh my Lord, put him onto the bed over there and elevate his leg,' Dr Batty said as he realized the urgent condition of his surprise visitor. 'How's he done this?'

'With a scythe, Doctor. It was an accident.' Ivy felt as weak as Bob as he lay down on the bed and waited for the doctor to look at his leg.

'Just as well you got him here quickly, as he's lost a lot of blood. You need stitches, Bob. The cut is deep, but no main artery is cut, thank heavens, else you wouldn't be here.' Dr Batty threaded a curved needle and carefully cleaned the wound with iodine, making Bob wince at the sting.

'Aye, well, I can thank my Ivy for getting me here. It was a bit hairy at times, but we made it.' Bob smiled wanly at Ivy and realized how much he loved her, and how strong a woman he was married to. He closed his eyes and felt grateful she was such a good wife and that she loved him. He realized, as he was helped back to his legs, exactly what he'd put his wife through of late when she nearly cried in relief at the sight of him, patched and mended and still alive.

'Let's be away home, our lass. Can you manage to drive the bike back again?' Bob asked and looked at the worry on her face.

'No need, Bob. I'll take you home in the car. I'm sure it will be safer for the two of you than the bike,' Dr Batty replied, much to Ivy's relief, as he told his nurse to explain to his waiting patients that he would be back shortly.

Once home, Bob sat with his leg resting on a stool and watched Ivy as she busied herself about the house.

'Come here, lass. I've something to tell you that I

should say more often,' he said quietly and held his hand out for her to take.

'What is it: don't waste all the tattie-peelings and to save them for the pig?' Ivy asked, then realized that Bob was looking too serious for it to be something as flippant as that.

'Nay, I just wanted to tell you that I love you, and that I'd be nowt without you.' Bob pulled her towards him.

'Bloody hell, you must have bumped your head and all. You've not told me that for years, you silly devil.' Ivy smiled and kissed him on the lips. 'And I love you, although you are the most pig-headed fella I could have married. For the next day or two you'll sit in that chair and let everybody else run after you, and the stock. Do you hear, Bob?'

'Aye, I hear, and we'll see. I don't aim to be off my feet too long. Now promise me you'll never doubt that I love you, no matter what my mood,' Bob said and held her tightly.

'I know, Bob, and the same goes for me. Now stop talking so soft and drink your tea.' Ivy grinned; they were the words she had been waiting to hear for so long. And even though, in her heart, she knew Bob loved her, it was still nice to hear it.

The grass had been lying in the warm sunshine for three days and now, thanks to everyone scaling it with their hay forks, it was dry and sweet-smelling. The clover within it made it even more appealing to the cattle in the dark days of winter, bringing a reminder of the summer days to come in the New Year.

'My hands are covered with blisters,' Sally said as she looked between her thumb and fingers, and at the blisters that had formed on the palms of her hands from holding the wooden hayfork and lifting the hay up with it, to get the warm air drying through it.

'Mine are too, but never mind, it's nearly over. Your father's gone for the horse and sledge; at least he can manage them, and his leg looks like it's healing nicely. I'm only thankful that I still have him with me. We'll load what we can before dusk, and then the billycocks for the rest until morning.' Ivy took a swig of the ginger beer that she had made just before haytime, in preparation for the hot work in the field. 'I bet our Ben helps now – look at him jumping over the hay rows. But he'll soon come running when there's a chance to have a ride on the horse or on top of the sledge full of hay.'

'It's the best part of haytime, Mam, along with hay-field teas. You know that the hard work is over and the hay is in for winter, and it's lovely lying back with the sweet-smelling hay around you and the blue skies above.' Sally smiled as Ben raced to walk next to his father and the horse and sledge.

'See, told you – always turns up when most of the work is done. Never mind, Ben hasn't got the strength in his arms to help for too long and, as you say, most of the work is done now. We'll have to see how Brian next door is coping. Your father said he'd seen two of the Winn lads helping him out, so he's not on his own, like he was worrying about. Now our hay is nearly in, your father will help Brian once he's finished his work for Jim Mattinson of a morning.' Ivy looked at her husband and son. They were both hot and sweaty, but a good wash with carbolic soap in the tin bath would soon get them smelling fresher, once the hay had been stored.

'Well, that's it for another year. I'm always thankful when all's gathered in,' Bob said as he stood back exhausted, with his pitchfork in his hand, and looked up at the full haymew. 'Just as long as it doesn't combust and fire; it shouldn't, although this year it's as dry as a bone. If folk haven't got good hay this year, there's something wrong, because it's been good weather for us all.'

Ben looked at his father and quoted a local saying – 'All is safely gathered in, except a bit at Rivelin' – and laughed.

'Nay, I think they've even gathered it in at Rivelin farm this year. There's only Brian next door who's still got some grass lying, and that will be gathered in tomorrow, with the help of the Winns and me. He's managed, and I think if there's been one neighbour's wife there with baking and suchlike, there's been twenty. It's at times like this that everybody bands together, so he needn't have worried.'

'He's got more to worry about than his hay this year,' Ivy said. 'Marjorie won't be far off having that baby, and Dora hasn't returned. I don't know what Brian's going to do.'

'I don't know what any of us are going to do, come to that. Neville Chamberlain keeps trying to make peace with that mad man Hitler, but it's all in vain. Even if the hay is in and gathered, it will be the least of our worries, lass, as war is on its way. But right now I'm going to have a shave and a wash, then go and down a pint at The Sun and have a game of dominoes with the lads. Prove to them all that I'm still alive, because there will have been some fair tales about me coming into Dent half-dead, with you riding the motorbike.' Bob grinned as the dusk started to come down over the farmyard, and bats flew out of their roosts in the barn. The summer was coming to an end, and with the approach of autumn came a feeling of uncertainty about what the future held for everyone.

'Oh, Mam, do you think that's why Edward is coming home? The army is letting him come before he goes and does his duty?' Sally asked as they walked across the yard and into the house.

'I reckon it might well be doing so, lass. The army didn't call him up for nothing, but you will see when he comes home next week.' Ivy smiled. 'He'll be alright, Sally. Edward will be able to look after himself, and hopefully this war will not be the same as the last one.' She hoped Sally couldn't read her true thoughts, because from what she had read and heard, the Nazi war machine was just as ruthless as the one Kaiser Bill had led. Heartache and hard times were coming to every household, and there was nothing the ordinary folk of the country could do about it.

Bob sat in his usual corner in The Sun inn, with the group of friends that he usually sat with, and played dominoes and had a drink. His pint of locally brewed ale was going down a little too well as he played his

284

dominoes and chewed the fat over local problems, after all of them had made fun of his predicament and were glad it had not been too serious.

'Ivy drove that bike of yours like a bat out of hell! Lord, I'm glad I didn't meet her. But she saved your life, that's for sure,' Jim Baines told his old mate. 'She'll be enlisting as a dispatch rider, if you aren't careful, the way things are going.'

'Aye, it'll either make us or break us these next few weeks. If bloody Germany marches on Poland or France, that will be it. All hell will break loose,' Ronnie Oversby said and sat back.

'Aye, it'll come to that. Hitler thinks he and his are better than any other race. Look at the poor Jews!' Bob replied. 'Our lass's fella is coming home next week, and that's a sure sign we are about to go to war, but I daren't say owt to her.'

'Well, I don't know if it's right or not, but I heard the army came looking for that Jonathan Birbeck up at his parents' home – and that of the Redmans. He's deserted from Catterick Garrison. As if both houses haven't had enough bother from him. He's worth nowt,' Ted said and played his next domino.

'That wouldn't surprise me. A rat deserting a sinking ship. The lad's no backbone – he is worth nowt. Thank the Lord our Sally had nowt to do with him. Instead she's given her heart to the young Riley, and it's going to be broken. She'll not be the only one, though, and there's not a thing we can do about it. Bad times are around the corner, so we had better have another pint while we can.' Bob picked up his glass and caught the barmaid's eye. 'The government will put a stop to any enjoyment in life at any time now, lads. So drink up and we'll have another, and then I'll away home to my Ivy.'

'She might have run off with Thompson's salesman, if he's brought Dora back to Brian,' Ted joked and winked.

'Nay, she's more sense than that. My Ivy would never be tempted by someone as flash as that. She's got all the man she wants in me.' Bob winked at the barmaid as she put the next tray of drinks down.

'She's got a cocky bugger who can't hold his drink,' the barmaid ventured and smiled. And the rest of his mates laughed, as Bob sat and didn't reply for a minute.

'Aye, but I'm a good catch, and she knew it back then when we married; and still knows it now. So you can hold your whisht.' Bob grinned as he enjoyed his haytime pint among good company, as darkness fell over the small town.

The young lad from the farm next to Redman's bent double and tried to catch his breath as he looked up at the sergeant major who towered over him.

'Please, sir, Mrs Redman says can you come quick to their farm. She says you are looking for Jonathan Birbeck and he's with them, but to come quick, before he decides to jigger off.' The lad gulped for breath as the sergeant major asked for directions and, along with armed guards, got into the army jeep and rode off up the dale.

* * *

286

Alison watched as her onetime lover, and the father of her baby, was cuffed and roughly handled by his fellow officers. She had loved him once, but now she realized Jonathan loved nobody and that she had been used, along with Marjorie Harper and any other girl who took his eye. It was her time to see him hurt.

Jonathan Birbeck looked back at the lass and the family that had dobbed him in and swore. How could they let him be taken away? He'd told them he had come back to support the girl he should have married. Perhaps he would have done, if they hadn't given him away. He'd do anything to get out of going to war.

'Shut it, boy, you are in enough trouble as it is.' The army captain pushed Jonathan's head down and shoved him into the jeep's back seat, with his wrists handcuffed.

'Oh, Mam, have we done right? Perhaps we shouldn't have told them?' a blonde-haired and blooming Alison said and put her hands on her stomach. 'This one might never get to know its father.'

'It'll be no great loss, my lass – you'll be better off without him,' her mother replied and put her arm around Alison, as they stood at the garden gate of the long, whitewashed house that was covered with a rambling red rose. 'Now, don't think about him ever again. The baby will be looked after; the faults of the father are not its faults. We are a strong family, and it'll not be the first baby that hasn't known its father.'

Chapter 18

Sally studied herself in the mirror in her bedroom. She wanted to look her best for Edward and if she had tied her hair back once, she had tied it back three times and then decided to keep it loose over her shoulders. She wore a Fair Isle cardigan knitted in heathery colours and a brown corduroy skirt. It might not be as attractive as Marjorie would have worn, but it showed off her curves, without being too obvious that she was dressing for her man. Besides, it might only be the end of August, but the weather was beginning to change, as were the hedgerows and trees outside. Another few weeks and the dale would be a-glow with the oranges and russets of the turning leaves on the trees.

She gave herself one more look in the mirror and felt her stomach churn, then went downstairs into the kitchen and faced her parents and young brother, all of whom knew she was to meet Edward at the end of the lane, as arranged.

'Now don't you look bonny. Edward will not want to leave when he sees you.' Ivy tried to hold back the tears that she could feel welling up in her eyes. Her daughter was going to feel pain and anguish as she watched Edward head off to war, which everyone knew was going to come.

'Do you think I look alright? I looked at some of Marjorie's clothes, but they were not really what I feel comfortable in, so I thought I'd wear my favourite jumper that you knitted me,' Sally said, standing in front of her family.

'You look grand, lass. He couldn't wish for anybody better and prettier,' Bob replied. And Ben puckered his lips, kissing the air and then sticking his fingers down his throat, pretending to be sick, as he imagined his sister and Edward courting.

Ivy gave him a clout around the head with her tea-towel. 'Behave yourself! Another few years and you'll be walking out with somebody, and then you'll understand. Now if Edward wants you to bring him in home for a cup of tea, you know he's welcome.'

'Oh, I don't know. I might tan his backside,' Bob said and then smiled at Sally. 'No, you bring him to see us – the lad's welcome, and you know he is.'

'I will, if Edward says he's got time. He's been at his mother and father's all day yesterday, he's already said goodbye to them and he's arranged to be picked up here by his detachment at the lane end this afternoon.' Sally noticed her father and mother glance at one another. 'He's not said anything about going to war in his letters, so I hope that it's not going to happen. Surely he would know, wouldn't he?'

'Aye, he probably would, lass. Don't you worry, he'll be alright,' Bob said as Ivy went over to Sally and kissed her on her cheek.

'Take care, love, and enjoy yourselves – but not too much.' She watched as Sally left the kitchen, and could have cried for her daughter.

'That doesn't make sense, Mam. Enjoy yourself, but not too much! What are you on about?' Ben piped up.

'Never you mind. But you'll be getting the same advice when you are her age and all,' Ivy replied, as Bob looked at her over the top of his newspaper. 'Poor Sally, she's saying goodbye to her fella today and then attending Annie Mackreth's funeral tomorrow. It's a bad few days for her, so you be kind to that sister of yours.'

Ben said nothing and decided that he was best out of the way, so he resolved to go and look for some field mushrooms, which were beginning to appear in the top pastures. At least that way he would get into his mother and father's good books, bringing back something tasty for supper. Today he couldn't compete with the attention they were both giving his sister, and all because she was walking out with a soldier.

Sally made her way down the farm lane. The leaves on the hedges were about to turn and she noticed the nuts on the hazel trees were nearly ready for picking. But her mind was not on foraging, unlike Ben, as she walked down to the end of the lane and waited for Edward.

Her stomach churned and her heart beat fast as she sat on the wall top on the other side of the road from her farm's lane. She looked around her. There was a slight chill in the air, but the sky was blue and cloudless and she watched as the last signs of summer, swallows flying south, soared above her head. They were not bothered by war or rumours of war; they were going where the sun shone and summer was just beginning, and she envied them. They twittered and ducked and dived, and Sally watched their path until they were out of sight.

'What's a nice girl like you standing at the side of the road for? Any Tom, Dick or Harry could pick you up,' Edward shouted as he rounded the corner and saw Sally sitting, waiting for him. A huge grin was on his face as he strode towards her in his army uniform, carrying his kitbag over his shoulder.

'Edward, you are here! And look at you, don't you look smart.' Sally went willingly into his arms as he dropped his kitbag in the middle of the road and held her tightly.

'Oh, I've missed you, my Sally. I've missed you so much, and I'm going to miss you again.' Edward held her tightly and then put her chin in his hand and reached down and kissed her on the lips, which she returned and she didn't want to stop kissing him.

She put her hands on his shoulders and felt the roughness of Edward's khaki uniform, and saw the badges on his sleeve ends and on his buttons. Her farmhand was now a soldier, she thought, as he took off his company's cap and she noticed his short-cut hair.

'I've missed you so much, Edward. There's not a day gone by that I haven't thought of you,' she said. 'I don't want you to go back. My mam and dad say there's war coming. They haven't said anything, but I think they believe you'll be leaving England to go and fight the Nazis, so please tell me they are wrong.' She gazed at the lad she had fallen in love with.

'Those in charge haven't said as much yet, but you can tell they are getting ready for something. I heard a rumour that there's an Expeditionary Force going to be sent into France, if war is declared. I hate to say it, but we are already trained, so they would send us, my love.' Edward put his arm around Sally and picked up his kitbag. 'Come on, we'll go and sit down by the river and have some time together, while we can. The wagon is picking me up at two, so we have three hours, and I don't want to waste a second of it.'

'I don't want to lose you. Tell them you can't go,' Sally protested as they held hands and made their way to a secluded place on the banks of the Dee.

'If only I could, my love.' Edward patted a sandy patch on the riverside for them to sit down on. 'I don't think they would let me get away with that.'

'Then run away, like Jonathan Birbeck. My father said the army was looking for him up the dale, and that he'd deserted.' Sally clung to Edward's arm and looked up at him.

'Aye, and now he's in the clink. A rumour was going

around the camp that they picked him up at Alison Redman's farm – the Redmans and his own family handed him in. Everybody hates him.'

'Oh, poor Alison. That must have been a terrible decision to make, to watch the father of your child marched off and perhaps never see him again.' Sally hung her head.

'Oh, he'll be back, just like a bad penny – and like me,' Edward said and beamed.

'Please don't go, Edward. I don't want to lose you.'

'No, my love, I'll do my duty. And if I have to fight, then I have to fight. But while I'm away, I'll write as often as I can and I will always be thinking of you.'

'And I will write and think of you, but how I wish and hope war does not come and that you'll be returning soon,' Sally replied, as they sat with their arms around one another and planned for the future. Life had been so happy a few months ago, and now the world had turned on its head and both of them were going to suffer the pains of being apart, no matter how fast their love for one another was growing.

Sally watched as Edward climbed into the back of the truck along with all the other recruits, who were dressed in army uniform and looking the part. She had listened to all the shouts and wolf-whistles as Edward held her tightly and kissed her, whispering into her ear his love and promising that he would write every day.

Now, as she walked back up the lane, her heart was aching. She knew she was unlikely to see Edward for quite a while. He had never said as much, but he knew that war was coming. Every minute together had been spent looking at one another and lying on the banks of the Dee, simply happy to be in one another's company, without many words being said. She felt guilty as she reached her home, as she knew her parents had wanted to see Edward, but every second between them had been so precious that she had not wished to share him.

Both her mother and father looked up at her as she entered the kitchen and noticed that the best china had been placed on the table, in readiness for Edward's visit.

'Well, I take it he turned up?' Ivy said. 'Is Edward outside? Tell him to get himself in here – we don't bite.'

'He's gone, Mam, and I don't think he'll be back for a long time.' Sally couldn't help herself as tears fell down her cheeks and she sobbed and sobbed.

'Aye, lass. These lads, they come along and break our hearts. But he'll be back – he's got you to come back to, and his family. He'll be alright. I'm sure he'll be alright, no matter what happens.' Ivy hugged her daughter, while Bob looked at them and spat a mouthful of chewing tobacco into the fire, in disgust at the war they all knew was upon them.

'He was talking about perhaps having to go to France, Mam. I don't think I'll ever see him again.' Sally buried her head in her mother's shoulder and savoured the security and warmth that had always been there for her.

Bob looked into the fire. He'd seen this once before, when his brother had gone to war – the war that was supposed to end all wars. But they had lied then, and they would lie again, of that he was sure. That was the way of the world, and that was how it would always be.

Chapter 19

Annie Mackreth's funeral was well attended and although she had been a good age at eighty-two, neighbours and friends shed tears for her as her body was interred in the churchyard that her home had overlooked.

'We'll miss Annie. She used to sit on the edge of the fountain many a day,' Jim Mattinson said as he put his trilby back on his head and walked with the Fothergill family across the cobbled street to the village hall, where a funeral tea was to be held, in grand tradition.

'Aye, our lass is going to miss her – and the bit of pin money she made there.' Bob smiled at Sally as she wiped her nose and tried to look unflustered.

'Annie was never the same after she lost her husband. It must have broken her heart, because there was only them two; it was a shame she had no family.' Jim took his hat off again as he entered the hall and made his way to sit down at one of the small round tables, indicating for Bob, Ivy and Sally to join him, as the young lass from the local tea room poured well-stewed tea from a huge aluminium teapot; she told them all to enjoy the sandwiches and cakes that the tea room had provided for the occasion. The air buzzed with people talking, remembering the good times of Annie's life and discussing the dale's affairs and whether they had all had a good harvest; but also the announcement that Germany was rumoured to have invaded Poland, and the consequences that would have upon the country.

'Your father tells me you've been walking out with young Edward Riley. He'll be a grand lad. His mother and father are good people, but they must be bothered to death with all this talk of war being bandied about. Like yourself, I'm sure.' Jim could see the worry on Sally's face. 'It may all come to nowt. Hitler won't have the nerve to attack Poland, and that fat, bloated Eyetie, Mussolini, is only his puppet. Your lad will be home before you know it. Are there to be wedding bells when he comes back? I hope I'll be asked.' Jim smiled as Sally blushed and put her head down.

'It'll not be for a while yet, Jim. You are forgetting that our Sally is only sixteen. I hope she will have the sense to wait just a little while longer. Although I must say, Edward seems a grand lad, from what we have seen of him.' Ivy sipped her tea and reached for a brawn sandwich that had taken her eye.

'Well, at least he's better than that Jonathan Birbeck – leaving two lasses expecting and then absconding from the camp at Catterick. They got him, you know? Edward told our Sally that the Redmans and his own family handed him in; they'll make that coward pay,' Bob said and gazed around him. 'It's not looking good, is it, Jim? Sally's fella has heard that there are moves afoot for them to be shipped to France, although he shouldn't be telling us that,' he continued in a quiet voice as Ivy gave him a dark look, while Sally wiped her mouth and made the excuse of wanting a bit of fresh air.

'Look what you've done now, Father. She was upset enough at the graveside, and now you've gone and said that,' Ivy admonished sharply and watched as her daughter made her way to the open door of the village hall.

Bob said nothing, but sat back in his chair.

'I doubt she'll not be on her own. There will be thousands of young men sent, if war is declared,' Jim replied and dropped his head. Usually a funeral tea was a good time to catch up and share some banter, but somehow the room full of locals seemed a little subdued, as they knew that dark times were coming over the horizon and there was nothing they could do about it.

Sally leaned against the village hall's wall. The last time she had stood there for any length of time was when Edward had been conscripted. She remembered him walking out of the hall, with a pair of boots hanging around his neck and a cheery smile. The cheeriness was still there, but so was a deep worry about what was to come, she thought, as she remembered his kisses and the soft words spoken to her on the banks of the Dee.

'Please let him come home. Please don't let any of our lads go to war,' she whispered and felt a tear trickling down her cheek as she looked across at the steep fellside and down the dale to her home. Germany and Poland were countries that were miles away. Why should some farm lads from Dent have to be made to fight there, she thought, and felt her stomach churning at the idea of it. Nothing was right in her world, and she had a feeling that things were only going to get worse.

It was Sunday 3rd September and it was a quiet morning at the Fothergills'. The stock were still out grazing in the fields, the hay was in the barn, and Bob was enjoying smoking his pipe of Kendal Twist, while Ivy chopped up some fresh mint from the garden to go with the mutton roasting in the oven. Ben and Sally were both in the front room listening to the wireless when an announcement came over the airwaves that made them run into the kitchen and drag both parents in to listen.

Sally's heart beat fast and she felt sick, as her father sat smoking his pipe and her mother sat in the armchair, wiping her hands on her apron and shaking her head as she heard the grave words spoken by Neville Chamberlain: 'I am speaking to you from the Cabinet Room at Ten Downing Street. This morning the British ambassador in Berlin handed the German government a final note stating that unless we heard from them by eleven o'clock that they were prepared at once to withdraw their troops from Poland, a state of war would exist between us. I have to tell you now that no such statement has been received, and consequently this country is at war with Germany.'

'Oh Lord, that's it then – we are at war. God help us all.' Ivy bowed her head.

'Aye, it would seem that we are. The bastard won't back down, so we will have to give him a good kicking and put him in his place.' Bob looked across at both his children. 'Let's hope we come out of this unscathed, and that lads like your Edward are kept safe and come home to the ones they love.'

Silence fell over the family as the wireless that had delivered the message was turned off. The war years had come to Daleside, and things would never be the same.

Marjorie lay back, with sweat dripping down her face and the sheets bloodied around her. It was over, she thought, as she turned and looked at the newly born baby in the sister's arms. 'I'm exhausted,' she said and wiped away a tear.

'Well, you had your pleasure and now you've suffered the pain. No good comes of sin,' the nun commented.

'May I see him? Is he healthy?' Marjorie asked weakly.

'He's a bonny wee fella, that he is, and he's healthy. But go and get yourself some rest now, after we have cleaned you up. He'll be fine in the nursery. The sisters will see to him.' The hard-faced nun left Marjorie with no idea what her newborn son looked like, as she'd never been given a chance to hold him and look at him for even a minute.

Marjorie curled up as another of the sisters cleaned around her and then told her that she needed bedrest for a day or two. Nobody asked her how she felt or gave

her any comfort, as she lay in bed and wondered what to do next and whether she should insist on seeing the baby she had just given birth to. Never had she felt so low, but she had to make plans for her life now, and never again would she be tricked by the likes of Jonathan Birbeck. Shortly before her baby's arrival, her mother had written to her saying that she was now living in Liverpool with John Blades and that there was a room ready for her upon Marjorie's return, provided she left her child for the nuns to take care of.

Perhaps it was for the best that she had not seen her baby, as she would only have felt love for it, of that she was sure, as she lay alone, with nobody to confide in. She'd leave him in the nuns' care and make a new life in Liverpool, well away from Dentdale. After all, Liverpool was a city where she could do and be whatever she liked. And her mother was right: a baby would only drag her down. That was what she would do – it was all going to be alright. She'd get a job, spend money on pretty clothes and enjoy her life. She didn't love the baby or Jonathan bloody Birbeck, and she could live without both of them.

Sally sat on the edge of her bed. The postman had handed her a letter with a sympathetic glance, knowing that he had delivered the same envelope with the same hand-writing on it to Edward's family that morning.

She felt her hands tremble as she opened the letter and read it in the privacy of her own room. There was no return address upon it, just a few hasty words written to her before Edward had boarded the ship that was to take him to fight with the British Expeditionary Force, whose main task was to keep the Germans from invading more of Europe. She felt her heart aching as she read his words:

Dear Sally,

Well, the day has come and we are about to be shipped out across the Channel. Don't worry too much, my love. I'll keep my head down and will be constantly thinking of you. I'll soon be home, and then I can hold you in my arms and tell you exactly how much I do love you. There will be better days soon, my love.

Your ever loving,

Edward

Sally kissed the letter and whispered, 'Take care, my love; please come back to me,' as she looked out of her bedroom window across the farmyard at the green hills and woods of her home. In the yard she watched as her father showed Ben how to service the motorbike, and their mother stood and laughed at both of them as they got covered in oil. At least her parents were happier now, even if her own heart was breaking. Edward would be back – he had to be, because she loved him too much for him not to be – and the war would not last forever.

The Mistress of
Windfell Manor

DIANE ALLEN

Charlotte Booth loves her father and the home they share, which is set high up in the limestone escarpments of Crummockdale. But when a new businessman in the form of Joseph Dawson enters their lives, both Charlotte and her father decide he's the man for her and, within six months, Charlotte marries the dashing mill owner from Accrington.

Then a young mill worker is found dead in the swollen River Ribble. With Joseph's business nearly bankrupt, it becomes apparent that all is not as it seems and Joseph is not the man he pretends to be. Heavily pregnant, penniless and heartbroken, Charlotte is forced to face the reality that life may never be the same again . . .

OUT NOW

The Windfell Family Secrets

DIANE ALLEN

Twenty-one years have passed since Charlotte Booth fought to keep her home at Windfell Manor, following her traumatic first marriage. Now, happily married to her childhood sweetheart, she seeks only the best for their children, Isabelle and Danny. But history has a habit of repeating itself when Danny's head is turned by a local girl of ill repute.

Meanwhile, the beautiful and secretive Isabelle shares all the undesirable traits of her biological father. And when she announces that she is to marry John Sidgwick, the owner of High Mill in Skipton, her mother quickly warns her against him. An ex-drinking mate of her late father who faces bankruptcy, Charlotte fears his interest in Isabelle is far from honourable. What she doesn't realize is how far he's willing to go to protect his future . . .

OUT NOW

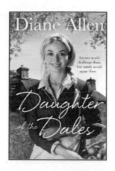

Daughter of the Dales

DIANE ALLEN

The death of Charlotte Atkinson, the family matriarch, at Windfell Manor casts a long shadow over her husband Archie and their two children, Isabelle and Danny. With big shoes to fill, Isabelle takes over the running of Atkinson's department store but her pride – and heart – is tested when her husband James brings scandal upon the family and the Atkinsons' reputation.

Danny's wife Harriet is still struggling to deal with the deaths of their first two children – deaths she blames Isabelle for. But Danny himself is grappling with his own demons when a stranger brings to light a long-forgotten secret from his past.

Meanwhile, Danny and Harriet's daughter Rosie has fallen under the spell of a local stable boy, Ethan. But will he stand by her or will he cause her heartache? And can Isabelle restore the Atkinsons' reputation and her friendship with Harriet, to unite the family once more?

OUT NOW

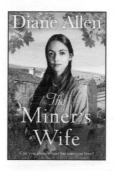

The Miner's Wife

DIANE ALLEN

Nineteen-year-old Meg Oversby often dreams of a more exciting life than the dull existence she faces at her family's farm deep in the Yorkshire Dales. Growing up, she's always sensed her father's disappointment at not having a son to help with the farm work.

So when Meg dances all night at the local market hall with Sam Alderson, a lead miner from Swaledale, a new light enters her life. Sam and his brother Jack show Meg a side to life she didn't know existed. But when her parents find out, she's forbidden from ever seeing them again.

Although where there is love, there is often a way. When Meg's uncle offers her the chance to help run the small village shop, she leaps at the opportunity, seeing it as a way to escape the oppressive family farm and see more of her beloved Sam. But as love blossoms, a darker truth emerges and Meg realizes that Sam may not be the man she thought he was . . .

OUT NOW

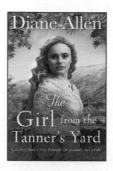

The Girl from the Tanner's Yard

DIANE ALLEN

After facing the horrors of the Crimean War, Adam Brooksbank returns to Black Moss Farm filled with regret over the path he has chosen in life. Starting anew, he decides to focus on rebuilding his family's rundown farm and making it a home again.

Lucy Bancroft lives with her parents near the local tannery, and is the most beautiful girl in the village. But unfortunately her wealth doesn't match her looks, and she soon realizes that nobody wants to court a girl from the filthy flay-pits, let alone marry her.

Yet when Lucy comes to work for Adam as his maid she finds herself falling in love with the farm, set high upon the wild moors of Haworth. Furthermore she begins to imagine a life with her new employer that goes beyond just being his maid.

As they spend more time together, their feelings develop for one another despite her parents warning her nothing good will come of it. As rumours swirl around the village, igniting jealousies and unearthing deeply buried secrets, will love find a way?

OUT NOW

A Precious Daughter

DIANE ALLEN

When Ethan Postlethwaite, his wife Grace and their daughter Amy announce that they will be leaving the family home in the Yorkshire Dales, Grace's parents are heartbroken. Hoping for a new life prospecting for gold in the wilds of Canada, the young family say goodbye and set sail across the Atlantic in search of a brighter future.

The journey there proves hard and treacherous, however, and upon arrival it becomes apparent that the riches they had been promised in the gold fields have already been plundered. So when the family is devastated by the death of Grace, Ethan decides he must take his daughter back to England.

Arriving in Liverpool, Ethan and Amy soon find work in a dairy as cow-keepers, but Amy is restless and struggles to settle into yet another new life. And when a chance encounter at a cattle show ignites an old friendship, she must decide where her own future lies and what she must do in order to find happiness at last . . .

OUT NOW

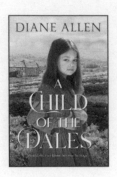

A Child of the Dales

DIANE ALLEN

Abandoned as a baby on the steps of a remote inn, Ruby Blake was raised by the innkeeper's wife, unaware of the family searching for her. One stormy night, Ruby is reunited with her long-lost father, who whisks her away to Banksgill Farm for a happy life with her true family. However, Ruby is quickly outcast for being born of Romany blood by everyone but the charming stable hand, and she seeks friendship and love with him. As their relationship blossoms, Ruby is faced with the temptations of a handsome local miner, and when rumours begin to spread, Ruby feels more lost and confused than ever.

With his daughter now safely under his wing, Reuben Blake is still desperately searching for Ruby's mother, and vows he will not rest until he finds his true love. But Reuben's mission shows only signs of heartbreak and despair. As neither father nor daughter feel quite whole, will either finally find where they truly belong?

OUT NOW